D1239481

The
Pink Flamingo
MURDERS

Elaine Viets

A Dell Book

Published by
Dell Publishing
a division of
Random House, Inc.
1540 Broadway
New York, New York 10036

The trademark Dell® is registered in the U.S. Patent and Trademark Office.

ISBN: 0-440-22445-4

Printed in the United States of America

Published simultaneously in Canada

July 1999

10   9   8   7   6   5   4   3   2   1
OPM

To Lee the Rehabber,
and all the other rehabbers who
saved St. Louis one house at a time

Acknowledgments

Special thanks to Willetta L. Heising, author of *Detecting Women*, who gave this fledgling flamingo its name.

To my husband, Don Crinklaw, who listened even at three A.M. when I asked, "Do you think it would work better if . . ." Discussing plots is grounds for murder, or at least divorce, with ordinary sleepy spouses.

To my agent, David Hendin, who's the best.

To the staff of the St. Louis Public Library, who answered a zillion nitpicky questions, and to Anne Watts, who knows that writing is murder.

Many other people in St. Louis and around the country helped me with this book. I hope I've acknowledged them all. I certainly appreciate their help.

They include Ira Bergman with Bergman, Schrairer & Co. PC; Elizabeth Braznell; the Broward County Library; Susan Carlson; pink plastic flamingo inventor Don Featherstone and his St. Louis wife, Nancy Featherstone; Jinny Gender; Jay "the Stark Raving Rehabber" Gibbs; Jane Gilbert; Kay Gordy; Karen Grace; Gerald Greiman; Esley Hamilton; Debbie Henson; George W. Johannes; Pam Klein; Marilyn Koehr; St. Louis Police Officer Barry Lalumandier; Cindy Lane; Edward Lulie; Betty Mattli; Paul Mattli; Tracy McCreery; Kathy McDaniel; the ever-hip Alan Portman and Molly Portman; Charles E. Raiken, Division Chief/Fire Marshal, Broward County Fire Rescue; Dick Richmond; Janet Smith; Martin Walsh; and Linda Williams with Mary King and Associates Realtors.

Finally, thanks to all those sources who must remain anonymous, including my deadly accurate pathologist, who explained it is indeed possible to commit murder by pink plastic flamingo.

1

We approved of the first murder.

We applauded the second.

By the third murder, I think we would have given the killer a ticker-tape parade.

But the fourth death, that was different. Now the killer was going after one of our own. People like us.

By the fifth death, everyone was so frightened, they asked me to solve the crimes. I told them the police would do a better job. I said I'd never solved a murder. I told the truth, but no one believed me. Maybe if they had . . . well, it's too late for maybes now.

My name is Francesca Vierling, and I'm a columnist for the *St. Louis City Gazette*. I'm six feet tall, with dark hair, dark eyes, and a smart mouth. Or maybe not so smart, since it's always getting me in trouble. Today was one more example. If I'd just kept it shut and not answered the phone. There was no reason to answer it at seven-thirty at night. I should have left the office hours ago.

I was at the *Gazette* at the end of a steamy St. Louis summer day. Even with the air conditioner running full blast, there were heat pockets in the corners. My hair was flat and frizzed. My face felt like it was coated with vegetable oil. My summer suit was damp and crumpled. It was definitely time to go home. But as I was heading for the door, I picked up my ringing phone. My life began to unravel with one question:

"Hi, wanna go forking?" It was a woman's voice, with a smoky whiskey-and-cigarettes sound.

"Who *is* this?" I said. Did she say forking? Was that something obscene?

"You don't know me," she said.

"Certainly not well enough for what you proposed."

"It's not what you think," she said. Her laugh sounded like it had been rubbed with sandpaper, but it was oddly pleasant. "My name's Margie and I live in your neighborhood."

Forking, she swore, was the latest city fad. "You have to see it to believe it," Margie said. She wanted to show me. Margie sounded harmless. I'd have an easy column if I could be at her house on North Dakota Place, which was only two blocks from where I lived, by eight o'clock. I called Lyle, the man I almost live with, and canceled dinner for the second time this week. He didn't seem too unhappy. That should have made me suspicious, but I was eager to get to Margie's.

The heat hit me in the face when I walked out of the *Gazette*, but considering the rundown area, I was lucky that's all that hit me. The drive was so short, the car barely cooled off before I got home. I parked Ralph, my blue Jaguar, and walked over to Margie's street.

North Dakota Place was an almost grand boulevard, off not–so–Grand Avenue. A hundred years ago it had been one of the city's handsomest streets, on a par with Flora Place or Utah Place. The South Side of St. Louis was the blue-collar part of town, the old German section, the home of the Anheuser-Busch brewery. South Side places were not as extravagant as the West End private streets. They featured large homes rather than mansions. But they had been beautifully built by German craftsmen. Margie's house on North Dakota Place was typical. It was sturdy red brick and white stone with a gray slate roof. The stone porch was as big as a bungalow. I climbed Margie's stone steps, and pressed the old-fashioned brass doorbell. Margie answered on the first ring. Inside, the foyer was flooded with fiery golden light from a red-and-gold stained-glass window. It was twenty feet tall with a surreal tulip-and-peacock design, a turn-of the-century opium dream. The wide oak staircase had mellowed to a rich honey gold. Margie had piled the parson's seat with green velvet pillows that I'd seen on sale at Pier 1 Imports. In the large room off the foyer, I caught a glimpse of a dark fireplace mantel with hunter green tile, green paisley wallpaper, and a coffered ceiling.

I could also see that plants and clever picture arrangements were trying to hide wallpaper that was faded and peeling. The white molding needed paint, and there wasn't quite enough furniture to fill the vast room. Like most people on North Dakota Place, Margie had a little too much house and not quite enough money. I'd bet she was rehabbing the place one room at a time, and from the size of it, she had years of work ahead of her.

But Margie looked cheerful. She seemed to enjoy the challenge of being a rehabber. In St. Louis, that word meant more than someone who remodeled old homes. Most people associated rehabbing with saving someone from drugs or alcohol. St. Louis rehabbers saved houses. The city had some of the loveliest, and most unappreciated, architecture in the country. Few other cities let ordinary people live in such low-cost stately homes. Too bad the old homes were being torn down by the score in St. Louis. Each house saved became a small, personal victory. Rehabbers saved the city one home at a time. We needed more of them.

Margie was a big-boned, comfortable woman of forty or so, who looked at home in jeans and T-shirts. She combed her well-cut, shiny brown hair straight back, which emphasized her wide green eyes. She looked attractive and easygoing.

Forking, she explained, in that raspy voice I thought was so intriguing, meant covering a lawn with hundreds of white plastic forks, tines up.

"Why would anyone want to do that?" I asked.

"You have to see it to understand," she said. "That's why I called you."

She introduced me to her two helpers, Dina and Patricia. Patricia was tall and lean, with straight, smooth dark hair and serious eyes the color of new blue jeans. She sold what Margie called "earth-friendly products" out of her home, so I wasn't surprised that her T-shirt said "Earth Day 1997." She carried a beige canvas bag from a health food store filled with white plastic forks.

Dina was just the opposite: small, round, blond, and friendly. But I didn't want to underestimate her. Under that soft manner was one smart woman. She ran a successful PR consulting company out of her home on North Dakota Place. Dina had the professional woman's haircut, a soft wedge, that would have gone perfectly with a tailored suit. But she was wearing a "Love me, love my cat" T-shirt.

"How late are we going to be?" she said. "Stan likes to be fed at eight-thirty."

"Is Stan your husband?" I asked, wondering why a woman with so much going for her would be married to such a tyrant.

Margie laughed, a brash barroom bray, and said, "Stan's her cat. If Dina waited on men the way she waits on that hairy beast, she could have ten husbands."

Dina didn't seem offended by Margie's remark. "One husband was enough for me," she said. "I got rid of him for tomcatting, then got the real thing. My man Stan is handsome, affectionate, and intelligent. He never comes home drunk and never leaves the lid up on the toilet seat. He likes his dinner on time, but all I do is open a can. Couldn't serve meals like that to my ex." Dina went to a round inlaid table in the foyer and examined an Art Nouveau vase in a glimmering sea green and silver. "This is lovely," she said reverently. "How much?"

"Fifteen hundred, and it's a steal at that," said Margie.

"Is it now?" Dina said dryly. I stood there, puzzled, wondering why this Dina woman was asking the price of something in Margie's home.

"I'm a picker," Margie said to me. "I go to junk shops, estate sales, and garage sales and look for bargains to sell to antique shops. Sometimes I find things I especially love and keep them for a while, but they're all for sale to my friends."

As we walked to Kathy's house, a few doors away, Margie explained their mission. "We're going to fork Kathy's house for her thirtieth birthday. Her husband Dale says he'll keep Kathy out until eight-thirty tonight. Wait till you meet them. They're rehabbing that whole house themselves and they're adorable. Fortunately, they have a small lawn, and it rained yesterday, so the ground is soft. Plus I bought plastic forks with pointed ends. They're easier to stick in the ground than flat-end forks. We can put two hundred forks in a lawn in ten minutes. We'll do this job quick."

"I like a quick fork," Dina giggled.

Kathy's lawn looked small, about the size of a living room carpet. But it seemed bigger when you were about to fill it with forks. Good thing a rose garden took up lots of room near the porch. Patricia opened the beige bag and gave the other two women a big bundle of white plastic forks. They each took a section of the yard. Margie got into a squat and systematically planted the forks about eight inches apart. Round, fluffy Dina did an efficient duckwalk, leaving rows of forks in her wake. Tall, thin Patricia bent at an awkward angle that hurt my back to watch. If you asked me, the woman in the Earth Day T-shirt should get closer to the earth. But I had to admit her method worked. The yard was quickly filling with white forks. The effect was eerie. The forks looked naked and needy in the lush grass, their long sunset shadows reaching out for us.

"The ghost of picnics past," Margie intoned.

"Don't you think all those forks should be topped with marshmallows, or dipped in some colorful paint?" Dina asked.

I thought they looked more haunting the way they were, white and empty.

"Try it," said Patricia, and gave me a handful of forks.

"I should fork around to get an idea of what it's like," I said. I put my reporter's notepad on the front steps, knelt in the damp grass near the rose garden, and felt a run open in my panty hose and go all the way up my leg. Oh, well, I never liked that color anyway. I broke one fork on the tough roots of Kathy's zoysia grass. But once I got the hang of it, forking was strangely satisfying. I liked shoving forks in the dirt, feeling the sharp snap of the grass roots. Weird. Very weird. I did two rows in the time it took the others to do ten. Patricia even had time to stop and give me a lecture. "The good thing about forking is it's recyclable," she said. Somehow, I knew her fun would be politically correct. "You can remove all the forks and use them again. We'll come back tomorrow night and take these out, then fork someone else's lawn."

"A friend's lawn," Dina said. "We don't fork strangers."

By eight-thirty P.M. we were finished. We stood back, admiring our handiwork in the gathering dusk. The effect was oddly eerie, as if the earth were hungry. If this was New York, some performance artist would charge thousands to fork a lawn. In St. Louis, we forked it over for free, for the sheer joy of doing something wacky.

A battered blue pickup truck pulled up in front of the house. It was a typical rehabber's truck with dented doors and a cracked side window repaired with masking tape. The truck bed was littered with paint cans, White Castle bags, paint-speckled wooden window screens, and drywall scraps. A youngish couple got out. She laughed at something he said, and he grabbed her around the waist and kissed her on the lips.

"That's Dale and Kathy," said Dina.

Both had khaki shorts, white shirts, and caramel-colored hair draped over their eyes. Their eyes were a dark brown, like chocolate syrup, and they looked so innocent and trusting, I wanted to sell them ocean-front real estate in Arizona.

"What's on our lawn?" said Kathy, running forward for a closer look. "Dale! We've been forked. I've heard about this. Awesome! What a great birthday this is! Dale bought me a Dremel Multi-Pro and took me to Ted Drewes," she said, "and now this."

I knew Ted Drewes was St. Louis's favorite frozen custard stand. But I had no idea what a Dremel Multi-Pro was.

"It's like a Swiss Army knife for rehabbers," Kathy explained. "It has all these cool attachments you can pop on, drill bits and cutters and sanders and, best of all, a wire brush." She said it in a breathy voice, as if it was every woman's desire. With anyone but this clean-cut couple, I would have evil visions of things to do with a motorized wire brush. But they were so innocent, they still had zits. No, what were those little red spots? Measles? They couldn't be that young. Whatever those red dots on their faces and arms were, I hoped they weren't catching.

Margie recognized the symptoms immediately. "You've been stripping woodwork, haven't you?" she said. "I told you both to wear long sleeves, gloves, and something over your face. That stripping compound is acid, and it splashes everywhere. Look what it's done to your skin."

"It's too hot for all that," Kathy said. "We can't close the windows and put on the air conditioning when we use woodstripper—it's too dangerous. Besides, the spots go away in a few days, and I think we look kind of cute with matching spots."

They did, too. "You have to come see our house," Kathy said to me, when we were introduced. "We still have a lot of work to do, but it's a wonderful old home with stained glass and an antique mahogany fireplace and—"

"And antique wiring and plumbing and really old plaster," her husband said with a grin, but he recited these defects as if they were desirable.

It was hard for Kathy to stand still for long. She danced around the edge of the yard, backed up for a better look at the forks, came in closer to examine a row. She was in constant motion, like an enchanted creature. Just like one, she made a wish.

"I love my forks," she said. "I wish I could keep them here forever."

The spell was broken by a deep, harsh voice demanding "How long are those plastic things going to be in that lawn?"

"It's the witch!" said Dale and Kathy, and fled into their house.

Margie and Dina made sour faces when they heard the voice. Patricia looked distressed. Margie rasped, "Relax, Caroline, the forks will be gone in twenty-four hours." All I could see in the lengthening shadows was a woman with her hands on her hips. Every line of her chunky body expressed outrage.

She spoke slowly and deliberately. "I hope so," she said. "I have a group of West County real estate agents coming to look at my showcase houses the day after tomorrow, and I wouldn't want them to see this. They might think we're . . ."

"Interesting?" Margie asked, snidely.

"I'm fighting a battle here," Caroline said, marching forward. "It took me months to get these realtors into the city. You know they won't come to this neighborhood. Now when I've finally arranged it, you've done this."

"I said the forks would be gone, Caroline," Margie said impatiently.

"We'll fork them over when the tines are right," Dina said, unable to control her hopeless punning.

"Go ahead and laugh," Caroline said. "You'll thank me when property values go up. I'm trying to be serious."

She was fully visible now in the dying light. So this was Caroline the Rehab Wonderwoman. At least, that was what her friends called her. I'd seen her around the neighborhood, but only from a distance. That's how Caroline kept most people—at a distance. Unless she wanted something. But I knew about her. Everyone did. Caroline was the subject of countless adoring profiles in the *Gazette* and the city magazines. The neighbors hooted at the inflated prices Caroline claimed to command for her houses in those stories. But we had to admit Caroline was good for property values. She always looked serious, or as serious as you can look in paint-stained cutoffs, a floppy straw sunhat, and a stretched T-shirt. Caroline was thirty-something, with short, cropped dark hair, thick eyebrows, a large, sunburned nose, and beat-up work boots. She was a short, muscular woman who made me feel that fashion was for the frivolous. I tried to remember what I'd read about her and heard from neighborhood gossip.

I knew Caroline was divorced with no children. Her ex-husband, a lawyer, complained that Caroline took him for every last cent. I certainly hoped so. I never had much sympathy for lawyers. At any rate, Caroline seemed to have an endless supply of money. She lived in a grand house on North Dakota that looked like a centerfold from *Architectural Digest*. Unlike most homes in the area, hers was completely rehabbed, from the expensive slate roof to the refinished hardwood floors. There was plenty of furniture, too, pricey pieces from Milan that looked like wire-and-stick sculptures. The chairs and couches were striking to look at, but neighbors complained they hurt your backside if you sat in them during one of Caroline's interminable improvement association meetings. The walls were decorated with a colorful Klee and other names usually seen in art museums. It was a showcase house in a hopeful but down-at-heels neighborhood. To protect her fine rehabbed house, Caroline bought houses up and down North Dakota Place as if she was playing Monopoly and rehabbed them. And to protect her investments on North Dakota, she started buying up houses and flats on the surrounding streets and rehabbed them. Then to protect those investments, she bought the flats and houses behind them. It was a never-ending process. The neighbors were pleased. They repeated, like a mantra, "Caroline has done a lot for the neighborhood."

For one thing, she restored the angels of North Dakota Place. A hundred years ago the street was a showplace for the city's prosperous German doctors and lawyers. The families lucky enough to live there looked out their wide wainscoted windows at a fountain in the center of the boulevard. Beaux Arts angels held an

Or, since she lived with Stan, maybe it was cattiness. Tall, serious Patricia shifted uneasily but said nothing.

"*Caroline* walks up and down the streets and points out our flaws for us," Margie said, sneering the woman's name each time she said it. "*Caroline* took it upon herself to tell her neighbor Mack it was time to mow his lawn."

"Mack needed to be reminded," Caroline said stiffly.

"*Caroline* took it upon herself to tell Sally her boyfriend was not allowed to park his pickup in front of her house," Margie said.

"It looked bad," said Caroline.

"The next time he did it, he got a twenty-dollar ticket. And he quit seeing Sally."

"He wasn't the sort of person we want on this street, anyway," Caroline said. "And Kathy and Dale better move that beat-up truck around back before *they* get a ticket."

"You must be really proud of your work with Mrs. Grumbacher," Margie said. "What is she, eighty? Ninety? *Caroline* sicced the city inspector on that poor old woman."

"She's a vigorous seventy-five," Caroline said. "And there's nothing poor about her. Her late husband left her quite well-fixed."

"*Caroline* pointed out that the wooden trim was peeling on Mrs. Grumbacher's house," Margie said. "Mrs. Grumbacher told Caroline to go to hell, she wasn't painting anything this year. Two days later the city inspector was all over Mrs. Grumbacher's house like white on rice, finding this violation and that one. She had to get a new roof, new gutters, new concrete steps, and a new wrought-iron railing."

"That railing was for her own safety," Caroline said righteously. "The gutters and steps should have been done years ago. And nobody would have called the city inspector if she'd just painted her trim."

"You mean *you* wouldn't have called the city inspector," Margie said. "By the time the city finished with her, it would have been cheaper if Mrs. Grumbacher had had Rembrandt paint the place."

Margie raked Caroline with the ultimate South Side weapon, the glare. A full-bore glare could make a grown man shrivel like cheap bacon in hot fat. Caroline didn't flinch. The two strong women locked eyes and sent out laser strikes of hate, like alien starships.

Tall, thin Patricia slipped between the furious women and bravely tried to give Margie's incendiary facts another interpretation.

"Caroline's done a lot for the neighborhood," she said, defending Caroline with the same thing everyone said. Patricia's sticklike form vibrated with anxiety. "Mrs. Grumbacher was old but tightfisted. She could afford to do a little repair work. It improved the appearance of the street so much."

Patricia's courageous move didn't work. Margie continued talking as if Patricia were invisible. "After that," Margie rasped, "when *Caroline* made a suggestion, the neighbors did it, because no matter how expensive it seemed up front, it was cheaper than what a city inspector would do to you."

But Caroline had quit paying attention to Margie. She was peering into the purple dusk at a house two doors down from Kathy's. Suddenly she screamed, "Otto, what are you doing!?" and ran toward the house, her stocky body shaking with anger.

"Something awful, I'm sure," Margie murmured. "Do you know him?"

I shook my head no.

"Otto Bumbaw is the only person on North Dakota Place who stands up to Caroline," Margie explained. "He's a City Hall worker who lives in a big old house that used to belong to his mother. She's been dead for years. Otto lives alone with his yappy little dog, Hansie, a miserable animal that's part Schnauzer and part Scottie."

"And ugly all over," interrupted Dina, but with the cats frolicking on her chest, I knew this was a biased opinion.

"With a piercing bark," Margie confirmed. "Otto let his house repairs slide. Caroline's threats to complain to City Hall didn't bother him. He's worked there for more than thirty years. I don't know exactly what he does for a living, but he seems to know all the city inspectors. City Hall would never touch him."

"But even Otto had to recognize that his place was falling down," Dina said. "If he didn't do something soon, he'd live in a leaky house."

"Caroline keeps up a constant campaign of harassment," Margie said.

"Oh, I wouldn't call it harassment exactly," Patricia said, mildly.

"I would," Margie said. "Otto can't step outside without running into the woman. Look how she acted now. Maybe she can't complain to the city and get anywhere, but she can complain to Otto. And she did. The man can't leave the house without Caroline stopping him. If he sits in a lawn chair in his yard, she'll march right up to the fence and say 'Otto, this house is a disgrace. What would your mother say?'

"'Nothing. She's dead,' Otto always growls, and chomps on his big smelly cigar. Hansie, that nasty little dog, yaps nonstop but Caroline talks right over it. Not that Otto ever listens."

"Yesterday she finally made some headway," Patricia said proudly.

"Well, I'll give her that much. She did seem to get through to him with that last lecture," Margie said.

"What did she say?" Dina asked, as curious as any cat.

"I happened to be walking down the street . . ." Margie said.

Dina snorted in disbelief. "Come on, 'fess up, you were lurking around listening."

"Whatever," Margie said. "I heard it. 'Your mother was house proud,' Caroline said to him, appealing to the memory of the one woman Otto respected. 'When she was alive her home never looked like this. You need to have the bricks tuckpointed, Otto. The paint is peeling off your windowsills. Your gutters and porch trim should be painted, too. And you still have your Christmas lights up. In June. Otto, how could you?'

"Otto hung his head. For once, one of Caroline's lectures seemed to have hit home, if you'll pardon the pun. 'Okay, okay,' he said to her. 'I'll paint the damn thing. But you gotta promise, if I paint it, you'll shut your nagging and let me enjoy my yard in peace.'

" 'It's a deal, Otto,' she said, and stuck out her hand. He shook it solemnly. I saw it with my own eyes. That was yesterday. This morning Otto came back with his old beige Plymouth loaded up with paint cans, brushes, rollers, drop cloths, and other supplies, which he unloaded and left in the yard. The whole street waited for him to begin painting. I spent the day sneaking peeks through my miniblinds. Nothing—until Caroline came out for her evening Pretty-up Patrol. He must want her to see him doing his historic paint job."

"Caroline is patient but persuasive," Patricia said admiringly.

"She wears you down like water on a stone," Margie said.

"I think she's come up against that rockhead Otto now," Dina said. "Listen to the two of them fighting."

The shouts and angry screams all seemed to be coming from Caroline. We walked over for a closer look, not bothering to hide our curiosity. Caroline and

Otto weren't punching each other out, but they were squared off like a couple of prizefighters. Caroline looked ready to hit Otto at any time. He looked like he was enjoying himself. He was sloppy fat, with a Friar Tuck fringe of black-gray hair, baggy pants, and a beer gut. He'd set up two tall aluminum ladders on the side of his house, then spread paint cans, rollers, and brushes all over the ground.

Otto was painting—not the trim but the brick itself. This was a cheapskate solution some city people used to avoid expensive tuckpointing. But they usually painted the brick either brick red, a tasteful white, or soft gray. Otto was painting the bricks with huge swipes of color, and it was the most godawful shade of purple you'd ever see. Heliotrope, I guess it was. He was turning the gently timeworn house into a three-story heliotrope heap. It would knock the heck out of any plans to sell North Dakota Place as a street for the elite. No matter how many flowers and angel fountains it had, the street would have that huge pulsating purple eyesore. It would be a local laughingstock, and Caroline's dreams would be dead. He'd painted only a few feet of brick when Caroline came roaring over. Now her dark hair was flapping like wings and her face was a dangerous red.

"Otto!" she screamed. *"What are you doing!!!!"*

"Painting my house, the way you wanted me to," he said sweetly.

"Not that color!" she wailed.

"You never told me what color to paint," Otto said, and shrugged. "And we agreed, if I painted the house, you'd shut up. Well, I'm painting, so shut up."

Caroline's mouth gaped open, like a beached fish, but no sound came out.

"But you'll probably want to know my plans," he said. "I can't get much of a start on the bricks tonight, but I wanted you to see what it would look like. Next

I'll start the trim and gutter work. I'm going to make the gutters turquoise. I think they'll look real nice with my turquoise Christmas lights. Set them off. Should look real pretty for your real estate ladies."

Otto had perfectly calculated which parts of the house would be seen first when the West County real estate agents rolled down the street. They'd get an eyeful of purple and turquoise, ugly as a bruise.

Caroline said nothing. She turned on her heel and walked back toward her house.

"Probably going to call her lawyer," Margie said. "He does all her dirty work for her."

"Too bad Otto's paint job will ruin my property values, too," Dina said. "Otherwise, I'd be in favor of it. Caroline needs to be taken down a notch."

"She's done a lot for the neighborhood," said Patricia, who believed in recycling the local mantra.

"But she doesn't own it," Margie said, with more bitterness than I expected.

My evening, which began in such good humor, was ending in an ugly mood. It was time to leave. I thanked Margie for the story and started to walk back home. I checked my watch. It was a little after nine. I'd canceled dinner with Lyle earlier. Now I wished I hadn't. I felt so lonely. Maybe it wasn't too late to see him tonight. I dropped my things at home and called him. Lyle wasn't at the university or at his house. He'd found a way to spend the evening without me. I was too tired to fix dinner and too restless to stay home. I wandered over to my favorite Thai restaurant, the King and I, on South Grand. I loved the rich colors of the booths and walls, and the little golden shrine to Buddha on the wall. I had pad Thai noodles with pork. Delicious. I had a table by the window, and I watched the people going by. There was an Asian woman in black pajamas, a gay couple with their hands almost touching, and a pot-bellied man walking an equally pot-bellied pig. They proceeded at a stately pace, bellies swaying together. Lord, I loved this neighborhood. I wasn't sure what my German grandparents would make of the newcomers . . . yes, I did. They'd treat them the same way as the other older Germans. As long as you cut your grass and kept up your property, they'd tolerate you. That's why we had so many gays here. The toleration stopped where the paint and the weeds started.

My good mood was restored. I started walking home, taking the shortcut down the alley. Some would say that was stupid, but the alley was brightly lit, especially since the building next door had been torn down and made into that St. Louis architectural specialty, the parking lot. The old Ritz theater used to be there, and I missed it. I'd seen my favorite movie there, *The Attack of the Killer Tomatoes*.

The parking lot didn't have the entertainment value of the old movie theater, but it added several rows of much-needed metered spaces. Even late at night there were still cars in the lot, and one blue minivan, almost out of sight, near the Dumpster by the alley exit. Hmm. What was that odd movement? It looked like the van was bouncing up and down. Was there a small earthquake or something? I walked over in that direction. Bounce. Bounce. Bounce. Bounce-bounce-bounce. Omigod. I was slow, but I finally figured out what had the springs rocking in the minivan. I should back away and give the lovers a little privacy. Must be an extracurricular married couple. The minivan was a little middle aged for courting kids to use. There was no way to tell whose it was. Blue minivans were as common as dirt. There must be half a dozen driven by staff members at work alone. Even Charlie, the *Gazette*'s managing editor, drove his wife's to work sometimes, when his car was in the shop. Wait. Didn't this one have the orange Gazette parking-lot sticker on the bumper?

I moved in for a closer look. It did. It was someone from the *Gazette*, taking a late-night quickie in my neighborhood. But who could it be? The *Gazette* crowd stayed in the richer, older suburbs of Kirkwood and Webster Groves, or behind the gilded gates of the mon-eyed Central West End. They didn't bother with low-rent South St. Louis. That's why I lived there.

The van had stopped bouncing some time ago. I backed up behind the Dumpster and tried not to breathe in the rotting garbage aroma. I had to see who was stepping out. At that moment the side door slid open and out stepped Charlie, our managing editor, like a weasel popping out of a burrow. The little weasel was buckling his belt and straightening his tie. I should have known. That man changed girlfriends the way you changed socks. I wondered how his wife felt about his unfaithfulness. After sizing up Charlie's ever-expanding beer gut and bald spot, I decided she must be grateful. Most of his conquests were ambitious young reporters, who lowered themselves to sleep with Charlie, then rose to new heights at the *Gazette*. The affairs never lasted long, but they always gave the young reporter a leg up at the paper. Oh, dear, that didn't sound right. But before I could find a better phrase, Charlie put out his hand to help his inamorata out of the minivan.

"Here, Cupcake," he said, his voice as mushy as the Dumpster contents.

Cupcake? Charlie never used terms of endearment for the women he bedded. He'd called them "sleeping bags" in my hearing. Lord knows what he said about them when he was drinking with the guys at the Last Word, the newspaper bar. But now he sounded almost reverent and grateful. The arrogant Charlie grateful?

To a mere woman? Who was this temptress? Now I had to see her.

The streetlights revealed that she was short, no more than five feet, with a wide bottom, a flat chest, and narrow, sloping shoulders. She ran her fingers through her soft, shoulder-length curly hair, and fear clutched my heart. Was it red hair? Please, please say it wasn't. The parking lot's mercury vapor lights bleached the color out of everything. Then her small white hands began tying a pussycat bow under her chin. There was only one person at the *Gazette* who still wore that old yuppie emblem. Dear God, it was her. Charlie was having a fling with Nadia "Nails" Noonin! She earned her nickname because she was "hard as," not for her fingernails, which were bitten to the quick. "Give me just a sec, Dimpletoes," she said.

Dimpletoes? She called Charlie Dimpletoes? I could see Charlie puff out his chest. Uh-oh. After two decades of mindless skirt-chasing, Charlie sounded seriously smitten. I almost felt sorry for the lovers, trysting in such a tawdry spot. But what choice did Charlie have? He was married. He couldn't take her to his house. Motel bills would show up on his credit cards. Large amounts of cash would have to be explained at home. Three staffers lived near Nadia, which meant Charlie would be spotted there. Charlie couldn't keep a love nest in my neighborhood, either. The neighbors watched everyone and everything. They'd recognize him in a minute.

Nails didn't seem to mind. She stepped out of the minivan like a star emerging from her private trailer. In a strange way, the match made sense. It was as if you'd fixed up Jack the Ripper with Lucretia Borgia on a blind date. I was tempted to congratulate them, but the last thing I needed was for Charlie and Nails to know I'd witnessed their duet as Cupcake and Dimpletoes. I stepped farther back into the smelly shadows of the Dumpster and kicked a soda can. It sounded like I'd overturned the Pepsi plant. They looked up, a pair of startled predators. And saw me. "Hi, Charlie," I said politely. "Hi, Na—Nadia." I'd almost said Nails. Well, better she should think I stuttered.

"In the trash as usual," Nails sneered. "Looking for column material? Or yesterday's column?"

I was trying to think of an appropriately snide retort when Charlie stepped in smoothly with "I was just taking Nadia for a little ride around the neighborhood. To show her some things she's never seen before."

"Oh, I'm sure she's seen them," I said. Love must have melted his brain. Charlie was better at cover-ups than this. But he kept fumbling around like a teenager.

"I mean the South Side," he snapped.

"Me, too. Good night, Charlie. Night, Nadia." I sauntered down the alley, which was dangerous, but not as dangerous as what I'd just done. I'd better enjoy this moment, because the rest of the summer was going to be hell. Nails would not forget this encounter.

2

I woke up to sirens screaming past my flat at seven A.M. I ran to the window. A fire truck was roaring down the street, fast and furious as a charging rhino. Two police cars, their sirens echoing off the brick walls, followed. If that wasn't enough noise, the fire truck let go with a window-rattling blast of its air horn. That brought out Mrs. Gruenloh, three doors down, in a blue seersucker robe. Good heavens. Her gray hair was bristling with Spoolies, those pink rubber curlers that folded down on themselves. I hadn't seen them since I was a kid, but I still remembered how much they hurt. Mrs. G. must be a masochist. I quit wondering about her pain threshold when a third police car screamed down the street. Something seriously bad had happened. I threw on some jeans, sandals, and a shirt. As I ran down my front stairs, I could see the EMS ambulance, with more flashing lights and sirens. I ran after it.

They were all on North Dakota Place, at Otto's house. The police and emergency vehicles were parked as if a careless child had dropped them. The medics were trying to revive Otto. I could see them working on his fat, rubbery body, but it seemed useless. Otto was an odd gray-green. He clashed horribly with the purple house paint. His little dog, an ugly black imp, was yapping so hard it was almost bouncing in the air, but no one paid any attention. One of Otto's ladders was up against the house. The other was sprawled out on the ground, along with Otto and a spilled bucket of purple paint. It looked like Otto had had a heart attack. I wasn't surprised. The beer cans and cigar butts littering the yard proclaimed Otto was no heart association poster child.

The North Dakota Place neighbors were clustered together on the sidewalk. Dina the punster was wearing striped Kliban cat pajamas and carrying a matching striped cat. Jeez, that woman even accessorized her sleepwear. That must be her man, Stan. He was a handsome dog, if I can say that about a cat.

Patricia, the tall drink of water, was wearing a navy T-shirt that made her dark blue eyes look like huge blue lakes. Today her shirt said she was saving wetlands waterfowl. Caroline the Rehab Wonderwoman was pushing her usual wheelbarrow. This one was loaded with dead leaves. Her paint-splotched cutoffs and stretched T-shirt looked like the same ones she wore last night. Maybe she never stopped working.

Margie was in an egg-stained pink cotton bathrobe, carrying the *Gazette* she must have just picked off her lawn. She moved very carefully, as if it hurt to walk. Her brown hair needed a wash, and she looked like she needed her morning coffee. I grew up with drunks and thought I recognized a hangover. Maybe whiskey really did give her voice that sexy rasp. By this time the EMS crew had loaded Otto into the ambulance. They drove off with their lights flashing and sirens howling. Hansie, the ugly little dog, added his own howl, a single sad note that made the hair stand up on the back of my neck. None of us expected to see Otto alive again.

Dina had no puns for this occasion. "Otto was a slob and a troublemaker," she said, and looked solemn, even with Stan under her arm and cats cavorting on her pajamas.

"I don't think anyone will miss him," Margie said. "I certainly won't."

"Maybe now we'll get a nice couple in Otto's house," Caroline said, parking her wheelbarrow in the middle of the sidewalk. She was almost chatty. "His passing will do a lot of good for the neighborhood."

"Does he have any relatives?" I asked. I had visions of fat, rude junior Ottos polluting the neighborhood with more cigars and noisy dogs.

"Just a grown nephew who lives in Columbia," Caroline answered. "Richard is a tenured professor at the University of Missouri. He'll stay there. He's not interested in uprooting himself a hundred and twenty miles to St. Louis."

Caroline seemed surprisingly well informed about her old enemy. But before I could ask how she knew all this, both she and Margie said, "Look at that!" and pointed in different directions. I followed Margie's pointing finger to a glorious sight: a muscular male jogger, glistening with sweat and wearing the briefest possible running shorts. He glided straight down the grassy boulevard. I thought he looked like Daniel Day-Lewis in the opening scene of *The Last of the Mohicans*.

So did Dina. "Holy Hawkeye," she said, almost dropping Stan in her excitement. The perfect man gets dumped for the perfect bod every time. "That's why God made running clothes." The jogger was a dead ringer for Hawkeye, right down to the perky pecs and long dark hair. All he needed was a loincloth. Or maybe not. He'd upped the local temperature enough in this outfit.

"Is he gay?" the practical Margie rasped. She wasn't going to waste her time admiring a man who couldn't ask her for a date.

"That is an offensive question," Patricia said. I took another look at her. I'd considered her scrawny and rather plain, except for those startling blue eyes. But now I saw how pretty she was. Her cheeks were flushed pink, and her mouth was as moist as a lipstick ad. She seemed slender and fit rather than stringy. Then it dawned on my morning-fogged brain: Patricia had a major crush on this man.

"He comes by here at exactly eight o'clock every morning," she said, checking her watch as if he were the incoming Metroliner. "He runs five miles a day and takes the same route through the neighborhood. He's into recycling, holistic medicine, and natural foods. He gave me excellent advice about a whey protein drink."

"I like mine shaken, not stirred," Margie rasped.

"Whey to go, Hawkeye Hunk," Dina punned. Her cat Stan squirmed.

"You are both too silly to have a serious discussion," Patricia sniffed, and waved to the jogger, who slowed down to talk to her. He looked very serious. She looked very happy.

Caroline sounded unhappy and angry. We turned in her direction, now that the distraction of the jogger had run its course. A muscular young black man in baggy gang clothes was shouting "You talkin' to me, bitch?"

"I am," Caroline yelled. "How can you sell that poison to your own people? You are destroying your race. Get off my street."

"You don't own this street, bitch," the menacing young man snarled.

"Fat lot he knows," Margie muttered, but she ran over and grabbed Caroline by the arm. "Come along, Caroline, we've already called the police," she lied. By the time Margie tugged at Caroline's arm the second time, the young man had melted down the street and was lost in the shadows of the angel fountain, a devil hiding among the angels.

"He was selling crack on my street. In broad daylight. To another young black man, who ran off when I shouted at them," the outraged Caroline said.

"So call the police," Margie said. "If you get shot, what will it do to property values?" she added wickedly. Patricia gave her a dirty look. Dina held Stan closer. He struggled to get away, and I didn't blame him.

"The police won't do anything," Caroline fumed. "By the time they get here, he'll be gone. They know where he lives and where he operates. They have to. *I* know."

"Where?" I interrupted. Inquiring minds had to know.

"The first brick rowhouse on Ratley Street," she said.

"How do you know?" I asked.

"He's running a drive-up operation," Caroline said in a superior tone. The semi-friendly Rehab Wonderwoman was gone. She couldn't bother hiding her contempt at my ignorance. "Drive by there any night after midnight and you'll see him in action. He's using underage kids as runners to the cars, taking orders and money and delivering the drugs. He has everything but kids behind the counter asking 'May I help you?' "

"McDrug," Dina chirped.

"Why don't the neighbors complain to the cops?" Margie asked. I thought it was a reasonable question. Caroline did not.

"On that street? You've got a handful of terrified elderly women, some working couples who are never home, and a boardinghouse for people who are no better than he is. They're probably his customers. If you ask me, somebody ought to clean his house out, the way you'd clean out a nest of cockroaches. I'd crush him the way I'd crush a roach, too," Caroline said, grinding her foot into the grass. Her face was cold and hard. "He is ruining everything, and the courts coddle his kind and let them destroy the city for decent hard-working people."

She looked frightening in her fury. I realized this was the second day in a row I'd seen Caroline pick a fight with someone on North Dakota Place.

"What's he doing up here?" I asked. "He's way off his turf. It's a little early for someone who usually operates at night."

"He's expanding his territory," she said impatiently. "He's going after the shift change at the furniture factory. They drive right by that corner. I don't want him on my street." Caroline didn't say this street. Or our street. My street.

"And it's time I had a talk with that jogger, too," she added sharply. "He's running on the boulevard grass."

"That's what it's for," Margie snapped. She was coming to life at the prospect of a rematch with Caroline: Margie the Mauler against Caroline the Rehab Wonderwoman. "Believe me, Caroline, Hawkeye is part of the beautification program. If I could display his bod in the parkway, I would."

"Not me," Dina said, looking wicked. "I'd take it home and give it a workout in my bedroom gym. Love those pushups."

Patricia flushed but said nothing. Caroline picked up her wheelbarrow and rolled off toward the angel fountain in search of stray sticks and beer cans, but she didn't make it very far before we heard the wheelbarrow thud loudly on the sidewalk. "No! No, no, no!" she cried. I ran over to the other side of the angel fountain, half expecting to see another body. Instead, I saw a crumpled Caroline, making anguished cries, like a new widow in a war-zone news video.

An outraged Margie said, "You're carrying on like that over a tree?"

"Six trees!" Caroline cried. "He broke my trees! My

babies. My babies are dead." The sobs were so heart-broken, they could have been for real children. Dina rolled her eyes. It did seem a melodramatic outburst for six broken saplings.

"For heaven's sake. Get a grip," Dina said. There was nothing soft about her now. "You got those trees free from the city."

"But they were doing so well," Caroline wailed. "Then that no-good . . ."

"How do you know he even did it?" Margie cut in.

Caroline squared off into her fighting stance. "You're defending a drug dealer?" she said. Her rage was frightening. Her whole body trembled.

Margie stayed irritatingly calm. "I'm just trying to find out if he really did the crime."

"When I watered those trees this morning, they were fine," Caroline said. "Not that *you* would notice. All you do is take advantage of my hard work and contribute nothing."

"It's true," Margie said sarcastically. "I'm guilty. I've got a life. No thanks to you," she added mysteriously. I had to admit I was curious about what had happened to the trees, but Otto, the other most likely suspect, had a fairly airtight alibi. So, I said my good-byes to the women, gave the sensible Stan a pat, and left them with the weeping, seething Caroline.

As I headed toward my street, Dale and Kathy came out on their porch. She was wearing the top of a pair of men's striped pajamas. He was wearing the bottom. "What's all the noise?" Kathy asked. "This was the one day we could sleep in."

I told them about Otto's heart attack and Caroline's encounter with the drug dealer.

"That guy is pretty brazen," Dale said. "I've seen him selling in broad daylight."

"C'mon on inside and see our place," Kathy said. "Dale's making coffee. It will just take a minute." I didn't know if she meant the coffee or the house tour, but I wanted something to take the bad taste of this morning out of my mouth. Their house looked like a smaller version of Margie's—red brick with a wide, pillared porch—but it wasn't as well maintained. The porch railing felt rough with rust. The wooden pillars, decorated with leaves and curlicues, were crusted with peeling paint. Kathy must have seen me staring at them. "We'll have to burn that paint off with a blow torch," she said.

"Caroline is pressuring us to do it now," Dale said. "We want to finish some inside projects before we start on the outside."

"But we're afraid she'll call the city on us if we don't start soon," Kathy said. They were so in tune, they finished each other's sentences. "We don't have a lot of money, and we're afraid. She can make real problems for us." Her pretty face looked ready to cry. Dale kissed her neck in a tender way that made me miss Lyle. "We'll be okay," he said to her. "We call Caroline the witch," he said to me.

"But we mean something else," Kathy giggled, her good mood restored by his kiss. She threw open the oak-and-beveled glass front door proudly. Inside was a desolate sight, about a half acre of dull, scratched hardwood floor, crusted with gritty gray plaster dust. The main hall led to a double parlor with pocket doors. I saw a drab, dusty staircase and a crooked doorway leading to a back kitchen, where I heard Dale clattering around with the coffee things. The walls were papered with a depressing gray-and-white scroll design that must have been classy fifty years ago. The brown water stains didn't help.

"Isn't it beautiful?" Kathy sighed.

"Uh. It has great potential," I said. For disaster. For bankruptcy.

"That's what everyone says," Kathy said, looking

pleased. "Just look at that fireplace." I did. The wood had about sixty coats of white enamel. The mantel was covered with coffee rings, foam cups, and soda cans.

"It's mahogany," she said. "The other owners covered it with deck enamel. All we have to do is clean it off."

All? She'd blithely dismissed months of painstaking work. "We're doing the woodwork now," she said, pointing to a four-foot section of stripped wood. There were miles of ugly, brown-painted woodwork, coated with dirt. The main rooms had three pieces of furniture: a dusty black Naugahyde couch decorated with white paint drips, a television on a listing stand, and a pressed-wood coffee table covered with cans of spackle, paint brushes, and paint samples.

"We'll get good furniture when we finish everything," she said. "Right now we're working upstairs. We just love this staircase." The wood looked dingy under its coat of gray dust. My fingers were gritty and gray with dust. But then the shifting sunlight touched the wood, and just for a minute, I saw what Kathy and Dale did: The mellow honey-gold wood glowed in the summer sun. Then the light shifted, and the staircase was once again dingy and depressing. I followed Kathy upstairs, past dark, closed doors, stacks of wallboard, tools, and paint cans. One door was open. It was obviously their bedroom, and the room had been finished. I caught a glimpse of sheer, gauzy curtains, soft yellow candles that had burned low, and a fullblown yellow rose on a bedside table. The bed was scrolled ironwork and the sheets looked rumpled from love. The sight pierced my heart. That could have been my morning, but I'd canceled my time with Lyle and chased ambulances instead. Kathy blushed and pulled the door shut. "Let me show you the bathroom," she said. "We're trying to figure out what to do with it."

The bathroom walls were covered with bright,

blinding blue cabbage roses the size of dinner plates. They looked like some awful tropical fungus. "We think it's wallpaper," she said. "It may be vinyl. It sure is stuck on there."

It was stuck on the clawfoot bathtub, too. The previous owners had covered the outside of the tub with the rank blue cabbage roses and painted the toenails on the clawfeet blue.

"First bathtub I've ever seen with a manicure," I said.

"I was wondering," Kathy said. "Do you know how to get wallpaper off a bathtub?"

I was still laughing when I walked to my flat. Dale's fresh cinnamon decaf sweetened a morning that had started sour. I changed into one of my spiffiest Donna Karan suits. Before I went into the office, I decided to drive by Ratley Street to see the alleged crack house. It was only four blocks—all downhill—from North Dakota Place to Ratley Street. Ratley looked like a handsome man invaded by cancer. The street was deathly silent. Not even birds sang. Caroline said the drug house was the first rowhouse. It was a nasty place, with a weedy front yard fenced with rusty chain link. A little alley ran alongside the building, making it easier for the dealer to do business. The unpainted plywood front door had burglar bars, and there were more bars on all the first-floor windows. Evidently the owner had never heard the term "second-story man." He didn't believe burglars could climb to the second floor. The basement windows were boarded. A rusty FOR SALE sign dangled by one hook from a post. I looked at the sign and saw the real estate agent's name. I knew that woman. Poor Tracy McCreery. She was new to the company and got the worst listings. No one in their right mind would ever buy this place.

The rooming house next door was just as bad.

Dingy curtains flapped out of the open, unscreened windows. The yard was a depressing mess of uncut crabgrass and chickweed. The only lawn decoration was a seatless toilet, with a tire leaning on it. On the front porch was a beige couch with ripped upholstery. The farther away the houses were from these two eyesores, the better they looked. By the other end of the street, there were little pots of geraniums and concrete birdbaths in the yards, and I could see how Ratley Street used to look. I shook my head at the sorry sight and left.

I had half a mind to skip breakfast at Uncle Bob's Pancake House, since I'd already had coffee, but I didn't go there for the food, anyway. I didn't like to admit, even to myself, that Uncle Bob's was my refuge. It was my office away from the *Gazette*, and readers knew they could find me there most mornings. The waitresses even took messages for me, and they were more efficient than our department secretary. Uncle Bob's was a good source for juicy city scandals. The police, the city workers, the city attorneys, and the people they plea bargained all ate there. By the time I sat down in a booth, Marlene the waitress was waiting with my usual. About eight years ago I'd ordered one egg scrambled and wheat toast. That became my permanent breakfast, for better or worse. But along with the skimpy food came a generous serving of gossip.

"Your boss Charlie was in last night with another of his cookies," Marlene said, holding two pots of hot coffee and pouring the decaf into my cup. She has wrists a tennis player would envy.

"Short? Red-haired? Has a pussycat bow?" I said.

"And a snippy attitude," Marlene said. "Charlie's brought in some doozies before, but this one was the limit. That woman expected to be waited on like the Queen of Sheba. Sat on her fat ass—I should talk, but at least mine is in proportion to the rest of me—and pointed at me and then at her cup when she wanted more coffee. Didn't even deign to say 'Waitress.'"

"That's Nails. This is bad news. I think he's serious about this one, Marlene."

"I think he is, too. He's got that look. People in my profession always know when someone is cheating," she said.

"No offense, but it wouldn't take a genius to figure out Charlie was up to something," I said, waving a piece of wheat toast at her.

"Yeah, but a lot of folks fooling around think they're clever. We always know. Even if a cheating couple is just having lunch, I can tell."

"You don't believe in a business lunch?" I asked.

"Of course. But monkey business looks different from business. People at business lunches bring brief-cases. At the very least, they have a notebook or an agenda. But it's more than that. There's a pattern of behavior. Cheating couples always arrive in two cars. Married couples sometimes use separate cars, because they've been working or running errands. Cheating couples never arrive or leave together."

She was warming up to her subject now. She set the coffeepot on my table and began ticking other points off on her fingers. I took notes. This was a column. "Cheating couples sit side by side in a booth. Married couples sit across from each other. Some dating cou-ples sit side by side. But two weeks after they marry, they'll be sitting across from each other.

"Cheating couples hold hands under the table. There's lots of whispering. It's obvious they are sneak-ing around. Charlie and Nails were doing that."

"Smooching, too, I bet."

"You bet wrong," Marlene said. "Cheating couples never kiss in a restaurant. They can explain away lots of things, but not that. The parking lot is another matter. They were going at it hot and heavy in his minivan."

"Again?" I said. If Charlie put that energy into his work, the *Gazette* would be *The New York Times*.

"The busboy saw them fooling around in the front seat. She had his . . ." Marlene looked up and saw two gray-haired members of the St. Philomena Ladies' Sodality staring at her in horror and fascination.

"Coffee, ladies?" Marlene asked. She poured for both and came back to my table. This time, her voice was much lower. "Anyway, they walked into the restaurant, and butter wouldn't melt in their mouths. But the busboy had told everyone what he saw. The staff was sneaking looks at them out the kitchen door."

"Charlie probably thought it was because he was such a famous newspaper editor."

"He sure didn't act ashamed. Oh, well. Sooner or later, Charlie will get his."

"He's getting hers. Now," I said, as Marlene walked away chuckling. I figured deserts, just or otherwise, would be a long time coming for Cupcake and Dimpletoes. Charlie had made Nails queen of the newsroom, and her life was a banquet. She was surrounded by courtiers who laughed at her jokes and brought her juicy tidbits of information. Her chief courtier was Babe, the *Gazette* gossip columnist who had a face like a deceased mackerel, white and haggard from too many late nights at too many unimportant parties. He was skeleton thin and always wore a tux after six, so he looked like Bela Lugosi after the blood banks closed. It was clear from the way Babe was hanging around Nails's desk that she was definitely on his A-list. I guess Babe forgot that only two months ago he always referred to Nails as the Bitch. So I reminded him when I saw him in the *Gazette* offices that morning.

"Oh, Babe," he said, in his mournful lost-calf

voice—that's how he got his nickname, he called everyone Babe—"Nails has changed. She's so much more
. . . more . . ." Sometimes words failed even Babe.

"Powerful?" I said. "Obnoxious?"

"Don't be a bitch," he said. "She could do you some
good."

"She's never done any woman any good," I said.
Babe sidled away, afraid my rebellious thoughts might
contaminate him. Rebellion was in the air. This morning the newsroom was more restless than usual. People were gathered into little whispering groups that
stopped talking when anyone approached. I went over
to Tina's desk. Imagine Whitney Houston at a computer, and you had Tina, our City Hall reporter. The
woman had class and brains. Also, information.
"What's going on?" I asked her.

"This," she said, and shoved a computer printout
under my nose. "Milton found this little memo to
Charlie from Nails. Those two are so busy doing the
wild thing you wonder how she has time to put down
us poor fools who are dumb enough to do the work
here." Tina knew about Charlie and Nails, too? Was I
the last one to find out anything?

"Oooh. Another bitter Gazetteer," I said.

"With reason," Tina said, her tip-tilted eyes brim-
ming with anger. "It's bad enough this place has more
clowns than Ringling Bros. Now we have to know their
opinions."

"Wow. This must be some memo," I said, grinning.

"Wait till you get to the part about *you*," she said.
My smile slipped sideways. I tried to pretend I didn't
care. Like most aging newspapers, the *Gazette* was topheavy with management. It had five editors for every
reporter. Instead of actually putting out the paper, the
editors met to talk about problems, such as staff morale, which to my way of thinking were caused by too
many editors holding meetings—but no one ever asked

me what I thought. Morale had taken another dip a few weeks ago when the Boston publisher came into town and let everyone know there was "too much crime news" in the *Gazette*. He said it was "unnerving the business community," and he wanted crime reporting "deemphasized." The editors read that as "don't give me no bad news." Murders, carjackings, and especially muggings, burglaries, and robberies at major malls went unreported. This led to rumors of cover-ups in the community. On the upside, the publisher wanted increased arts reporting, so St. Louis seemed a lot more gracious and crime-free, if you read the *Gazette*.

The reporters were outraged. Their reporting was dictated by a bunch of accountants. The reporters may have been lazy and demoralized, but they did feel a duty to report any story they stumbled over. Bitter signs were plastered all over the newsroom: "Floggings will continue until morale improves." "Hear no evil, see no evil, speak no evil—read the *Gazette*." Now Nails was writing memos and sending them to Charlie's secret computer desk. Didn't she know we'd cracked the code to it months ago?

I leaned against Tina's desk while she fiddled on a story and started reading through Nails's memo. My, my. Nails thought our sports columnist, Big Buck Bailey, "spent too much time working for other media." Nails must be jealous of his popular radio show and TV commentaries. She cited the religion writer for six typos in a story, then whacked two cityside reporters for convoluted sentences they probably didn't write— the copy desk was notorious for combining several short, concise sentences into one long, tangled one. Nails complained the education writer missed a story and the feature department did too many PR-generated stories, which was true, but since the Family section only had one reporter, the guy couldn't be everywhere. Nails didn't have a good word for anyone, particularly the women. But she saved her worst venom for me.

"I rated three paragraphs," I said to Tina, pretending to be pleased.

"She had a lot to say about you, girl. Your column is 'silly, frivolous, it offends people, it serves no useful purpose.'"

"Here's a good line," I said. "'I see no reason for this column to exist.'"

Jasper, the surliest cityside reporter, came over and patted my shoulder. "Don't let her get you down," he said, and stumbled off to snarl at someone else.

"What got into him?" I said. Jasper never said anything nice to anyone.

"The staff hates Nails so much, they may actually start liking one another," Tina said, digging around on her desk for a current phone book.

"Nah, Charlie would never permit that," I said. "He'd feel threatened if we all got along. Charlie believes if we're fighting each other, we won't be after his job."

"Worked so far," Tina said, shoveling a stack of newspapers aside and diving for the Yellow Pages.

"How long do you think Charlie and Nails have been fooling around?" I asked.

"Long enough for it to get serious," she said. "Charlie's had more one-night stands than a Motel 6, but I don't think this is one of them. I've heard an ugly rumor at the courthouse I want to check out. I think our court reporter's been asleep at the wheel."

"What ugly rumor?" I said.

"It's too frightening to spread unless it's true. Call me this afternoon." Tina's phone rang, and she turned back to her work. I took the printout and headed straight for Georgia's office on Rotten Row. Georgia was my mentor and the only senior editor I've ever trusted. She was short, smart, funny, and foul-mouthed. A newswoman of the old school, Georgia had had to show she could drink and cuss like a man—and report like one, too. Usually I didn't hang around her office, but now I was too upset to care. I needed some comfort. I pushed some papers off her old leather club chair and sat down. She was wearing another of her ugly expensive gray suits. This one had lapels sharp enough to saw redwoods. The silk blouse was the color of dirty teeth.

"What the fuck is it now?" she snarled when she saw me.

"Good morning to you, too," I said.

"It's afternoon and nothing in this day has gone right. Charlie has just started a fuckin' book club," she said.

"Like Oprah Winfrey?"

"I wish. We have to read some goddamn college professor's ramblings on journalism, then discuss it with Charlie. He says it will give us perspective. I've got a newspaper to put out. I don't have time for this crap. This professor guy's never been in a daily newspaper in his life. Look at this title."

She pushed a fat book the size of a St. Louis phone book at me. The cover had a typewriter and an American flag on the front. I read out loud: "*Ensheathe and Ensnare: Equitable Essence of Power in the Press Corps in Post-Modern America.* What's that mean?"

"Beats me," Georgia said. "I'm on page two-ten and still can't figure out what this asshole is saying."

"Where'd Charlie get that idea?"

"From his latest squeeze, Nails. She said it would improve the tone of the paper. So now we're doing book reports. I sure hope he breaks up with this bimbo soon."

"Listen," I said a little desperately, "that's what I came to see you about. Have you seen this memo she wrote and the stuff she said about me? I'm worried, Georgia."

"You been shootin' your mouth off again?"

"Well, maybe a little," I said.

"Francesca," Georgia began, eyeing me shrewdly, "how many times have I told you to shut up? But I wouldn't worry about the snippy opinions of one of Charlie's many girlfriends. You sell newspapers, she doesn't. She'll be gone by next week. And you should be gone now. Shoo. I have reading to do."

I found something gray and soggy in the office vending machine and ate it for lunch. The label said "turkey," but if you work at the *Gazette,* you don't believe everything you read. At least I could look forward to a good dinner at Lyle's tonight. I turned Marlene's discourse on waiters and adultery into a funny column. Maybe the subject wasn't politically wise, but I slyly enjoyed the discomfort I knew it would cause Nails and Charlie. At four-thirty I called Tina, to see if she found out anything.

"I need to take a walk," she said. "Want to come with me?"

This must be sizzling news if she couldn't say it over the phone. The *Gazette* phones were all bugged and the computers monitored, but usually we ignored that, figuring management spies couldn't be watching and listening every minute. The *Gazette* was too cheap to hire enough people for that. It was serious if Tina wanted to walk in downtown St. Louis in the hottest part of the afternoon. I stepped outside, and the heat made me catch my breath. Downtown had the seedy, bleached look that comes after days of high temperatures. If the heat kept up like this another week, some TV station would start frying eggs on the sidewalk.

We walked half a block to a Burger King and got two large sodas. The counterman couldn't keep his eyes off Tina. I didn't blame the man. She was a sight.

"Sit down," Tina said. "You'll need to be seated when you hear this. Charlie filed for divorce more than sixty days ago. It slipped by our court reporter, as usual. Charlie is dumping his long-suffering wife. Something is up."

"Inside his pants," I said.

"Nope, this is serious. I'm serious, too. So you be serious."

"Maybe his wife wised up and left him," I said. "Do you even know that woman's name? He's always called her the Wife. Is 'the' her first name?"

"Wife isn't her name, it's her job," Tina said. "My theory is he needed a wife to protect him from his predatory girlfriends. Not only did he have someone to cook, clean, and keep house, but he could tell his current squeeze that he couldn't leave his wife. He used her as an excuse. A wife was the perfect protection for a philanderer like Charlie. If he's dumping her that means only one thing."

The thought was too horrible to contemplate: "Charlie is going to marry Nails," I said. As soon as I said it out loud, I felt a sickening sensation, as if some awful truth had been revealed. We dumped our drink cups in the waste barrel and walked back to the paper in silence. There was nothing left to say.

I was determined to leave the office at a decent hour, after two weeks of working until past eight every night. I was having dinner with Lyle tonight at his town house in the Central West End. At five-thirty I packed my briefcase and walked through the newsroom. There was a bouquet of flowers on Nails's desk big enough for a mob funeral. I didn't see any card, but one look at her smug face and I could guess who sent them. She and Charlie were going public.

About thirty feet from Nails's desk, the newsroom had developed a kind of black hole. Everyone suddenly avoided it, as if they'd be sucked in. The spot was the

desk of Geraldine, Charlie's official mistress, a rather
lumpy-looking blonde. Charlie may have played
around on Geraldine with his many girlfriends, but he
always came back to her. Geraldine wasn't my favorite
person. I got irritated at any woman stupid enough to
admire a slimewad like Charlie, but right now Geraldine looked pretty pathetic. She was packing notebooks and papers into a cardboard box. Tears ran
down her face and left eyeliner tracks as black as her
roots, but despite her obvious distress, no one in the
newsroom would go near her. I hated that most about
my colleagues. If you were in trouble, they acted like
you had Ebola. Cowards. Well, hell, I couldn't be in
any more trouble than I already was. I might as well
talk to her.

"Is something wrong, Geraldine?" I asked.

"I'm being transferred," she said, her voice watery
with suppressed sobs. "To the Ellisville bureau." Out of
sight and out of mind. The Ellisville bureau was a
grand name for a cheap storefront office equipped
with a phone and an ancient, cranky IBM 386 portable
computer. Ellisville was a far west suburb of St. Louis,
forty minutes from downtown on a good day. Geraldine would never cover another important story—it
would be school bond issues, Little League news, and
church fund raisers from here on. Charlie, that sawed-
off louse, had sent her into exile.

"Can I help?" I said. Geraldine shook her head and
continued silently packing and crying, like a banished
royal mistress.

A few desks away, Nails was queening it, her triumph complete. She was watching her final rival pack
up, and she was giddy with malice. Babe whispered
little nothings in her ear, and Roberto, our city editor,
stared at her as if she was Sharon Stone. Nails amused
herself by making snide comments about her colleagues.

"Did you read her column today?" Nails's voice was nasty and insinuating, and I knew she meant me. Her courtiers dutifully shook their heads no.

"I never read it," Roberto said, which was interesting. Two days ago he'd told me how much he liked my column. I was particularly proud of today's column. It was about a woman who had thirteen sure-fire ways to spot a dubious date. I thought it was funny. Until Nails began to read aloud the words I'd labored over. That's how they sounded now. Labored. Pointless. She interrupted herself to say "You know, if these people ever got a life, Francesca would be out of a job."

"Francesca Vierling, president of the Get a Life Club," Roberto sneered.

Then Babe said, "Did you know that she and Lyle . . ."

I didn't stop to find out what awful half lie Babe was spreading now. I didn't confront Nails. I didn't stop her with a snappy comeback. I fled. I hated myself for my cowardice, but I couldn't stay there any longer.

"What do you think, Lyle?" I asked over dinner that night.

"Huh?" he said. "Oh, yeah, sure, probably. Charlie will marry her. He's capable of anything. Do you think this mango pork is too dry?"

Lyle had picked up sesame green beans, mango roasted pork, and gingered sweet potatoes from his local deli. I thought it was all luscious. "I think we need a stronger wine," he added. "Maybe I should have gotten a merlot."

Despite the food, dinner with Lyle was not a success. He seemed distant and preoccupied, and bored by my endless speculations about who was doing what to whom at the *Gazette*.

"You're brooding," Lyle said, kissing my forehead.

"You are, too," I said, kissing him back.

"I wanted you with me tonight, not at the *Gazette*," he said. This time, when he kissed me, all thoughts of the *Gazette* went from my mind. We went upstairs to his bed, trailed by his enormous gray cat, Monty. For a while, Charlie and Nails and Babe and Roberto did not exist. It was just Lyle and me. And then he ruined everything.

"Francesca, will you marry me?" Lyle asked. I rolled over in bed and looked at the love of my life. He had a slightly crooked nose, pale blue eyes, and a cowlick in his blond hair that gave him a little-boy look I loved.

"Are you proposing to me in bed?" I asked. "That's a fine thing to tell our grandchildren."

"Francesca, I'm serious. I've asked you before, but you've never said yes or no. I want to marry you. I want to set a date."

I wanted to forget the whole thing. I loved Lyle. I even lived with him most of the time. But marriage was the last thing on my mind. My parents' marriage had been miserable, and all my friends who got married when we graduated from college were divorced now. Then there was Charlie and his band of buddies, every one of them a liar and a cheat. Who was I to escape the odds?

"Why can't we just live together happily ever after?" I said. I tried to distract him with jokes. I wrapped the white brocaded Ralph Lauren sheet around my waist like a train and stood up. "Can you imagine me as a bride? I'm getting a little long in the tooth for a white wedding."

"You'd make a beautiful June bride," he said. "Let's get married this month."

"June is almost over," I said. "I don't want to rush into this."

"Okay," he said, "what about August?"

"In St. Louis? We'd swelter," I said.

"October then. It's a beautiful month. We could

have a wedding in Tower Grove Park, your favorite place. The ginkgo trees are gold. It would be lovely to get married in a Victorian gazebo."

"I can't get any time off in October," I said.

"December then. We'll have a winter wedding."

"Too cold. I hate cold."

"We'll get married in the Caribbean, on an island on the beach. It will be warm and romantic."

"But my family couldn't be there."

"Your cheap West County cousins would be relieved they didn't have to buy you a present. But if you don't want to get married in the winter, we could get married in the spring."

Spring sounded comfortingly far away. In fact, it might never happen. "Spring has possibilities," I said, gathering up my underwear and heading for the shower.

"So name a date," he said.

"I need to check my calendar and make sure there's nothing going on in spring."

He sounded exasperated. "Dammit, Francesca. You know there's nothing. You just don't want to marry me."

Lyle was right. I didn't want to marry him—or anyone else. But I didn't want to lose him, either. And besides, he always looked so cute when he was angry.

"No," I said, dropping my drawers for what wasn't the first time that night. "I can't give you a date this minute. But there is something I would like to do right now."

I didn't stay the night. I was afraid he'd try to get me to set a wedding date again. So I told him I had an early appointment near my house, and it would make sense to go home. I could tell he didn't believe me, but he let me go. As I went out the door, I heard him playing that sad Jim Croce song about how we never have enough time to do the things we want to do, once we find them. The song sounded even sadder when I realized that Croce was dead. Time had run out for him. Maybe it was running out for us, too.

I drove home in a night black with storm clouds, with an ominous cool wind under the heat. The wind whipped the street trash in circles. Tornado weather. I spent a restless night, filled with the sound of tornado sirens, then police sirens and wind and rain. My sleep was so full of screaming sirens, I couldn't tell if they were real or in my dreams.

3

The next morning I awoke to a day so deliciously cool, I wondered if I'd had a blackout, climbed aboard an airplane, and flew to some other city during the night. La Jolla, maybe, or San Diego. St. Louis in mid-June does not have perfect days like this, and usually we're glad we don't. Otherwise, everyone would want to live here. The city would be overrun with tourists, prices would go up, and there would be no parking.

But this California weather was a little different. There was a haze and a curious burned smell in the air, like someone had had a huge campfire. I wondered about that. Was there a fire nearby? I remembered vaguely hearing sirens in my dreams. Maybe they were real. Instead of heading straight for work, I wandered over to North Dakota Place. All the trouble these days seemed to be centered on that street, so maybe a stroll there would find the source of the sirens.

But the place looked like the entrance to paradise. The angel fountain was wrapped in fresh rainbows. The trees rustled like taffeta petticoats. The leaves were a tender yellow-green. Lord, this was a pretty place. How could anyone who lived here be unhappy?

Suddenly a wild-eyed, white-faced Kathy came rushing out of her house. "Come quick, come quick," she cried, and clamped her hands on my arm like it was the last lifeboat off the *Titanic*. "There's been a terrible accident. It's Dale! It's awful." She was near tears and could not tell me what was wrong, except to repeat that it was Dale and it was awful. I had horrible visions of broken ladders, broken necks, and bloody electric saws. She threw open the front door and began crying again. "I can't look," she said. "It's too awful."

I entered slowly, wondering if I'd find Dale drowning in a pool of blood. I heard him groaning near the staircase. Okay, Francesca, I told myself, get it together. These people need help. I walked over there on hundred-pound rubber legs. Dale was squatting on the floor, staring at the gritty wood. I didn't see any blood. "I can't believe I was that stupid," he said in a flat voice, and then he stood up. All the major parts seemed to be moving.

"What happened? Are you okay?" I asked.

"I'm fine," he said, but he didn't sound happy about it. "I've ruined our staircase." With that, Kathy let out another heartrending wail. Then I saw the damage— huge scooped-out gouges on the upstairs floor and three steps, then a football-size hole through the spindles on the staircase. It looked like a small flying saucer had gone through it.

"I did that," Dale said. "I rented a sander to do the second floor and it must have overloaded our electrical system. It tripped the circuit breaker and shut the electricity off. So I went downstairs to turn it back on, but I forgot to turn off the sander and . . ."

I could see its path of destruction carved into the wood. When Dale flipped the circuit breaker back on, the machine began merrily sanding the upstairs floor by itself, cutting potholes into the floor. Then it bounced down the steps, taking more chunks of wood, and finally flung itself through the staircase spindles. I bit my lip to keep from laughing. "I'll get Margie," I said. "She'll know what to do."

Margie answered her door in her pink bathrobe. The egg stains were gone and her green eyes were unclouded and alert. "Those kids," she said, when I told her the problem. She smiled and shook her head and followed me back to Kathy and Dale's house, where she was all sense and sympathy. "Don't cry," she rasped to Kathy. "It can all be fixed, and it won't cost that much, either. There's a shop on Cherokee Street that sells these spindles. I wish you had talked to me, anyway, before you started. You shouldn't sand these upstairs floors. The wood is too soft. I know where we can get you some nice wall-to-wall carpet to cover them."

Poor Dale. He must have felt like some sitcom boob. Yet I'd had a glimpse of his and Kathy's restoration in the bedroom, and the work seemed carefully crafted. And from the way those bed sheets were rumpled, he could perform well there, too. But rehabbing was a kind of modern frontier, where one slip could bring disaster. Still, Margie the urban pioneer assured us the damage looked worse than it was. By the time Margie and I left ten minutes later, Kathy had dried her eyes and Dale looked sheepish but cheerful.

"Amazing," I said to Margie. "You've solved a crisis before eight o'clock."

"Correction," she said. "It's eight exactly. Here comes Hawkeye." We paused to watch the magnificent jogger skim down the boulevard before he made his usual turn up the alley at exactly eight-oh-five. The motion was so fluid, he seemed to glide over the grass.

"Makes your heart—or some other body part—positively twang," Margie said.

Our conversation was interrupted by an unearthly screech. *Get off my grass. Get off now. You're ruining it. You're ruining everything.* It was Caroline, a short, sturdy tower of outrage, clutching a wheelbarrow filled with fertilizer.

Hawkeye stopped dead. "Your grass? Your ass!" he said, sounding disconcertingly ordinary. "Listen, lady, this boulevard is city property, not your private park, although you seem to think you own everything around here. It's not new sod. It's just grass."

"It's not just grass," Caroline said, as if she was pleading for the life of each blade. "Do you know how hard it is to grow grass on that boulevard? I put it there with my sweat. I watered it with my blood. Day after day and night after night. While everyone on this block watched me and didn't lift a finger. You have no right to run on it, or walk on it, or even look at it. None at all." Her tanned face was blotched white, and she was literally trembling with rage. She clamped her hands on the handles of the wheelbarrow to stop the shaking and took some deep breaths. Was she going to hyperventilate, right there on the boulevard? Hawkeye stepped backward, then plucked three blades of grass from where he had been standing.

"What are you doing?" Caroline shrieked, as if they'd been plucked from her own hide.

"Showing you that I am not hurting your sacred grass," Hawkeye said. He held out the grass blades on his palm. "See? No damage. No cuts. No bruises." He jabbed his finger at her to punctuate each sentence. "Believe me, lady, I plan to run here every single morning. I am never changing my route now. It is set in stone. You can look for me at eight tomorrow."

Their loud voices were attracting a crowd. Tall, lean Patricia came running from her backyard, a pronged garden tool in one hand and grass stains on her knees. Today her T-shirt said she was saving the manatee, which was definitely endangered in Missouri. At least, I'd never seen one. Dina came out of her house wearing a tailored pale-gray power suit with a silver cat pin on the lapel. Her cat Stan was not with her. Caroline saw the women, plus Margie and me, and softened her tone. To me, this soft insinuating voice seemed scarier than her anger.

"Besides," she said to Hawkeye, "I'm worried about you. You could get hurt. Kids have been doing prankish stuff around here lately. They've been setting traps to trip people. I think it's the boys who live in that rundown house behind us. I'm just giving you a warning. Be careful. Runners get killed that way. Maybe you should vary your route."

"And stay off your fuckin' grass?" Hawkeye said, his voice a harsh bray. "Is that supposed to scare me? Well, it doesn't, lady."

They had squared off and looked like a confrontation between a fireplug and a heroic bronze statue. The fireplug was determined to have the last word. "I'm warning you, stay off—or I can't vouch for your safety," Caroline snarled.

Before she could stop him, Hawkeye reached over and broke off a yellow flower on a plant near the angel fountain. He stuck it rudely under Caroline's nose. "Why not take the time to smell the flowers, instead of covering them with horseshit?" he sneered. Then he grabbed her wheelbarrow and upended its load of manure into the angel fountain. Caroline's mouth was a perfect O of surprise, but no sound came out. I laughed. I couldn't help it. We all did: Margie, Dina, even Caroline's defender, Patricia. We knew it was mean. We knew Hawkeye the Hunk shouldn't have done it. But he'd stopped the female tank in her tracks and we all enjoyed it.

"Do you put up with that bullshit all the time?" the jogger said, turning to us. Sigh. Hawkeye was losing his appeal with every word he spoke. But that was only my opinion. Margie, Patricia, and Dina seemed dazzled.

"Well, your ass is grass with Caroline," said Dina, flirting outrageously. Once again, her striped sweetheart Stan was forgotten. So much for cats replacing men. Patricia frowned, but I didn't know if she was unhappy because of what Dina said or the way she was carrying on with Hawkeye. I could tell Caroline heard them. She pretended she didn't, but I saw her square her shoulders.

"That woman has taken over the neighborhood," Margie said, her rasp cutting into their conversation. "She won't let us do anything. Do you know she complained when Dina and I were standing on the parkway talking? We were just standing there—and she told us not to. She said it *looked* bad. She chases away kids who want to play ball on the parkway and goes ballistic if anyone walks on the grass."

"The bitch is nuts," Hawkeye said, not sounding like Daniel Day-Lewis at all. I wished he wouldn't open his mouth. He was destroying all my illusions. "I'm going to run down that boulevard every day now, just to make her crazy. Right now I'm going in that alley she warned me about. Traps for joggers, what a crock. This should send her right over the edge." And off he went, such poetry in motion, so prosaic when he opened his mouth.

Caroline was over the edge. She was standing inside the angel fountain, water up to her sturdy calves, shoveling the last of the wet manure into her wheelbarrow. Then she stiffly wheeled the barrow to the other side of the fountain, making a wide detour so she could avoid us. But I knew she'd heard every seditious word.

"It's time to fight back," said Dina, who didn't sound like her fluffy, friendly self anymore. The shrewd political strategist, suited up in power gray, was making her first public appearance in my presence. "We need to take back our turf. No one asked Caroline to be the unpaid monitor of North Dakota Place. Or the gardener, either. We need to rebel with a party in the parkway."

"We need to have a Take Back Our Own Place party. And damn soon," Margie said. "How about this Saturday? We can dance all over her precious grass."

"I'll go skinny-dipping in the angel fountain," Dina said.

"Let's fill the fountain with tea and have a modern-day Boston tea party," Margie said. From that rasp in her voice, I was sure she had no interest in tea.

"Why don't we go to my house and discuss the party plans?" Patricia said. That surprised me. Patricia had always looked uncomfortable when anyone criticized Caroline. Maybe she was fed up with her, too. Or maybe Patricia thought she could contain the malice in her own home. "I have homemade gooey butter coffee cake," she said.

Patricia the health food nut had gooey butter cake? This was the city specialty that made St. Louis one of the nation's centers for heart bypass surgery. Gooey butter coffee cakes, with their soft butter-rich centers and snowdrifts of powdered sugar on top, had been clogging St. Louis arteries for generations. Janet Smith had shown me her recipe for gooey butter, which is as close as two friends can get short of swapping husbands. The one-layer cake had two sticks of butter, a package of cream cheese, and a whole box of powdered sugar, which made a sweet, sugary swamp. Rich? Bill Gates should be so rich. SnackWells would never make a low-fat gooey butter. There was no such thing. I was glad. Some things are worth dying for.

None of us could resist the lure of gooey butter. Besides, I figured I'd get a column out of the party plans. North Dakota Place was becoming a continuing soap opera, and I didn't want to miss an episode. We followed Patricia to her house, a well-kept three-story brick-and-stone next door to Caroline. After we admired her organic garden and compost heap, we went inside. Patricia was rehabbing her house in stages, but the kitchen was definitely finished. The cabinets and woodwork were a rich gold. The countertops had deep-blue ceramic tile, and the floor was a rough, peachy Mexican tile. The underpaid peasants who made it would probably have killed for linoleum. Herbs were growing in the windowsills. Tall, lean Patricia looked precisely in proportion in this long, high-ceilinged room. She was truly at home here.

Fried eggs were my sole culinary accomplishment, but even I had to admit Patricia's kitchen was impressive. Countless kitchen machines were on display. I recognized a blender, a food processor, four-slice toaster, assorted steamers, pasta and bread makers, and stainless steel items I couldn't identify if you beat me until stiff with an egg whisk. I watched Patricia fill a streamlined stainless steel tea kettle that looked like it came off the Space Shuttle.

"Do you really use all these things?" I asked.

"Of course," she said. "But not all at once. Caroline and I have a good arrangement. She has all the tools I need to borrow to rehab my house, and I have the cooking utensils she needs. We share all the time. I run into her garage to take tools, and she comes into my kitchen for things. Neither door is locked during the day, because Caroline is always watching the street."

Dina was examining a pantry filled with home-canned vegetables, jams, jellies, and relishes, each jar labeled by hand. Green beans. Peas. Peaches. Green tomatoes. Red tomatoes. Cucumber pickles. Cha-cha relish. "Look at that," she said, awestruck. "Did you do all that yourself?"

"I grow most of my own vegetables and some fruit," Patricia said. "The rest I get at the Soulard farmers' market. But here's what I'm most proud of." She threw open the door to the old butler's pantry, revealing a huge recycling center, with compartments for newspaper, white paper, foam trays and cartons, and three colors of glass. There were places for aluminum foil, cardboard and plastic jugs, and lots more I couldn't see. "There is absolutely no need to throw anything into a landfill," Patricia said. "It can all be recycled properly."

"Even aerosol cans?" Dina asked.

"There is no excuse to buy aerosol cans. Not ever. They . . ." But then the tea kettle started making a racket and cut off the lecture. Patricia made herbal tea and poured it into handmade blue pottery mugs. Then she cut huge squares of gooey butter cake and put them on blue plates. We sat down at the round oak kitchen table to plan the protest party. Three bites into the cake, we all had powdered-sugar mustaches, which we all ignored.

Patricia insisted that Caroline be invited to the party and that her invitation be a gracious recognition of her work. "I am not comfortable criticizing Caroline," she said. "I must ask you not to do so in my presence. She's done a lot for this neighborhood. But I agree she needs to relax."

I admired Patricia for her little speech. I'd seen too many hatchet sessions at the *Gazette* to be comfortable with this one, even if I didn't like Caroline.

Dina was ready to bury the hatchet—right between Caroline's shoulder blades. "You bet she needs a rest," she said. "Caroline's obsessed. I heard a noise last night and went out to investigate. I saw her wheeling a barrow full of mulch. At three in the morning! She must have been really working, because her clothes were dripping sweat and filthy black. She was . . ."

Patricia interrupted Dina firmly. "Caroline's been working almost around the clock, and I'm concerned that she is stressed. Maybe if we hold the party to celebrate our street in a positive way and invite her to share our enjoyment, she won't feel so threatened."

I thought Caroline was more interested in control

than celebration but said nothing. It wasn't my street. I was just scrounging for a column. Margie looked like she was biting her tongue until it was bloody, but she stayed civil. For about twenty minutes everyone discussed plans for the celebration. The rebellion fizzled out, and soon Dina, Patricia, and Margie were figuring out how many lawn chairs, cold-cut platters, and carrot cakes they'd need. The anger toward Caroline was dissipating like a summer shower.

"I have to go to City Hall today—that's why I'm wearing this suit—but I'll be home the rest of the week to help with the details," Dina volunteered, sweet and fluffy again.

"Time for me to go," I announced, suddenly eager to be away from the shifting moods of North Dakota Place. "Can I use your kitchen phone, Patricia?" Of course I could. I called Cutup Katie, my pathologist friend in the city medical examiner's office. She would have the last word on Otto's death.

"Can't talk now, I'm busy," said Katie, sounding genuinely rushed. "Just finished carving up another one of your neighbors. Two murders in two days are a bit much, don't you think? Gotta go."

Two murders?

"Wait! You can't do this. What murders? Otto? He was murdered? I thought he had a heart attack. And who's the other one? We have to talk." Patricia, Dina, and Margie were clearing the table and pretending not to listen.

"I came in early and I'm off in an hour," Katie said. "Meet me at the city golf course in Forest Park. Two of our usual foursome canceled at the last minute."

"I don't golf," I said.

"Good," she said. "You can be a golf babe. Wear leopard Spandex, gold sandals, and lots of nail polish, and you can ride around in a cart and cheer Mitch and me on. Practice saying 'Ooooh, you're so strong.'"

"Over my dead body," I said.

"That can be arranged," Katie said with an evil cackle. Then she hung up.

"Was Otto murdered?" Margie asked, not bothering to hide that she'd eavesdropped.

"I don't know," I said, "but I'll find out." It looked like I was meeting Katie at the golf course or not at all. I called the *Gazette* and told Scarlette, one of Charlie's former afternoon delights who now answered our department phones, that I was on assignment. I just hoped no one from the *Gazette* saw me in the park on a nice day.

Katie acted less like a doctor than any doctor I knew. She was a country girl, with a practical attitude toward death. She didn't have any of the standard doctor trappings. She drove a pickup and she had a big old used hound—his previous owners sent him back to the pound and she saved him from death row. Her one medical weakness was golf, but she refused to join a country club. Instead, she played on the public golf course at Forest Park, an old city park about the size of Liechtenstein. She was waiting by the clubhouse with her friend, Mitch, another doctor who worked on some research project at Washington University he wasn't anxious to discuss. Mitch was a big gray-haired guy who didn't say much, which was okay because Katie talked for two. Both wore jeans and golf shirts, instead of funny-colored outfits. Before I could say anything, they grabbed me and ran for the tee.

"We have a once-in-a-lifetime chance to tee off as a twosome," said Katie. "This *never* happens on crowded public courses. We've got to get going before they change their minds and pair us with a couple of geeks. Mitch and I usually walk, but we'll rent a cart for you."

"I'll walk," I said. "I can use the exercise."

"Good. We move quickly," Katie said. "A round takes us about four hours for eighteen holes."

"Four hours! How do you stand the boredom?" I was never going to make four hours. The grass looked short and dry, and there were heat waves shimmering on the course. And this was a cool day.

"You were never in med school," she said. "Besides, I like golf. Mitch and I are relatively closely matched, but I'm the better driver."

"I thought you walked," I said.

"Drives," she said. "As in long shots. He drives about two hundred yards and my good drives are two-twenty. We shoot between eighty-six and ninety-five. I'd rather play with old guys like Mitch, because they're not intimidated by a good woman golfer." The fifty-something Mitch acknowledged this with a snort. "The young guys get into arguments and accuse you of being a lesbian if you beat them, and want to bet for big money. We bet for beer."

She proceeded to explain a complicated betting game where the first time someone three-putt they were "holding the snake." This sounded like something a lonesome teenage boy did, and the rules were too complicated for me to follow. I did figure out the loser bought beer for everybody.

I never understood how people as interesting as Mitch and Katie could play something as dull as golf. I know Tiger Woods has made the game cool again, but before him the nation's best known golfer was Dwight Eisenhower, which said it all for me. Forest Park was very crowded, so we waited on every shot, broiling in the sun like hot dogs. I wanted to set my buns down somewhere. I kept wishing I was in a cool booth at Uncle Bob's. Not only was golfing dull, it was dangerous. While we stood around and talked, there was a *whump!* noise, and some fool lobbed a golf ball right in the middle of us.

"He could have beaned us," Katie said.

Mitch looked disgusted. "All because he's too impatient to wait for us to move," he said. "Some idiot shot with people around. He should be banned from the course."

"I'll fix him," Katie said. She picked up the ball and wrote "Nice shot, asshole" on it with a Sharpie pen, then put it back down. "He can play it where it lays. I gave him a little souvenir."

I figured I better start asking about Otto and the other murder before one of us got killed in action. Or nonaction. I paced around while we waited, to make more of a moving target. "What's this about two murders in two days? Didn't Otto die of a heart attack?"

"That's what I first thought," Katie said. "But then I saw the small, telltale marks of electrocution—a black hole in the palm and sole. That's where the current entered and came out. The victim broke his arm and one leg falling off the ladder, but he was probably dead before he hit the ground because there are marks on his face. Live victims—at least the ones who are alive before they land—put out their hands to protect their face."

She was right. I remembered a South Side friend who was painting his gutters forest green and his window trim white—the only acceptable neighborhood colors—one Sunday. His ladder went over backward. Out of respect for the Lord's Day, he yelled, "Oh, SHOOOOOOT," on the way down. He broke a wrist when he put out his hands to protect his face.

At last, Katie got to make a shot. She whacked the ball soundly a good long way and looked pleased. Mitch looked impressed. Then he did the same thing, but he wasn't as happy about it. We walked on a little more, stood around like we were in a checkout line, and then Katie and Mitch made a bunch of short shots. I gathered some of those short shots should have been long ones, because neither one was very happy. I was going to have to sit through four hours of this. Good thing there were two doctors present. I might die of boredom. When we started walking again, I started my questioning.

"I still don't understand why it's murder," I said. "Otto was standing on a metal ladder, getting ready to paint metal gutters. They were festooned with a cheap set of Christmas lights he'd bought on sale at Kmart at Gravois Plaza. He left those lights up all year. I'm not surprised the wire frayed and electrocuted him."

"That was *not* normal wear and tear," Katie said. "After we found he'd been electrocuted, the police went back and looked at those lights. The plastic coating had been peeled down to the wire. It was murder."

"So Otto was the first murder," I said. "Who was the second? I didn't know someone else was killed. When did it happen?"

"Last night. A drug dealer with the imaginative name of John Smith. His friends called him Scorpion. He died wearing a gold-and-diamond scorpion necklace valued at two thousand dollars. That thing had a gold rope chain and a gold pendant the size of a small candy bar with a diamond scorpion on it. His family tried to claim the necklace and his three gold-and-diamond teeth before EMS even got his body out of the ambulance. They had their priorities straight."

"Not exactly grieving, were they?"

"No. But Mr. Scorpion Smith should get the usual bang-up drug dealer's funeral."

"He was shot?"

"He was an arson death," Katie said. "Fire investigators say someone set fire to his house. The arsonist got up on the flat roof, probably used the fire escape belonging to the rooming house next door, walked across the roof, and poured gasoline down all the vents. Got a little careless and dribbled a little gas on the roof, so the investigators saw the burn pattern and figured it out. Mr. Smith died trapped inside. Nasty way to go."

So was drug addiction. I wasn't wasting much sympathy on him. As far as I was concerned, one less drug dealer was no loss. Katie and Mitch stopped to take a few more short whacks—excuse me, putts—and from what she said, Mitch was buying the beer. Maybe I wasn't getting the point to this game, but at least I was getting information.

"How do you know something inside the house didn't start the fire?" I asked. "Those guys don't work under the safest conditions."

"Yeah, but an explosion looks different. And drug dealers also don't padlock their own door on the outside. Mr. Smith had a hasp on his back door, because that's the method he probably used to secure the door when he left the house. His back door was padlocked and there were burglar bars on his front door and all the first-floor windows."

"I don't see how he got trapped. Most houses around there are at least two stories. Were the second-floor windows barred, too? Couldn't he run up and climb out those windows—or get up on the roof?"

"It was a gasoline fire," Katie said, "and gas is a really fast accelerant. Fire races up staircases. It looks like he tried to get out the back door, then headed for the front when he couldn't get the back door open. By that time smoke inhalation got him. Most burn victims die of smoke inhalation. I found soot in his trachea, so he was alive when the fire started. If he were dead before the place was set on fire, I wouldn't find that soot."

"Do you remember where that drug dealer lived in my neighborhood, so I can check out the location?" I asked.

"Yeah, sure, it was a weird name," Katie said. "He lived on Ratley Street. I don't remember the address, but the house should be easy to find. It was badly burned." A fire in my neighborhood. That explained the haze and the burned smell this morning and the sirens in my sleep. They weren't dreams. They were real.

A little cart driven by a little blonde in little shorts headed toward us. "It's Bev Cart!" Mitch and Katie said together and started laughing, although I couldn't see what was so funny.

"That's a beer wench dead ahead," Katie said. "They are mostly college women, who drive around the course in little carts, selling beer and other refreshments and flirting outrageously with the male golfers. We were at this course where one golfer kept calling the beer wench Bev. The beverage cart had the license plate Bev Cart, and he thought Bev was her name. This is one area where golf needs to improve its treatment of women. We need more male beer wenches."

"A male wench?"

"Okay, a beer stud, or a beer hustler. I want to see cute college guys in tight shorts riding around selling beer and flirting outrageously with me for big tips. Buying beer is one of the great golf rituals, and we women are denied participation in it by our fellow women."

I thought I knew what she meant. "You watch now," she said. "Little Bev here will act like I'm invisible."

Bev the beer wench looked more like a beer cheerleader. The word "wholesome" was made for her, from her blunt-cut hair that was almost natural blond to her bouncy little body. Bev pulled up in her cart and giggled at Mitch. "I bet you're thirsty," she said. "I have beer, Powerade, bottled water, and soda."

"I bet she never asks me," Katie muttered.

Bev got Mitch a beer and asked about his game. Finally Bev said, "Oh, does she want something?"

"Respect," Katie shouted. "Equal time. I'm a doctor just like he is. My wallet is as big as his."

"She'll take a Bud," Mitch said. "Can I get you anything, Francesca?"

"See," Katie said to me. "We need male beer wenches. Beer studs, if you will."

"It would definitely improve the view," I said. "The average golfer here is about the same as the temperature—somewhere in the high seventies." Mitch snorted again.

Male beer hustlers would give me something new to watch. We weren't even to the third hole yet, and I'd seen more grass and trees than I wanted. Now I saw some kind of commotion up ahead. Katie broke into a lope and Mitch moved pretty fast for a fifty-something guy. I brought up the rear. Soon we were close enough to see three middle-age guys flapping their arms and a fourth one lying motionless on the ground. Even from this distance he looked unnaturally white and clammy. One of the standing and flapping guys was yelling "Is there a doctor on the course?"

"Shit, Mitch, look at that guy in the fairway," Katie said. "I bet he's had a heart attack. We'd better check him out and see if he's still alive. He could be gone by the time EMS can get in here."

Gee, I thought, that was heartwarming.

"God, I hope he's not dead," Katie said fervently. "I'm on call. I'd have to cut him up on my day off."

My freshly warmed heart chilled pretty quick. But I saw a chance for escape. I had almost all the information I needed, anyway. "Listen," I said magnanimously as she and Mitch galloped along the pathway, "if this is an emergency, I'd just be in your way. I can walk back to my car."

"Good idea. You got a phone with you? No? Then call 911 from the clubhouse."

"I'm on my way," I said, my heart leaping like a

young lamb. I was sorry my freedom was bought at this price, but that golfer did not flop down in vain. I was grateful for his sacrifice. Katie and Mitch were closing in on the downed man in the fairway. I ran off to find the clubhouse. But even as I ran to bring help to that man, I couldn't stop thinking about the two murders in my neighborhood.

Both victims lived within blocks of each other, but they sure lived different lives. One was a city employee pushing sixty, who never smoked anything stronger than a cigar. The other was a drug dealer who'd never see twenty-five, wearing enough gold to stock a pawnshop. They didn't have much in common.

Except no one would miss them.

And they both had fought with Caroline.

4

Fighting with Nails was as deadly as fighting with Caroline. The gaping hole in the newsroom testified to Nails's power to obliterate her enemies. Geraldine, Charlie's ex-mistress, was gone—and so was her desk. All I saw was a dirt ring and a few twisted wires marking the spot. Every trace of Geraldine had been removed, but no one claimed this prime newsroom real estate. They avoided it, as if the area were contaminated.

I was amazed no one grabbed it. Space for reporters was in short supply at the *Gazette*. Although the paper had fewer reporters than at any time in its long history, it had less space for them. The editors built themselves bigger and bigger offices, until the reporters were squeezed like cattle into one open corral in the center of the room. The crowding frayed tempers. The staff oozed resentment and quarreled constantly, shouting curses and rude remarks at one another while other reporters tried to talk on the phone.

It wasn't always like this. I came to the *Gazette* at the end of its golden era. The paper hadn't had any major investigations or prizes for twenty years even then, but it still had the remnants of that prizewinning staff, although they were old and riddled with cancer, heart disease, and alcoholism. The paper spent money on its people back then—the *Gazette* paid some of the highest wages in the industry. Reporters traveled first class and stayed at the best hotels. When a reporter was gone for a week, the *Gazette* sent his wife a dozen roses. This first-class treatment paid off. Reporters produced first-class work. They ruined their health and their home lives, but they spent eighty hours a week laboring for their true love, the *St. Louis City Gazette.*

In those days, we had huge olive-drab metal desks of stupendous ugliness and dignity, and sturdy padded leather swivel chairs. The furniture was battered, solid and useful, and we felt like we'd stepped into *The Front Page.* But the *Gazette* got greedy in the mid-1980s. The easiest way to make more money was to cut wages and staff perks. The roses and first-class travel went first. Then the high wages. The final humiliation was when the *Gazette* switched to computers. The magnificent monster desks were replaced by the smallest, cheapest computer "pods," the tinny kind where the drawers stuck and the chairs creaked. We were crowded so close we heard everyone's phone conversations. There was no privacy. We didn't even have the proper tools for our job. Paper, notepads, and pens were locked up and rationed. Every reporter used to have a typewriter, but we did not have our own computer. Four to six reporters shared one terminal. Fights broke out at deadline as desperate staffers tried to find a computer. Editors had their own computers, which mostly went unused, but we weren't allowed to touch them.

The paper saved thousands with this cheese paring but lost millions in staff goodwill. The best reporters left or took early retirement. The rest no longer worked eighty-hour weeks. The story count dropped, and pep talks urging us to write "shorter, better, faster" were met with shrugs and "fuck it." The staff mantra became "You can love a newspaper, but it can't love you back," and anyone foolish enough to work late heard that chant a hundred times.

Geraldine had figured out one way to get some extra privileges. She took up with our runty but randy managing editor, Charlie. For accepting a few insignificant inches of Charlie whenever he felt like it, she got several extra square feet of choice space behind a pillar, where the city editor couldn't see if she was working or loafing, plus an undeserved promotion and her own laptop computer. But what Charlie gave, he also took away. Geraldine's empty spot was an ugly reminder. So was Nails's triumphant face and fawning courtiers. I passed them and heard snide whispers and giggles, which I pretended to ignore.

But I couldn't ignore the clumps of grumbling staffers gathered around the bulletin board. There must be some new, outstandingly dumb memo. I went over to look. There were two, actually, both from Charlie.

"The *Gazette* Sensitivity Committee has determined that the word *black* for *African American* persons is outdated, demeaning, and nondescriptive," it began. "Therefore, the term *African American* will be used at all times in place of this word. The term *black*, when used to mean *African American*, will not appear in the *Gazette*."

At last, a decision. The *Gazette* committee had spent six months and god knows how many hours in meetings to reach this conclusion. A managing editor with any guts could have decided the question in two seconds. But Charlie, the cowardly little shrimp, was not short on brains. He wouldn't make any ruling that might backfire later, and race in St. Louis was a quagmire. So he appointed a committee, and let them decide. If there was any controversy, he could blame them. In between, we'd waffled on which term was more politically correct. There were huge fights at deadline, as reporters argued for the right to keep quotes intact. Now at least we knew which word to use. I didn't care one way or the other, as long as the editors made up their minds. But trust the *Gazette* to screw up any sensible move. The rest of Charlie's memo read:

> In order to aid you to make the correct choice, the spell check on all *Gazette* computers has been reprogrammed to automatically change the word *black* to *African American*.

"What!" I yelled. "What moron dreamed up that spell-check stuff?"

"I did," Nails said, coming up behind me. Her voice was somewhere between a sneer and simper.

"It's a dumb idea," I said. "If the computer automatically changes black to African American, it's going to cause big problems at deadline. Black is used for more than race."

"It won't be a problem, if people are careful," Nails said. "But I wouldn't expect a racist South Sider to understand." That was a standard charge from people who hadn't been in my neighborhood for ten years—and I didn't count Nails's night of love by the Dumpster. The South Side was the old German neighborhood. But recent infusions of Korean, Chinese, Bosnian, Romanian, Russian, Thai, Ethiopian, and Hispanic immigrants had greatly changed its complexion. Improved the food, too.

"Racist? If you ever left your lily-white suburb, you'd know I live in a mixed neighborhood," I said.

"Kirkwood is not lily-white," Nails said. "We have a black physician living three blocks away. His wife is a college professor. Their house is as well kept as any of ours," she added, not realizing that she was patronizing the couple.

"Isn't he an *African American* physician?" I said. "I thought *black* was dated and demeaning." But I was talking to her back. She flounced off. I read the next memo with horror. I'd just insulted the first female head of the powerful All Business section. Charlie's memo announced Nails's promotion as the new business editor, effective immediately upon the retirement of the old editor, John Gannet. John's assistant, Joan, who'd been with him since women at the paper were called "girl Fridays," was being passed over for Charlie's main squeeze. Joan had been groomed for that job for ten years and now she would not get it. Worse, Joan would be Nails's assistant, which meant she'd do the scut work and Nails would get the credit. Charlie's memo also said the "multitalented and versatile" (his words, and he ought to know) Ms. Nadia Noonin would write a column on selected business issues "as she saw fit."

As I read this, an arm went around my shoulder and gave it a friendly squeeze. "We're all meeting at the Last Word at three o'clock to discuss Nails's latest power grab," said a voice.

"Jasper?" I said in disbelief. The paper's most misanthropic reporter was acting like my old pal.

"It's time to call a halt to the infighting," he said. "That woman is dangerous. We need to pool our knowledge of our common enemy." I was speechless, and Jasper didn't try to explain. He just stuck out his hand and said, "Truce."

"Truce," I said, and shook it.

Nails must be a powerful threat if the surly Jasper was bothering to sweet-talk me. I agreed to be at the Word, my least favorite bar, at three. But before then, I had a column to write. I wanted to try out the concept of Katie's beer stud on greater St. Louis. I went back to my desk, a landfill of old newspapers, notebooks, and papers. The day's mail had the usual fan mail and hate mail, plus an odd postcard. The spiky blue ballpoint printing was hard to read, but I thought it said the guy's mother had died recently. He seemed to be taking it hard. "My life is not the same now that my dear angel Mother is gone," he wrote. "Nobody cares."

The postcard was sort of creepy, but at least I could write the guy a condolence letter. Where did he live? I checked the return address. A few blocks down from me, on Utah. His name looked like Erwin Shermann. "Dear Mr. Shermann," I began. "I am very sorry for your loss . . ." The phone rang as I was licking the flap on Erwin's letter.

"Jinny!" I said. I loved calls from Jinny Peterson. She was a gossip—correction, unpaid reporter—of the highest quality. "Whatcha got for me?"

"A word to the wise," she said. "I saw your column about forking. I see you fell for Margie's charm. We all do, at the beginning."

I had that cold feeling of dread I always get when I've been bamboozled. I hated being a fool. "Is something wrong?" I asked carefully.

"Thought you'd like some background, my dear," she said. "Margie has made some enemies by cutting sharp deals with friends. And rumor has it she may have sticky fingers. You've met Julia. She lives on Westminster. Julia has one of those houses with hundreds of little knickknacks around. You can't imagine that she can keep track of them all. Well, she does. After a visit from Margie, Julia noticed her grandfather's silver cigarette case was missing. She's not saying that Margie took it, because there were other people in the house that day. But Margie would be the most likely person to know where to sell it. Julia couldn't see her Grandmother Edith hocking it, and Hilda has worked for her for years. Anyway, after Margie visits now, Julia counts the spoons."

"But there were no arrests, were there?" I'd checked the *Gazette* files before I did the story, but maybe I hadn't done a thorough enough search.

"Oh, heavens no," Jinny said. "There weren't even

any formal accusations. Just some bad feelings and a little cloud of suspicion. I just wanted to warn you, Francesca, before you turn that woman into a regular source."

I tried to tell myself that this was simply gossip. But Jinny's information was generally accurate. I felt uneasy and a little embarrassed. I finished my column a little before three and turned it in to the Family section editor, Wendy the Whiner. Wendy looked even frowsier than usual, her no-color hair sticking up in points and her burlap suit wrinkled and sagging. "I'm working on an important project for Charlie," she said. I noticed a fat book open in front of her: *Ensheathe and Ensnare: Equitable Essence of Power in the Press Corps in Post-Modern America*. It was the same book bedeviling Georgia. Wendy was a member of the *Gazette* book club, too. Well, at least it kept her out of my hair. Wendy was distracted and barely glanced at my column before she sent it without comment to the copy desk. I was pleased. Most *Gazette* editors were so bad, the best we could hope for was benign neglect. I wasn't so lucky when the column got to the copy desk. Cruella, the copy chief, grabbed it. Cruella had dead black hair and bright red nails. She wore tight, glamorous clothes, which looked out of place on her tubby body. Her real name was Peggy. She earned her nickname because she once sent some pound puppies to certain death when she pulled their "Pet Pick of the Week" feature to run a picture of a hunky surfer. Cruella and I had a long, unhappy history, and she was in a troublemaking mood today.

"Francesca," she said in a snippy school-marm voice. "I have a problem with your column."

"Yes," I said.

"I think it needs to be rewritten," she said.

Copy editors were supposed to check spelling, names, addresses, and grammar. They could not order reporters to do rewrites. Cruella was overreaching and hoping she could get away with it. She had picked the wrong woman.

"Why do you think that?" I said. "Have you found many inaccuracies or misspellings?"

"No," she said. "But I'm interested in quality. This column is not up to our usual standards, Francesca."

"What's missing, Cruella?" She frowned when I used her nickname. It was a direct challenge. "If you can tell me exactly what it needs, then I can fix it."

She couldn't. I knew it, and she knew it. She didn't like the column because she didn't like me. "It made me restless," she said. "I read hundreds of stories, and I can always tell when something is not well written. I start fidgeting in my chair."

"And this column caused you to fidget," I said.

"Yes," she said. "And if it happened to me, it will happen to readers, too."

"So all of St. Louis will be fidgeting while they read my column?" I said. "Could be dangerous, Cruella. Mass fidgeting might set off the New Madrid fault. St. Louis could have a major earthquake, all because my column made you fidget."

I studied her plump rump hanging over her chair. "Must be nice to have the whole city wired to your ass, Cruella. But if you touch my column, I'll kick your super-sensitive rear end all the way to the Mississippi River."

"You heard her," Cruella shrieked. "She threatened bodily harm."

Wendy the Whiner, deep into *Ensheathe and Ensnare*, pretended not to hear us, so the rest of the copy desk, a collection of doughlike creatures who did what they were told, acted as if they didn't hear anything, either. I got out of there and over to the Last Word for the Nails meeting.

The Nails session was in full swing. The inside of

the Word was pitch black, as usual, and that was a good thing. Otherwise, we might see the dirt—and god knows what else. The bar depressed me so much I avoided it whenever I could. It was where the *Gazette* staff went to cheat on their spouses and gripe about their editors. It was a hopeless place. Going there regularly was an admission that you'd given up.

Jasper, my new best friend, waved to me as I entered. Everyone was at four tables pushed together. The tops were littered with beer and Coke bottles, potato chip and pretzel bags. Staffers who ordinarily didn't speak to each other had agreed to drink together and discuss Nails. Jennifer, a timid young general assignment reporter who looked like a brown baby bird, was sitting next to Jasper. Normally she was terrified of him, but now Jasper was feeding her barbecued potato chips. On Jasper's other side was the glamorous Tina, whom I knew wasn't a Jasper fan. Next to Tina was our oldest female reporter and only genuine society type, Endora, handsome in an I-don't-give-a-damn way. Her hair was scraped back in its usual pony tail, which went well with her horse face. I spotted Matt, a jolly fat guy with a face like a potato, who was treacherous as a snake. I grabbed a chair and squeezed in next to Tina.

Endora was filling everyone in with high-level gossip. She knew the publisher personally. "Nails went to the best schools, Brearley and Vassar," Endora was saying in that lockjaw accent of hers. "Her father was a fraternity brother of the publisher."

"Hah! Nails always claims her family connections have nothing to do with her getting hired," Jennifer said.

"They didn't, I'm sure," Endora said, anxious to get off this subject, since her family connections got her the job at the *Gazette*.

"Probably didn't have anything to do with her making assistant city editor so fast, either," Tina said in her don't-give-me-that-stuff voice.

"You know what an assistant city editor is, don't you?" I said. "A mouse in training to be a rat."

Everyone laughed but Matt, who hoped to be a city editor. So many mice, all so eager to find a way out of the maze. Nails saw her chance to escape when she was made head of the Crime Team, as part of Charlie's new team reporting program. The two women on Nails's team were Tina and Jennifer. "We definitely got different treatment from the three men, Jasper, Matt, and Austin," said Tina.

Jasper rolled his eyes and said, "Oh, god, not another women's lib lecture."

"I know you guys didn't notice it, but she treated you better," Jennifer said. "We aren't making it up. Nails flirted and giggled with the Crime Team men, and when they turned in their regular assignments she acted like they'd done something special. Nails even brought you chocolates to sweeten you up, Jasper. That's what she said. Her exact words."

"So what?" Jasper snarled.

"Do you think she had any chocolates or giggles for the women?" Jennifer asked.

"You tell him, sister," Tina said.

"We never got any praise," Jennifer said earnestly. "We never even got an ordinary thank you. Finally I said the women might appreciate some appreciation, too. 'You're expected to do your work,' Nails told me. 'Your paycheck should be reward enough.'"

My respect for little Jennifer was rising by the minute. The new kid had guts.

"Nails expected the women to work longer hours with no overtime, no time off and no excuses," Jennifer said. "I called in sick one morning because I was having bad cramps from my period . . ."

"Oh, for chrissakes!" Jasper said. He could tell the

crudest jokes, but he was offended by any mention of female functions.

"Shut up, Jasper," we women said. Little Jennifer looked terrified but continued. "Anyway, I had these terrible cramps and Nails told me that women should not use their femininity as an excuse to avoid work."

"But I bet she excused Austin's hangovers," Endora said.

"Austin was going through a divorce," Matt said. "He was having a bad time."

"And I wasn't?" Jennifer said.

"Tell them about your evaluation, Jennifer," Tina said. "That's where you really saw the difference between the boys and girls. Nails took Jasper, Matt, and Austin each out to lunch to discuss their evaluations. They were *long* lunches, too."

"Do you think we enjoyed them?" Jasper asked incredulously. "Trying to talk to that simpering twit for two hours was hard work."

"I'd trade you any time, Jasper. My evaluation was handed to me at the end of the day on a Friday. Nails gave me low scores for almost everything, even though my Westfall series was nominated for the Ripplinger Reporting Prize."

"You're kidding," Matt said. "What did you do?"

"I steamed all weekend. She managed to ruin that, which was what she wanted. But I marched into the office Monday morning and told Nails I refused to sign the evaluation until she explained those low scores when my work was up for a prize. I also asked for an explanation, in writing, of why she took all the men out for evaluation lunches but handed the women sheets of paper."

"What did she say?" Matt asked, his voice soft and soothing. His interest made me suspicious.

"Nails never gave a reason," Jennifer said. "She said that she would reconsider my evaluation. Two days later I got a new, improved one. It wasn't exactly glowing, but it had enough praise that I was satisfied and signed it. Shortly after that Nails transferred me back to city desk, which was fine with me."

"I left the team a month later," Tina said. "I was the token, crime being a 'black thang.' Nails and I had serious philosophical differences from the beginning. Nails was your basic white-bread suburbanite, who thought she was a liberal. You know the definition of a liberal, don't you? If you're drowning fifty feet from shore, they throw you a twenty-five-foot rope and say 'I'll meet you halfway.'"

There was uneasy laughter. "Because she lived in the suburbs, Nails considered crime solely a city ill. Since St. Louis was mostly black, that made crime a black phenomenon. St. Louis County had more than its share of rapes, muggings, carjackings, and murders, and some of them took place at malls that were the *Gazette*'s major advertisers, but you never read about that in the *Gazette*. Nails knew better than to produce anything that would upset advertisers, not if she wanted to continue her upward climb. But after a carjacking at the fancy Clayton Park Mall in West County went unreported, I couldn't keep quiet any more. 'Don't we report white folks' crimes?' I asked her. Nails waved my question away, saying 'It's too hard to cover all those little towns. St. Louis County has ninety-one communities. We couldn't possibly keep track of them all.' She could, if she hustled. But the Crime Team took the lazy way out and only covered crime in the city. That was a smart move on her part. Kept the advertisers happy and appealed to the popular prejudice—white prejudice. After the Clayton Park Mall incident, I quit."

"What happened to the Crime Team?" I asked. "Was it ever officially disbanded?"

"No, it just fizzled out," Jennifer said.

"About the time the Crime Team quietly disintegrated," Tina said, "Nails latched onto Charlie, so its success or failure didn't matter anymore. We know what happened after that."

"Nails was promoted to the head of the business section," Jennifer said.

"She's also writing columns, don't forget," Jasper said. "I found her first column, due to run in a few days." Jasper was good at rummaging through the computer for interesting electronic tidbits. He produced a printout.

"Read it!" we all cried.

Jasper cleared his throat and began: " 'A grave injustice has been done to a working woman by the president of the Eichelberg Company.' "

"Wow," Jennifer said. "She's certainly going after the big guns, no pun intended. They're a major defense contractor."

Jasper continued, " 'Company President Adam Eichelberg allegedly promoted a woman he was having an affair with to the position of vice president and passed over the rightful female candidate for the job. That woman is now suing the company for sex discrimination.' "

"This line of Nails's is priceless," Jasper said. " 'The moment that he had a sexual relationship with the woman and then promoted her to vice president, he broke the law.' I think she's forgotten the circumstances of her own promotion."

"Oh, Lord, how am I going to hold up my head at City Hall when this gets out?" Tina groaned, and she said it for all of us. If news of the Nails-Charlie affair became public, the *Gazette*'s credibility was zilch.

"It's already out," said Endora, our most social reporter, and she would know. "It's all they talked about at the dinner party I went to Saturday night. They even have Charlie and Nails sightings. At the Opera Theatre he supposedly spilled champagne on her hand and then licked it off."

More groans.

"And do you know her pet name for him?" Endora added.

"Dimpletoes," I said, and told them about the Dumpster love scene.

As I talked, I knew I was doing something stupid. I was sure one of my colleagues at this table, listening so earnestly, would repeat every damaging word to Charlie or Nails. I suspected Matt was most likely to sell us out, since he showed the most interest but contributed the least. Also, Matt had managerial ambitions. It could also be Jasper. All he did was read Nails's column to us, and everyone in the city would read it in a few days, anyway.

It could be either of them. Maybe it was both. Judas would be a team player at the *Gazette*. Betrayal was a way of life. But I couldn't stop myself. I kept telling the story.

I could not change the *Gazette*, and I could not change myself.

5

"Lyle, I need you. Please stay with me to-night."

That's what I wanted to say when I called Lyle after the meeting at the Last Word. But I didn't. I am so good at talking at the wrong time and so bad at speaking up when I should. So I didn't say how much I wanted him. I just sort of casually asked if he wanted to go out that night. Lyle said, "I'm sorry. I have to work late, Francesca, and I'm tired. Let's make it tomorrow night."

I wasn't going to beg a man to spend the night with me. If Lyle said he had to work late, then he did. I'd said the same thing to him dozens of times. So why did I feel so rejected when he said it to me? With no reason to go home, I stayed at the *Gazette* until almost eight o'clock working on another column. And instead of driving straight home when I was done, I made a detour to Ratley Street to see the arson house. I had to know for sure if it was the drug house.

One look told me it was. The place looked worse than ever. The weedy yard was covered with broken glass and unidentifiable blackened litter. A burned couch had been dragged outside. The bars were pried off some of the lower windows by the fire department rescue squad. Window bars looked fierce, but they were surprisingly useless for protection. All they did was delay your rescue in an emergency. Most bars were attached to rotten, eighty-year-old wood frames that did not hold screws well, so the bars usually popped right out with a prybar. The bars over the illegal plywood front door looked like they had been cut with a rescue power saw. The door itself was blackened and charred.

The windows were boarded up with fresh plywood. Any surviving glass was a grimy, gray-black. The brick structure seemed surprisingly undamaged, but I couldn't get close enough to see inside. The small square of front yard was festooned with yellow crime scene tape, running from the rusty gate to the front porch. I might have opened the gate anyway to get a better look around, but a thin gray-haired woman came out on her front porch three houses up and stood there with her hands on her hips, watching me. Maybe with the drug house gone, the street's decent people were once more asserting themselves.

There was one other major change. The dangling FOR SALE sign was now hanging from two hooks, not one, and it had a fresh, new UNDER CONTRACT sign plastered across it in big red letters. Who would buy that burned-out building?

I took one more detour and drove slowly up North Dakota Place. The street was deserted. Caroline's grass glowed golden in the long-shadowed sun, and the angel fountain was a mass of gilded rainbows. At sunset, the street was paved with gold. It was an enchanted summer place.

I had no more reasons to avoid going home. I parked Ralph in front of my flat and waved to Mrs. Indelicato behind the counter at the confectionary on the first floor of my building. That used to be my grandparents' confectionary, and some of the same families still ran in for milk, bread, disposable diapers, and six-packs. When unexpected company dropped in, they still sent the kids out the back door for a pound of

boiled ham to dress up the everyday pickle loaf and
baloney on the cold-cut platter. I spent a good part of
my childhood in that store, helping my grandparents. I
sold penny candy to my classmates and dusted the
canned goods with a turkey-feather duster. I still liked
those pink and purple candy buttons on the long strips
of paper, even if I did wind up eating half a pound of
paper.

I unlocked my front door and spotted a cobweb
above the radiator. I'd get that before I went to bed.
My housekeeping wasn't up to my grandmother's standards, but I was still Scrubby Dutch to my soul, and a
cobweb could not be tolerated. Dutch was a corruption of Deutsch. The old beer-making and beer-drink-
ing Germans who built this section didn't think
cleanliness was next to godliness—they thought it was
better.

The flat was unchanged since my grandparents'
deaths. They took me in when I was nine years old,
after my parents died. Well, Mom and Dad didn't just
die—they went out in a pretty spectacular scandal.
They were supposed to be the perfect young couple,
except they were both boozers and Dad played around
a lot, but most people didn't know that, because they
were such big deals in the Catholic church. Then Mom
caught Dad with her best friend at a church party and
went kind of crazy. A week or so after she caught them
together, I came home from school and noticed my
dad's car was in the drive, but it was too early for him
to be home. I heard this dripping sound, like a water
pipe had broken. And Mom wasn't in the kitchen, fixing dinner. I followed the dripping sound upstairs to
their bedroom. At first, I wondered why Mom had a
new red bedspread and what she and Dad were doing
taking a nap in the afternoon, but then I realized the
sound was blood dripping, and they were dead, and
then I started screaming. The police said Mom had

shot Dad and then shot herself. After that, I got to live with my grandparents. I didn't tell anyone, but I liked that better.

I never changed my grandparents' place, because I admired them, and besides, their home was comfortable. There was the big old recliner, with my grandmother's hand-knit afghan. The TV was a huge, dark-wood Magnavox cabinet on skinny brass-bound legs. Over it was a picture of Christ where the eyes followed you. The kitchen had a gray Chromcraft table, a huge gas refrigerator, and a Sunbeam toaster with a skirted Aunt Jemima doll. The bathroom had a plaster fish blowing three gold bubbles and a top hat that Grandma knitted to cover the extra toilet paper roll. A decorator friend told me the place was the epitome of kitsch, so out it was in. He loved it, but I think it's safe to say most people didn't appreciate it.

I ordered up a fourteen-inch Imo's pepperoni-and-mushroom pizza, and when it arrived, I settled in to watch the tube. But I couldn't find anything worth watching. I switched from old movies to sitcom reruns and then, wait a minute . . . was that Charlie on TV?

It was. Our managing editor, the slimy little snake, had crawled on a show called *Press Pass,* the local version of *Meet the Press.* The show featured a host and a couple of local media types who sounded off on national politics without knowing much about the subjects. I preferred the political debates in the local saloon. They were just as informed, and I could get a drink while I was at it. Charlie was wearing his blue suit and a yellow tie to match the streak down his back. His red nose and bald spot had been carefully powdered, and he talked earnestly into the camera, as if he were talking each and every one of us into bed. Charlie could talk the balls off a pool table when he got wound up. And he was definitely wound up. But what about?

The host helpfully answered my question. "Tonight we're discussing the latest revelations about Missouri Senator Deaver Dulwich. The senator is alleged to have had an affair with a twenty-five-year-old intern, then promoted her to a forty-thousand-a-year job in his office," he said solemnly. He was wearing a good suit and a bad rug.

Oh, yeah, Not-So-Dull Dulwich, they were calling him, the photogenic I'm-for-Families senator who always posed with his blond wife and their two blond children. His dog was blond, too. The scandal came out when his wife decided to divorce him, instead of standing by her wandering man.

"In my day politicians had standards," Charlie was saying. "Such behavior in our leadership was not tolerated." What? I turned the sound up, in case I was hearing things.

"Absolutely," said the TV host, whose wife had kicked him out of the house for boffing an intern. "I couldn't agree more."

"If we excuse his infidelities, then we show our own lack of character," Charlie said. "The senator must resign."

"Our leaders should set standards for the little people," said a jowly syndicated columnist who was rumored to be having an affair with the wife of a prominent businessman.

Charlie grabbed the floor back. "I don't care if the young woman was promoted. That doesn't make the senator's actions better. That makes them worse. The minute an executive has a sexual relationship with an underling and then promotes her, he has broken the law," Charlie said, quoting his inamorata on the issue of infidelity.

The other two adulterers nodded smugly. I stared at this shameful display. Had my profession really sunk this low? Newspaper people were never angels—adultery and alcoholism were our two favorite vices, and we had lots more. But we didn't used to be such hypocrites. I shut off the TV in disgust, fetched a broom, and tied a clean rag around it. I got that cobweb, and any other one I could find. Then I started cleaning the house, as if I could scrub away the whole disgusting display on TV. I even dusted the gold bubbles on the plaster fish. Finally, at two A.M., I was so tired I fell into a dreamless sleep.

It was after eight-thirty when I was awakened by sirens screaming down my street. I peeked out the window. It was a repeat of Otto's death: first a fire truck, then a wailing string of police cars, and finally, an ambulance. Once again, they were heading toward North Dakota Place. I threw on some clothes and followed them. This was getting old.

This time, the police and emergency vehicles were at the entrance to the alley behind Dina's house. I saw Homicide Detective Sergeant Mark Mayhew's unmarked car, which looked so much like an unmarked car it might as well have UNMARKED POLICE CAR painted on the side. Mayhew was talking to Dina. The fluffy little blonde was alternately flirting with him and wringing her hands. Uh-oh. It finally penetrated my sleep-fogged brain. If Mayhew was here, that meant only one thing. There was a suspicious death. But all the principal residents of North Dakota Place seemed to be there. I saw Kathy and Dale, both in double-breasted khaki suits, standing at the edge of the alley. She was clutching a briefcase, and Dale had his arm protectively around her. For a moment I felt a pang and wished Lyle was here with me. But I turned my attention to the others. The usually cool Margie looked agitated, talking a mile a minute and shifting from foot to foot. Tall, thin Patricia was standing alone and very still. Her face was drained of all color. She looked like a pillar of salt in a T-shirt. Caroline wasn't saying anything, either. Short, strong, and wide-hipped, she looked like a primitive fertility carving, with a single stroke of the ax blade for the grim line of her mouth. She clutched her wheelbarrow with both hands. It was filled with dying weeds.

"What happened?" I asked.

"It's Hawkeye." Margie's voice rasped like a runaway chain saw. "Dina found him in the alley this morning. Dead."

"Was he mugged? Shot? Stabbed?"

"Here's Dina now," she said. "She can tell you."

As Dina joined us, I saw Mayhew walking toward the alley, freshly barbered and dressed like something out of a *GQ* summer fashion issue. He was a brave man, wearing a cream silk jacket in an alley on a St. Louis summer day.

Dina's eyes were red and puffy, as if she'd been crying, and up close her fluffy blond hair looked flyaway. Her woeful face contrasted oddly with her funny T-shirt. It said: "LOST—husband and cat. Reward for cat."

Dina couldn't wait to talk about what she saw, as if maybe that would push the awful picture out of her mind. "He wasn't shot or anything," she said. "I didn't see any bullet holes or knife wounds, but I didn't look real close after I saw the blood. I think he fell and hit his head on the bricks."

"I don't see how that can kill a big strong guy like Hawkeye," I said.

"I don't, either, but he was dead just the same," Dina wailed.

"What's a jogger doing running in an alley?" Dale asked. Now he was clutching Kathy for comfort.

"He used it as a shortcut to Tower Grove Park," Margie said. "Besides, Caroline told him not to run there, so of course he did."

"I told him it was dangerous," Caroline corrected. "Looks like I was right."

Patricia still said nothing. She just stared straight ahead. But Dina kept talking. "I opened the front door to get the paper this morning, and my cat Stan ran outside. He never does that. Well, hardly ever. He slipped through the gate to the backyard, and I ran after him, and grabbed him as he ran out to the alley, and then I saw poor Hawkeye lying on the bricks, blood all over, and the back of his head . . ." She stopped, took a gulp of air, and said slowly, "It was horrible. I didn't go to City Hall today. If I had, I would have been back by my garage when he was running in the alley. He always turned in there at eight-oh-five. That's when I used to see him, when I was getting my car out. Maybe if I'd been back there . . ."

"He wouldn't have fallen and hit his head?" Margie rasped. "Sorry, sweetie, there wasn't anything you could do. It was an accident."

"What a waste," I said, remembering Hawkeye's beautiful body, bronze as a statue, skimming across the grass.

Patricia was speechless until I said that. Then she made a little catlike mewing noise, which suddenly turned into wrenching, awful cries. But she never said a coherent word. Caroline patted her shoulder, said something soothing, and half guided, half carried Patricia back to her home. She must have stayed with her distressed friend for hours. Margie told me Caroline's wheelbarrow with the dying weeds sat in the parkway for most of the day.

I noticed Mayhew spending a lot of time examining the fence at Dina's house. While everyone was watching Caroline take Patricia away, I tried to get a closer look. There was no way I could get into the alley at this end. It was blocked with crime scene tape, police, and emergency vehicles. They still hadn't taken Hawkeye away, but there were too many people around him to get a clear look at the body. I walked around the block and approached the alley from the other end, but it was guarded by a cop I didn't know, and he waved me on. I walked some more, slipped into Dale and Kathy's backyard, and eased past their battered pickup. I still couldn't get out into the alley, but I was within shouting distance of Mayhew. I couldn't see much, because Dina's garage stuck out and blocked the view. Most garages in this alley were made for Model-Ts, and unless you drove something the size of a Geo, you had a hard time squeezing a car inside. But Dina had built a big, new garage. The rusty Dumpster next to it blocked more of the view, but I saw Mayhew squat down (first pulling up his perfectly creased trousers) and examine the brick pavement. I also saw two grass-stained running shoes and muscular tanned legs on the bricks, and felt really queasy. Fortunately, the Dumpster blocked the rest of Hawkeye's body. Then Mayhew checked out Dina's six-foot privacy fence, going over it carefully, inch by inch. Something was photographed and put in an evidence bag, but I couldn't see what it was. Then he went straight across the alley to an old white-painted garage and examined a nail about two-thirds of the way up in the door frame, and repeated the photographing and bagging routine.

"Find something interesting?" I yelled.

"Yep," he said.

"Want to tell me what it is?" I asked.

"Nope," he said.

Mayhew had that alert, concentrated look, and he was talking in one-syllable sentences. When he got that way, I might as well try to hold a conversation with a clam. I figured I'd find out anyway when I talked to Katie tomorrow about the autopsy results. Katie had no clamlike qualities. I closed the gate and walked back to where the group was. Kathy and Dale were gone.

"They got a little rattled when the police started questioning them," Margie explained, when I asked after them. "The cops were talking to all of us, just doing their jobs, but Dale and Kathy looked really spooked. They took the Toyota that Caroline lets them park in front of their house and went to work."

"I don't want to be mean," Dina said, being mean, "but Patricia is carrying on like the grieving widow. I don't even think they had a date."

"No, but they would have," Margie said. "There was a strong attraction there. Patricia blushed like a young girl around him, didn't you notice? And if he saw her outside, he always stopped to talk to her after his run. He didn't have to, either. He could have kept running. I didn't see her out this morning, though."

"Probably playing hard to get for a change," Dina said, waspishly. "I could see what she saw in him, but what did he see in her?" She sounded puzzled rather than envious. Round, blond Dina was so much prettier than Patricia. "He was a knockout, and she's so plain, except for those amazing blue eyes."

"I wasn't surprised that Hawkeye fell for her," I said. Dina flinched at my poor choice of words, but I kept going. "Stunning people aren't impressed with beauty. They already have it."

"There's more to it than that," Margie said. "He and Patricia had so much in common. They both knew the difference between soy and whey protein drinks and could talk compost until your eyes crossed."

Dina shook her head, as if she didn't want to hear any of this. We had drifted down the street by Otto's house. It looked different. What was it? I stared for a minute until I saw it: the purple paint patches had been painted over with a discreet brick red. The turquoise trim was gone, too. Now it was a respectable forest green. "Who covered up Otto's paint job?" I asked.

"Caroline," Margie replied. "She's already made an offer to the nephew in Columbia to buy Otto's house. I heard it's way below market price, but the place needs a lot of work. Anyway, the nephew accepted. He just wants the house off his hands and the estate settled. It will take awhile for the final details, but meanwhile, Caroline convinced him that she should paint over that purple spot on the brick. I'm trying to get the nephew's phone number from her, so I can pick the contents. Otto's mother had some nice old pieces I'd love to get my hands on."

Something else was different. I did a mental inventory. The backyard was still littered with dandelions and beer cans, and Otto's rusted metal lawn chair sat under the maple tree. Next to it was a pile of cigar butts and an old *Gazette*, yellowing in the heat and humidity. It looked as if Otto would come out the back door any moment. But something was missing. What was it?

"The dog," I said. "Where's Hansie?"

That's what was missing. The noise. The constant high-pitched, ax-blade-in-your-skull barking. The ugly little yapper was silent. "Did the nephew take Hansie?" I asked.

"Er, no," Margie said, and looked slightly ashamed. "Caroline relieved him of that burden. She called the animal shelter right after they took Otto's body away and had Hansie taken away, too."

"He's dead, isn't he?" I said. "She had the dog killed."

"Hansie was old and would pine for his master," Margie said.

"He's dead and I'm glad," Dina said, but her cat T-shirt said she was no dog lover. "He yapped constantly, and Otto wouldn't do a thing about it. Caroline lost at least one tenant because of that dog. I could hear him all the way up the street. His barking drove the neighbors out of their minds. Poor Miss Siemer went crazy when she was recovering from her shoulder surgery. She finally called Otto to complain about the noise. You know what Otto did? He let that dog outside even more, so it barked night and day."

"I'd never have had the nerve to send that dog to the pound, but I'm glad Caroline did," Margie rasped. It was the first time I'd heard her praise Caroline.

"She does all our dirty work for us," Dina said.

More death on North Dakota Place. The jogger, dead in the alley. The drug dealer, burned alive. The disgusting Otto, electrocuted. His noisy dog permanently silenced. The large, smelly piles Hansie left in the yard were his only memorial, and those biodegradable markers would soon be gone. Four deaths. I left. I was sick of North Dakota Place. Even the *Gazette* looked better to me right now.

It was another hour before I got into work. Mrs. Indelicato just happened to step out of the confectionary when I returned and wouldn't let me upstairs until I gave her the lowdown on Hawkeye. By the time I got dressed and made it into the office, it was after ten o'clock. As I walked into the *Gazette* newsroom, I braced myself for the usual sullen quiet. But for once, the place was convulsed in laughter. Even more unusual, the entire staff seemed to be reading the paper. Most Gazetteers were ashamed of the mediocre mush that went out under its masthead and rarely read it except to see what inaccuracies the copy desk had added to their stories. But now they were eagerly—no, gleefully—reading every word.

"What's so funny?" I asked.

"The new day has dawned on our politically correct paper," said young Jennifer, looking like a chirpy little brown bird today. "The new computer program, the one that automatically changed black to African American, went into effect yesterday, right before deadline. Now, in today's paper, in the All About Science section, scientists have discovered an African American hole in space."

"Instead of a black hole?"

"Yes!" She was laughing so hard, she could hardly get out that one word.

"Wait! Here's another one!" Jasper yelled. "Bet you didn't know that Nelson Mandela was an African American leader."

"We could use him," Tina said, but then she too collapsed in laughter. Tears were running down her face. She was pointing to another page.

"What's making you laugh?" I asked.

"The police report," she managed to get out, but she couldn't read it. She simply pointed at it.

Jennifer read it for us: " 'A blue Buick collided with an African American Cadillac,' " she said. "Sounds racist to me."

"This African American drives a Volvo," Tina said.

There were more whoops of laughter, which quieted when a grim-faced Charlie marched across the newsroom and into the glass-walled room where the editors assembled for the morning meeting. He slammed the door and pulled the blinds so we couldn't see inside.

We eagerly scanned Nails's business column for bloopers, but there were none. It was an endless story about the disposable diaper controversy, with information that had appeared before in a hundred other stories. For Nails, the definition of serious reporting was dull.

Enough fun for the day. I went back to my desk, answered phone calls, and checked my mail. It included a photo and press release for a new Mommy-in-the-Making doll that looked like a pregnant Barbie, right down (or up) to the nose-cone boobs and blond hair. She had to be designed by a man. Mommy's long, skinny legs were made for high heels, terrific for a pregnant woman.

There were two letters from readers who liked my column and one who thought I should hang it up—or hang myself, he didn't much care. There was also another postcard from Erwin Shermann, the man with the dead mother. If his last postcard was a little creepy, this one seemed downright threatening. "It's a dirty, lousy shame, isn't it?" it said in that spiky ballpoint. "No one really cares for anyone else. Everyone looks out for Number One. That's what you did. You didn't really care. I could tell in your letter that you didn't understand. Not like my lovely Mother. She understands, but she's no longer with me. It's not fair, is it? You are here, and she is gone. She cares and you don't."

Brrr. That's enough for you, Erwin. I don't want you as a pen pal. I stuffed his postcard in my Weirdo file, where I keep death threats and bizarre communications. Lyle had instructions to show it to the police if anything happened to me.

The phone rang. "Hi," a voice said, nearly breathless with excitement. "My name is Candy. I'm just a reader, but I have a great story for you. The talking virgin has been run over."

"I didn't think there were any virgins left, talking or silent," I said.

"This is a shrine to the Blessed Virgin that talks," Candy said.

Oops. I'd better watch the jokes. South Siders took their religious statues seriously. They treated lawns like knickknack shelves and decorated them with concrete bird-baths, swan planters, pink flamingos, and plastic sunflowers that twirled in the wind. But they always saved room for a shrine to the Blessed Virgin.

Some painted the statues, some made little shrines out of bathtubs sawed in half, and some put spotlights on the statues. But Candy's neighbors, Bud and Dorothy, went one step forward. Bud added sound.

"But not to defraud anyone," she said. "Bud wasn't faking miracles or trying to get money out of people. He just wanted to make the experience more devout. He and Dorothy bought a particularly large and fine concrete Madonna and painted it up real nice, with blond hair and a blue robe. Then they planted a garden of blue-and-white flowers around it. Those are Mary's colors, you know. Naturally, people would stop on the sidewalk to admire the statue and the garden. When they did, Dorothy said prayers in a muted voice into the mike. Respectful, Virgin-related prayers like the Magnificat or the Hail Mary. But if someone walked on their lawn, she'd hand the mike to her husband. Bud had a deep voice and he'd intone, 'WARNING: Do not tread on holy ground.' "

"Let me guess," I said. "The statue was hit by lightning."

"No," Candy said. "It was hit by an eighty-seven Toyota. Jumped the curb and went up on the lawn. Has Mary pinned under the car. You have to see it."

I agreed and rushed over to the unholy scene. It was just as Candy said. The gray Toyota was up on the neat little front yard. It had plowed through the garden, taking out a moon vine and several hydrangeas with softball-size blue flowers. The Virgin was under the crumpled front fender. The car owner said he swerved to avoid a kid on a bike, and "the next thing I knew, I ran over the Virgin Mary." Mary did more damage to his car than he did to her, but Bud and Dorothy said the concrete Madonna would be relocated to a safer spot in the backyard. "This is God's way of telling us to move his Mother," Dorothy said, which I thought gave new meaning to auto-da-fe.

I thanked Bud and Dorothy and counted my blessings. I had a column, and I had dinner with Lyle, and if I left now, I had just enough time to get there on time. We met at Rizzo's, an Italian restaurant in St. Louis Hills. For a so-called German city, we had far more Italian restaurants than German ones. Even Germans like me would rather eat pasta than sauerkraut. Besides, Italian food satisfied other basic St. Louis needs. It was cheap and filling. But it wasn't quite fried enough. After all, we were a Southern city, too. So the local Italian restaurants made a little alteration to their cuisine. They invented toasted ravioli, which are really deep-fat fried ravioli. We dunk them in a ketchupy red sauce. That's what I ordered for my appetizer.

"How can you eat those things?" Lyle asked, as he dug into his eggplant Parmesan. "They taste like a french-fried football."

"You didn't grow up here," I said. "Toasted ravioli satisfy a deep-seated need for grease. This is South Side soul food." He grinned his little boy grin, but I don't think he believed me.

The chicken speidini put a satisfying layer of garlic on top of the grease. For dessert, we walked hand in hand across the street to Ted Drewes, the frozen custard stand. Ted Drewes was wonderfully nostalgic. The white-painted building with the steep roof and wooden icicle trim looked like an elf's cottage. The yellow bug lights over the screened windows belonged to the summer of 1955. So did those fresh-faced kids working the windows, cheerfully calling out "May I help you?" and swiftly serving up our order. The lines were long at Ted Drewes. There were so many customers, the place needed police for crowd control every night, but the waits were entertaining. We had a chance to talk and meet with neighbors.

Lyle ordered a regular soft custard cone, and I ordered a chocolate dip, a foolhardy act, since I was still wearing a suit and dip cones dripped like crazy. But I couldn't resist that sweet chocolate coating. I bit into it, picked off a huge piece of chocolate that slid off, and ate it. Melting frozen custard dripped down my fingers and turned my paper napkins into a sticky mess.

"Here, take this," Lyle said, handing me his handkerchief. "Why do you eat those messy things?"

"More South Side soul food," I said. "I like it when you fuss. Reminds me of my grandmother."

"Thanks a lot." Lyle took the last bite of his cone. He didn't drip anything, depriving himself of the full Ted Drewes experience. We were sitting on the trunk of his car, Sherman, an enormous gold '67 Chrysler. Sherm was the size of a sun porch and made a comfortable seat.

"I like watching the West Countians, watching us," I said.

"How do you know they're West Countians?" he said.

"How many South Side women wear itsy tennis outfits and little socks with fuzzy balls?" I said. "Besides, most South Siders don't drive BMWs."

"Or Jaguars," Lyle said.

"Touché," I said. "I admit that Ralph is not your average South Side car. But those people are still West Countians. It's a thrill for them to drive into the big, dangerous city, even if they are only a mile or so from the city limits. They sit inside the sliding doors on their minivans and stare at us South Siders. Look at them, pointing at that family in the station wagon. That's rude."

"Those folks are kind of fat," Lyle said.

"West Countians aren't fat?" I asked.

"They are, but their fat is better tailored."

"Handsome is as handsome does," I said.

"Now you sound like your grandmother," Lyle said,

laughing. "Feeling superior is the favorite St. Louis sport."

"I can always go to the nontourist Ted Drewes on South Grand if the crowds bother me. No West Countian would venture that deep into the city. Do you believe in coincidence, Lyle?" I asked, abruptly changing the subject.

"Sure," he said. "Happens all the time."

"Do you believe four deaths could be a coincidence?"

"Which four?"

"The ones on North Dakota Place. Everyone who disagrees with Caroline dies."

"You've told me about Hawkeye, but refresh my memory about the others."

"The first death was Otto," I said. "He was electrocuted after an argument with Caroline. She even sent his dog to the pound. Next was that drug dealer who died in an arson fire after he killed six of Caroline's trees. The fourth death was Hawkeye, who ran on her grass."

"That's only three deaths," Lyle said.

"I'm counting Hansie, Otto's dog."

"Oh, come on, Francesca. A dog? Anyway, wasn't Otto involved in ticket-fixing and other illegal activities at City Hall?"

"That's the rumor."

"There would be lots of reasons someone would want to kill him, then. And it's no surprise when a drug dealer dies. Most never make thirty. You don't even know if Hawkeye was murdered."

"Katie will tell me for sure tomorrow. But Mayhew was crawling all over the alley where he died."

"I think you're reaching, Francesca," he said. "All you have is two murders—a crooked city employee and a drug dealer. Hawkeye's death is suspicious, but you don't know anything about him. He could have been doing something risky, too. All he did was jog on Caroline's grass. Do you think she'd kill him for that? She's a rich woman. Rich people don't commit murder. They sue you to death."

I laughed, though I knew very well that the rich could be just as murderous as the poor, and they could hire better lawyers to escape the consequences.

"You can't understand the tension on that street, Lyle," I said, losing another battle with my dip cone. "Rehabbers are free spirits, and Caroline is trying to control them like a cross between a prison matron and a high school principal. She doesn't want them parking their trucks out front. She yells at them if they walk on the grass. She calls the city inspectors if they disobey her. You can get by with that tight-assed behavior in the richer parts of West County. I heard about this Ladue subdivision where the neighbors go nuts if you didn't close your garage door. But city people won't put up with that kind of control."

"They're not putting up with it," Lyle said. "They're telling off Caroline."

"And winding up dead," I said.

"But you said Caroline has fought with just about everyone on the street. The others are still alive, aren't they?"

I mentally ran down the list. Mrs. Grumbacher, the widow who had the city inspector all over her house when she didn't paint fast enough to please Caroline, was alive. So was Mack, reprimanded for not cutting the grass. And Sally, whose boyfriend got a twenty-dollar ticket when he parked his pickup on North Dakota Place. Make that ex-boyfriend, thanks to Caroline.

"Yeah, they're alive," I said. "But they all did what Caroline wanted. Is that a coincidence, too?"

Another squiggly line of melting frozen custard escaped and ran down my fingers. I finished the last bite and licked my fingers. Then I licked Lyle's ear. He grabbed me and kissed me firmly. His lips were soft and sticky sweet, his tongue was hard and talented. "How's that for South Side soul?" he asked when we came up for air.

"Very nice," I said. "I think we're giving those West Countians quite a show. Now they're pointing at us."

"Let them find their own entertainment," he said. "My place, or yours?"

6

The next day I was sitting nervously in Katie's office at the city medical examiner's, wondering what horror was lurking here. Katie didn't have anything obviously awful in her morgue office, like jars of pickled people's feet. She was more subtle, but I knew it could be stomach-turning just the same. I was already unnerved by the faint smell of spoiled meat that seemed to seep under the door.

Katie sure didn't look like a morgue creature. Her short brown hair was shiny and springy and she had a healthy tan. She'd even remembered to change into a fresh lab coat, so I wouldn't be grossed out by any suspicious stains. I inventoried her office. The shelves still held fat, dignified medical books, the walls were covered with framed diplomas and honor society certificates, and her golf putter was in the corner. Then I saw it, in plain view on top of her desk. It was long and shiny, with a lethal-looking metal club on one end.

"Is that a murder weapon?" I asked.

"It's been used to beat a man pretty badly, but he'll survive," Katie said, and grinned. "It's my new putter." She stashed it in the corner, next to her old one.

"What happened to the guy who collapsed on the golf course?"

"He'll live," Katie said. "It wasn't a heart attack. He had heat exhaustion, which gave him severe muscle cramps and chest pains, which scared the heck out of him. Happens a lot on golf courses in the good old Midwest."

"So what did you and Mitch do for him?"

"There was only one bottle of water around, and a lot of beer, so we had his three pals dump their cold beer on him, which they thought was the ultimate sacrifice for a friend. That helped cool the guy down. Then we made him drink the water, something that hadn't passed his lips for a while. By that time EMS showed up and took him off to the emergency room. Mitch and I resumed our game, and it went a little faster with that foursome out of the way. I won, Mitch bought the beer, and then I called the ER. The guy had been treated and released. I haven't seen him in here, so I assume he's okay." Katie leaned back in her chair and stretched.

"That's the good news," I said. "Now for the bad. How did the jogger fall and kill himself?"

"He didn't fall," Katie said. "He was murdered. Your neighborhood is getting downright dangerous, Francesca. That's the third murder I've seen. The uniforms who answered the call saw something was wrong right away. I just confirmed it. Somebody did a bad job of trying to make a murder look like an accident. Your friend Mayhew figured out that a thin wire or fishing line had been stretched across the alley—he didn't find the wire, but he did find the nails the killer used to hang it on."

"That explained why I found Mayhew examining Dina's fence and the nail on the garage across the alley," I said. "How do you know it was wire?"

"That's the best guess, judging by the injuries. Fishing line has a better chance of breaking. Mayhew spotted the thin line the wire made across the guy's neck."

"And that killed him?"

"No, he was only stunned when he fell. Probably

knocked him out for a minute or so. But he died of repeated blows to the head, and they were not caused by the fall. They were inflicted later. Somebody beat the victim so hard with a brick or rock, it killed him."

I shuddered. What an ugly end for the hunky Hawkeye. "You're sure it wasn't a bad fall? That alley is paved with bricks, and some of them get loose. He could have hit one."

"No way," Katie said. "I examined his head and saw his X rays. Skull fractures look different when someone is hit repeatedly as opposed to when the person falls. The murderer probably used a brick, but the police didn't find the actual weapon. It would be easy to remove and toss away later. What a waste. Such a fine physical specimen, and now he's a hundred and ninety pounds of meat."

"The man was beautiful," I said. "You should have seen him running through the grass. I don't like Caroline much, but she was right to warn him to stay out of that alley. She said some kids were playing dangerous pranks back there, boobytrapping the alley."

"Kids?" Katie said. "This wasn't done by kids, and it wasn't any prank. Kids might have gotten lucky and knocked the guy out with the wire, but they wouldn't smash his head with a brick. He was killed by someone who was very angry. The killer literally beat his head in."

I shuddered. "We called him Hawkeye, but I know that wasn't his name. I don't know what he did for a living, either."

"I have that information," she said. She paged through the autopsy report. "His name was Johnny Morano. He had an apartment on Maryland Avenue in the Central West End. He was unmarried, twenty-nine years old, and a bartender at the Meet Rack, a singles' bar on Laclede's Landing."

Katie's beeper sounded. She read the number and jumped up. "Gotta go," she said.

So did I. As I walked outside to my car, the heat hit me in the face. It was like walking into a burning building. The temperature had to be near a hundred degrees. My suit jacket was soaked with sweat on the short walk. My panty hose felt like wet bandages. I wondered if it was possible to strangle from the waist down. Ralph's leather car seat burned my legs. His steering wheel was almost too hot to hold. Only after the air conditioning cooled off my car could I think about Hawkeye's death—excuse me, Johnny's. Now that he was dead, he at least deserved the respect of his real name.

Did Caroline kill Johnny Hawkeye? No, that was crazy. Caroline was a respected businesswoman. She wouldn't kill a jogger for running on her grass. Anyway, it wasn't her grass. It was the city's. But Caroline acted like the grass was hers. Heck, she carried on like she'd personally adopted each blade. And Johnny Hawkeye didn't just run on the grass. He humiliated Caroline—and she seemed fairly unhinged to begin with. She didn't sleep much. She worked almost around the clock. She made harsh, ridiculous rules and expected people to follow them without question, as if she were a queen giving commands. I'd seen her get into screaming fights with three people. Who were now dead.

Still, as Lyle said, rich people didn't kill, they sued you to death. But how could she sue Johnny Hawkeye? He wasn't doing anything illegal. He was running on a public parkway and in a public alley. Johnny had a mean mouth and a serious stubborn streak, both ideal for a feud with Caroline. South Siders loved feuds better than the Hatfields and McCoys. They could start over something as small as a grass blade and go on for decades. I knew a woman who didn't speak to her own sister for fifty years over a twenty-five-dollar savings bond. One of my aunts didn't talk to her husband for twenty years over a button he wanted her to sew on his shirt. She had three kids during that time, too, but that was her wifely duty.

None of the deaths, except Otto's, had actually occurred on North Dakota Place, and the *Gazette* had reported Otto's as an accident. There was no follow-up story when the autopsy concluded Otto was actually murdered, because the *Gazette* publisher did not like murder stories in his newspaper. So North Dakota Place's reputation was saved. Thanks to the publisher's desire for gracious living, nobody knew how deadly life was on North Dakota Place—or how profitable death was. Caroline would make a handsome profit from Otto's death. She'd bought his house cheap from his nephew.

I remembered that "Under Contract" sign on the burned-out drug dealer's house. Was Caroline buying that place, too? Why would she want it? Why would anyone want it? I knew who I could ask. Tracy McCreery, the real estate agent for the house. She'd given me a funny column once, and I'd helped her by talking to her real estate association when a speaker canceled at the last minute. Tracy owed me one. She could tell me who had the house under contract. I found a pay phone and was instantly sorry I'd left my cool car. The heat shimmered on the pavement, and my heels sank into the melting blacktop. One of these days, I'd have to give up my prejudice against car phones. Tracy was in her office when I called. I said I wanted to ask her some questions about rehabbing. She sounded extremely cheerful.

"Hey, Francesca," Tracy said. "I thought I'd take an afternoon off for a change and sit by the pool."

"Your city flat has a pool?" That was a rarity.

"Nothing but zoysia grass in my backyard," she

said. "But I'm house-sitting a friend's condo in West County, and it has a very nice clubhouse and pool. Might as well see how the other half lives. I'll have my kid with me, but Michelle will be in the water most of the time. There's always a nice cool breeze. Why don't you come along and ask me your questions there?"

"Love it," I said. "I can't go swimming, but I'll be happy to sit around and call it work." Tracy gave me an address in the far west suburb of Manchester. Forty minutes later I pulled off Woods Mill Road and into the condo subdivision. The condos were red brick with white balconies and shrubs just high enough to hide the air conditioner units. Tracy met me at the door wearing her swimsuit and holding two glasses of cold lemonade. She led the way to the pool. Her five-year-old daughter, Michelle, capered around us in her pink Little Mermaid suit, crying "Mommeee, look!" every thirty seconds. I wondered how Mommeee managed to act interested, but Tracy didn't seem to be faking it. I guess a real five-year-old was better than the people at my office, who just acted like five-year-olds. At the pool, Michelle ran off to splash around in the shallow end with two other girls in Little Mermaid suits. We found two white plastic lounges to watch Michelle while we talked. I took off my suit jacket, rolled up my sleeves, kicked off my shoes, and settled in. With a breeze to cool things down, the sun felt good on my face and arms, and the strong chlorine and coconut suntan oil smell conjured up lost summer days. The other folks at the pool were moms and retirees. Two of those old guys were going to step on their tongues if they kept staring at Tracy in her black suit. The woman was built, even if she did hide a lot of it with a modest one-piece suit. She'd really attracted the attention of a wrinkled old guy who sported a tiny leopard pattern Speedo suit, an enormous gut, and a neck full of gold chains. He looked like a mummy who'd escaped his wrappings.

"You'd think those gold chains would burn his neck in the sun," Tracy said.

"Keep America beautiful," I said. "Keep your shirt on, sir."

We both laughed. I don't think Mr. Leopard heard what we were saying, but he guessed it wasn't flattering. He retired to the other side of the pool to read his Tom Clancy and sulk.

"Congratulations for getting the contract on the Ratley Street house," I said.

"Talk about a fire sale," Tracy said. "The day after it burned, I had an offer."

"Who would buy a burned-out house?"

"There's no serious structural damage. If you were planning to rehab it, you'd have to gut it anyway. Before the fire, the owner had, shall we say, an optimistic view of its value. He refused my suggestions to fix it up and lower the price. He rented to that awful tenant without a reference check, because the guy paid him in cash. No buyers in their right minds would look at that dump. We only listed it as a favor to the manager, who went to church with this guy. I couldn't show it, and I thought I'd never sell it.

"Now the owner will take anything. He grabbed this low-ball offer and was grateful. He'll do all right. Better than he deserves, renting to a drug dealer and ruining that street."

"You sound angry," I said.

"I am," she said. "The owner lives in Chesterfield, did you know that? One of the richest parts of St. Louis county, and he has slum property in the city. The county is killing the city. Some of the worst city real estate is owned by people like him. Greedy doctors and lawyers and executives. They consider themselves good family people, too. They wouldn't rent to a drug dealer on their nice street in Chesterfield, but it's okay for city people to live next door to them. It's okay for city people to live in substandard housing. And it's certainly okay to collect those rents. There's a guy who comes into my South Side neighborhood in a Mercedes, to collect rents on a four-family flat with no hot water."

"Maybe if the city enforced the code," I said, "he wouldn't be doing that."

"How?" Tracy asked. "If he's cited for bad tuck-pointing and hauled into court, the most he'll get is a five-hundred-dollar fine. Replacing the washed-away mortar on that old brick building would cost him between two and three thousand dollars. Guess which one he pays?"

I took another sip of my drink. "Look, Tracy, I'm not going to defend scum like that. But since the tax laws changed, maybe that's the only way you can make money with those old buildings. Maybe there's no money in renting out a place that's fixed up nice."

Tracy snorted in a way that hurt my sinuses. "That's the irony," she said. "You can make money rehabbing, but only if you spend money. You have to do a quality rehab. Most people think of rehabbing the way it was in the seventies and eighties. Back then some naive young couple would buy an old house, teach themselves how to strip the wallpaper and the woodwork, patch their own plaster, and refinish their own floors. It was all trial and error. Then they'd move on and sell the house to another nice young couple."

I immediately thought of Kathy and Dale, the sweet young rehabbers.

"That's not how you make money," she said. "You need to know what you're doing these days. First, you buy the property cheap. Then you gut it and fix it up first class. You put in a new kitchen. You put in new bathrooms with period-accurate fixtures. The old plaster is removed and new drywall put in. The floors are either refinished or new ones put in. Outside, the wood trim is stripped or you buy new trim that's milled just like the old. Then, when it's finished, you don't rent it cheap to drug dealers. You charge good money, you do background checks, and you bring in first-class renters. Or you sell at high prices to quality people. Again, no cash deals to drug dealers.

"This kind of rehabbing is expensive, and it's time consuming, and it takes a lot of knowledge. But you can make good money. I know a couple who bought a derelict place from the city for one dollar, then spent a hundred and twenty thousand on a first-class rehab—and still made a hundred thousand when they sold it. Everybody did well on that deal. The rehabbers made money, and the home buyers had a fabulous house that would have cost half a million in the county.

"But this kind of rehabbing is risky. I also know people who lost their shirts because they did a quality rehab but misjudged where the DMZ was—the outer limit in the drug wars, where nice folks won't cross. They couldn't sell the building for six years. It ruined them. Rehabbing is a high-stakes gamble now. But there's no money in slumlording, as the Ratley Street owner can tell you. It's a dead end. He rented that place to that drug dealer for two-fifty a month, as is, because he was too cheap to make any repairs. He didn't even want to fix the toilet. If the owner had any sense, he'd have gut-rehabbed the property and fixed it up right. The good landlords are getting a thousand to fifteen hundred a month rent. But he was too cheap. And too prejudiced. He thought only black drug dealers lived in the city, so that's who he rented to."

"You really hate him," I said.

"I hate what he did to my neighborhood," she said. "The new buyer is shrewd and plans to do a quality rehab. And the house is on the right side of the DMZ."

"So who has the house under contract?"

"I'll ask the seller if he wants to reveal that information," Tracy said.

"You just can't tell me?" I asked.

"No, it wouldn't be ethical," Tracy said. "I can't reveal who has it under contract without the seller's permission."

"Come on, you can tell me. I'm the woman who helped you when your speaker didn't show."

"Sorry, Francesca, I can't. I just can't tell you."

"Okay, if you can't tell me, how about if I tell you? I'll name a name. If that's the right person, you don't have to say anything. If it's not the buyer, you can say I'm wrong." I knew I was pushing my luck as Tracy studied the ice melting in her almost-empty lemonade glass. "It's Caroline, isn't it?" I said. Her silence was louder than the laughing children.

Finally Tracy looked at me and said, "We're even, Francesca." Her voice was flat and her gray-blue eyes were angry. I knew she felt used. I thanked her, put on my shoes and jacket, and let myself out of the pool gate. Tracy did not say good-bye. I hoped that was because she was distracted by Michelle's latest "Mommeee, look!" I also hoped Tracy wouldn't stay angry with me. But I didn't feel too guilty. I was right. Caroline was buying the Ratley Street house. She had profited from Scorpion Smith's death. That was two murders she'd made money on.

Even going to the *Gazette* didn't dampen my mood. I was right, I was right, I was right, I told myself on the long, fast highway drive back downtown. I was right, I was right, I repeated, as I walked from the parking lot to the *Gazette* office. The sidewalks were as hot as a grease-joint griddle, and just as dirty, but I didn't care. I was right, I was right.

My song of triumph carried me into the *Gazette*. It was two-thirty, and most of the staff was still at lunch.

The Family section was deserted, except for O'Hara, a burned-out feature writer, sleeping off another liquid lunch at his desk. I could hear him snoring, and that cheered me up, too. He wouldn't be listening to any phone conversation I had with Lyle. The *Gazette* phones were bugged, but if the buggers wanted to listen to the spicy details of last night, that was fine with me.

"You were wonderful last night," I said to Lyle, my voice low and breathy.

"Yes," he said. His voice had a satisfied, purry sound to it, too.

"Modest, too," I said.

"Nothing to be modest about," Lyle said, teasing me. "But since we're handing out compliments, you were pretty good yourself."

"Only pretty good?"

"Who's being modest now? You were spectacular."

"So, want to see if you can exceed my expectations tonight?" I said.

The bantering tone stopped. "I'd like to, Francesca," he said seriously. "I can't tell you how much I want to be with you tonight. But I have to work late again, and it's important, or I wouldn't put you off. If we were married, we wouldn't have these conversations. I wouldn't have to drive across town to see you. You'd be there, waiting for me when I got home."

"Don't bet on it," I said, "I might be working late, too." I hung up the phone hard enough that O'Hara, dozing at his desk four cubicles away, popped up like a gopher out of his hole. I smiled and waved at him, and he popped back down and went to sleep again.

In the stack of letters and press releases on my desk was another bizarre postcard from Erwin, the motherless mother-worshipper. The spiky handwriting looked like daggers. The words themselves were even more threatening. "Nobody cares and nobody understands, not like my Mother. You don't understand. You don't care. You don't deserve to live in the same world as my pure angel Mother. You got lucky, but you don't deserve your luck. My lovely Mother saw the invisible people and made them real. She made me real. Now that she's gone, I'm one of the invisible ones. I'm not here. If my Mother isn't here, you don't deserve to be here, either."

Erwin was getting seriously strange. I started to stick this postcard in the Weirdo file, too. But then I grabbed all three and stuffed them into my briefcase instead. Maybe I should show them to someone. It was too early to leave for my four o'clock interview, and there was no point in hanging out at Uncle Bob's, since it wasn't on the way. I couldn't fall asleep like O'Hara, and with Nails holding court in the newsroom, I didn't want to be wandering around out there. Why be a moving target for that woman? I was so desperate, I read the *Gazette*. It wasn't as much fun, now that the spell check had been fixed so it no longer changed black to African American. The publisher's gracious living campaign continued, so the major front-page story was about the symphony conductor's contract. There was another long piece about the new art museum show. Amazing. The *Gazette* had eliminated crime and corruption. I flipped to the business pages and checked out my sister columnist, Nails. What was this? Nails had written another story about babies. This one was a puff piece about a new organic baby food company in St. Louis. Two baby stories in a few days. Ah-hah! Now I had news.

The newsroom was still almost deserted, so I risked going to Georgia's office. She was wearing one of her squared-off gray suits and eating a matching square gray-meat sandwich. She was frowning, but not at the sandwich. She was still reading the journalism tome *Ensheathe and Ensnare* and expected me to share her misery. "On page three-twelve, this so-called expert says, 'The individualization of the essential ideation has created an identifiable communications vacuum between the news generator and the news consumer.' Any idea what the fuck that means?"

"Why doesn't the guy speak plain English?" I said.

"Because then we'd know for sure he's not saying anything," she said. Then she fixed me with a knowing look. "I heard someone's been doing some plain speaking. You had a little run-in with Cruella."

"She started it," I said, sounding like a third grader.

"Why are you so eager to make another enemy, Francesca?" Georgia asked.

"Do you think she'd like me better if I let her butcher my column? The woman is a bully. The only way to deal with bullies is to bully them back."

"There are other ways. Now she's bad-mouthing you to management. You're getting a reputation as difficult."

I shrugged. To change the subject I said, "Nails is pregnant."

"Get out of here," Georgia said. "She's too smart to be pregnant." Georgia had a jaundiced view of motherhood.

"Nope, she's passed my infallible pregnancy test. Two baby stories in a week. When a newswoman is pregnant, she starts writing stork stories. She can't help herself."

"She has no interest in children. Why would she get pregnant?" Georgia asked.

"So Charlie will marry her—the oldest reason in the world. I'll bet you twenty bucks."

"You're on," Georgia said. "But I want proof before I pay up."

Proof was just around the corner. I almost stumbled over it, when I walked out of Georgia's office. "Baaabbbbe," a voice like a lost sheep said. "Baaabe, come here. I have something I want to show you." It was Babe, our gossip columnist, looking like a cod with a secret sorrow. He stuck a letter in my face. It was on Charlie's personal *Gazette* stationery, covered with Charlie's personal hen-scratching. "Dear Babe," it said. "Thank you for your sensitivity in the matter of my forthcoming nuptials to Nadia. We both understand that there is no need to mention in your column that my bride is expecting." Expecting? How Victorian for a sleazy affair in a minivan.

"You were going to print in your *Gazette* column that Nadia got knocked up?" I asked Babe. I was astonished.

"Even though he is the managing editor, I had to treat Charlie like anyone else," Babe said piously.

"Did you write that little item yet?" I said.

"No," Babe said, looking slightly shifty. "I felt I owed him the right to discuss it with me."

"Just like anyone else?" I said acidly.

Babe didn't have to explain the rest. He'd blackmailed Charlie. If Charlie had booted Babe out of his office during their little discussion, Babe would have written a column mentioning Charlie's pregnant bride. Once that explosive topic was in the computer system, the whole staff would know about it, thanks to the newsroom hackers. Of course the item would never make the *Gazette.* Any editor with a rudimentary sense of self-preservation would kill it. Then someone on the staff, maybe even Babe himself, would slip the killed item to the *St. Louis Media Critique,* the media watchdog, which would gleefully make it public. The resulting scandal would get more attention than if the item had actually run in Babe's column, in between the fertile doctors and salon-jumping hairstylists. It might even make the national journalism journals. Charlie couldn't risk that. It was shrewd of Charlie to respond to Babe quickly, but it was stupid of him to put it in writing. Usually he was too crafty to leave a paper trail. His brains must have leaked out between his legs. He'd just guaranteed Babe employment as long as Charlie was in power. Now Babe was bragging a bit by showing it around. I couldn't wait to get back to Georgia with the good news. She was still struggling with page three-twelve of *Ensheathe and Ensnare*, the unending journalism tome, and not happy about it. "What the hell do you want now?" she asked.

"Pay up," I said. "I have confirmation," and told her the whole Charlie and Babe story.

"I'll be damned," Georgia said. "The woman is fuckin' pregnant."

"Usually how it happens," I said, and held out my hand for the twenty. Georgia paid up, and I shoved the bill into my jacket pocket just as Smiley Steve, the assistant managing editor for scummy stuff, walked over to us with a big insincere smile on his face. That wasn't his real title, but Steve handled all the nasty jobs at the *Gazette*, and from his extra-wide smile, this one must be particularly unpleasant.

"I'm collecting for a wedding present for the upcoming nuptials of our managing editor and Miss Noonin," he said. "Suggested donations for those in management positions are twenty dollars."

"Can't get the troops to shell out for a gift for our beloved leader?" I asked. I didn't bother to look at Georgia. I could feel her glare.

"The staff has the greatest respect for our managing editor, but many have families to support," he said.

"Maybe if Charlie paid them more, his staff could afford to give him a gift," I said. Steve would carry this conversation right back to Charlie, but I didn't care. My career was trashed anyway if he was marrying Nails.

Georgia handed Smiley Steve two tens. She'd pay anything to get him out of there.

"What about you, Francesca?" Steve asked.

"I'm not management," I said. "Besides, I don't have twenty dollars."

"She has it," Georgia said, and took the twenty out of my pocket.

When Smiley Steve departed, she added, "Consider that a tax on your big mouth. Maybe next time it will pay you to shut up."

7

"Isn't this heat awful?" Margie said when she met me at her door. "I can't remember a summer this hot."

Spoken like a true St. Louisan. We were heading into July. It would be hotter than the hinges of hell from now through September, but we always acted like the heat was a surprise. St. Louis has two nice days a year, and we'd had both of them. The rest of the time the weather was extreme: extremely hot, extremely cold, extremely wet, or extremely dry. It was raining, hailing, sleeting, or snowing, sometimes all on the same day. Just to add color and texture to our weather, we had tornadoes, where the sky turned sickly green and black, and floods, where the Mississippi looked like a roiling river of mud. We were proud of our bad weather. It built character. St. Louisans were convinced that California was filled with wackos, wimps, and weaklings because it had perpetually nice weather. An accurate response to Margie's question would be "Of course it's hot. It's almost July." But I gave the polite St. Louis answer: "It's just awful. How did people live here in the summer before air conditioning?" (They didn't. The rich went to Michigan. The poor went to their basements or slept on blankets in the park.)

Margie looked like a slightly demented Ethel Mertz from the old *I Love Lucy* show. Her hair was tied up in a jaunty flowered scarf, like Ethel and Lucy used to wear. She wore cutoffs and a saggy, stained T-shirt. I could still read the writing on the shirt. It said "You can't get rid of me—I've tried." If that wasn't unnerving enough, her sweaty face was streaked with dirt and she was covered with gritty, gray dust, as if she'd clawed her way out of a collapsed building. Or maybe beat her way out. She was also holding a dusty baseball bat.

"How did you get so dirty by seven A.M.?" I asked.

"You're late to my demolition derby," she said. "I've been up working since five-thirty this morning. You can't have the air conditioning on when you're taking out plaster—you need the windows open for ventilation, or you'll choke on the dust. It's so hot, you can only do this early in the morning or late at night."

"It is hot," I agreed. "Seventy-eight degrees at seven A.M. It will be up near a hundred again today."

"Come on up," she said. "I've got most of one wall out already."

I'd volunteered to help Margie knock the plaster off the walls in her third-floor bedroom. I knew my friend Jinny didn't quite trust Margie, but I did. I wanted to talk to her about my suspicions about Caroline, without Dina and Patricia, and this was the only time we both had for the next few days. Besides, I thought clubbing cracked plaster might make a column. I'd never been to what rehabbers called a gutting party. Margie told me the dress code: Wear old clothes, wrap my hair, and I could shower and change for work at her place.

"Bring your weapon of choice for cracking plaster," she said. "I use a baseball bat and an old pipe wrench."

I brought a tire iron from the back of Ralph. I hung my work suit in a downstairs closet and then followed Margie upstairs to the third floor. She'd sealed off the landing using masking tape and big sheets of clear plastic, but the plaster dust still seeped out and drifted all the way down to the first floor. It coated the round table and the parson's seat, and Margie left gray-white footprints when she climbed the steps to the third floor. Dust-streaked plastic hung like a gray curtain over the door to the room. When we pulled it aside, it was like stepping into a sauna. A really dusty, dirty sauna, with chunks and crunchy piles of plaster on the floor. I took a deep breath, a real mistake. The air was almost solid, there was so much dust. Margie pulled a once-white paper filter mask out of a tool chest. "You can use this, if you want." I waved it aside. I wasn't getting much air as it was. Three walls were painted a sickly mint green, set off with brown water stains, kid-size handprints, and light patches where pictures used to hang. The fourth wall, an outside wall, had about half the plaster gone, so the brick was exposed.

"All you have to do is hit this so hard, it breaks," she said. "Some of it is old and crumbly and falls right off. Some of it, you really have to pound. It's a great way to relieve anger. I pretend I'm beating someone I really hate. I use the heavier pipe wrench for beating Caroline to a pulp and the lighter ball bat for smashing antique dealers." She picked up a three-foot pipe wrench that had to weigh ten pounds and slammed it against the wall. A flat, frying-pan–size chunk of plaster fell out. "Take that, Caroline," said Margie, and swung the pipe wrench. There was a clanging *CRAK!* and a star-shaped crack appeared in the plaster. "Take that!" *CRAK!* "And that, and that and that!" With a noise like a minilandslide, about four feet of plaster slid off the wall. There was a choking cloud of dust.

I chose another outside wall, with a dormer window, and began beating it with the tire iron. With each swing, I imagined I was hitting another Charlie body part. The first shot went right to the managing editor's wobbly fat gut. Nothing much happened. Next I kneecapped him and got a huge crack in the wall. Then I slammed him across the chest. That felt so good that I hit him on his thick head. I got in a few whacks for the *Gazette* staffers, hitting the wall until all of the plaster had broken off. But I didn't feel any better: I knew Charlie would be at the *Gazette* forever.

"Hey, you're really getting into this," Margie said, admiring the huge hole I'd created. The plaster dust had turned her rasp into a croak. "I need to wet my whistle. Let's take a break." We crunched out into the hall and sat on two yellow webbed lawn chairs. Margie opened a box of glazed doughnuts and offered me either coffee from a Thermos or a cold drink from the cooler. I munched on a doughnut and washed it down with bottled water. My mouth was full of grit, my nose was clogged, and I had plaster chunks in my bra.

Margie talked a little about her plans for the room and then the subject switched to Caroline. "Did you hear the latest? Now she's after those poor kids."

"Dale and Kathy? What's she want with the world's sweetest rehabbers?"

"Caroline wants them to paint their porch. That's a major job. That paint has to be burned off. I don't think they can do it themselves. Not at their current skill level. They'll probably have to hire someone, and they don't have any money. But Caroline is really pressuring them."

"Why is she putting the screws to Dale and Kathy?" I asked.

"Remember when she brought those West County real estate people through on the tour?"

"How can I forget? That's when Otto almost painted his house purple."

"The real estate agents ate this buffet at Caroline's and then went up and down the street, making snippy comments about our homes. The plantings around the fountain were outdated. They didn't like the on-street parking. Caroline could put in a forest of fountain grass and Japanese maples, and hide all the cars, and you still wouldn't get those people showing houses on North Dakota Place. They made up a bunch of reasons why our houses wouldn't sell, because they couldn't say the real reason: They didn't like all those black people walking around, not wearing maids' and waiters' uniforms. You don't see any black people walking around their part of West County, and they like that just fine.

"Anyway, one touring real estate agent remarked that Dale and Kathy's porch needed paint. That set Caroline off. She told the kids they were ruining the street. Caroline gave them until the end of July to fix the porch, or she'll call the city inspector. The kids are frantic. That house has already eaten every dollar they have, and they were putting off painting the outside until next spring. Dale and Kathy told Caroline they were short of money, and do you know what she said? They didn't need two vehicles! Caroline said they could sell either their car or their truck, and she hoped it would be the truck. Of course, Caroline claims she's doing this for the good of the neighborhood. I think she wants to drive them out, so she can buy their house cheap, too."

That sounded a little far-fetched, but not as wild as what I was about to propose. I tiptoed into the subject carefully. "Did you ever wonder about all the people turning up dead after Caroline fights with them?"

"I think she's killing them," Margie said flatly.

My soul sister. "You really believe that?"

"Sure," Margie rasped. "I told Dina that I thought Caroline had killed Otto, and she thought I was out of my mind. After her reaction, I shut up. But I think Caroline is coming unglued. I think she killed Otto, for sure. It would be easy for her to set up that accident with the Christmas lights. She's handy, and she hated Otto."

"She made money off his death, too," I said. "She got his house cheap."

"You saw how she yelled at that drug dealer," Margie said. "You'd have to be crazy to confront him like she did. And the way she carried on when he broke her trees. She's lucky that's all he did. He could have shot her, and us, too. Instead, she said he should be crushed like a cockroach. Here's something else. Dina told me she saw Caroline out late the night the drug dealer's house burned."

"She's buying the drug dealer's place," I added.

"If I had any money, I'd buy it," Margie said. "It's perfect for a gut rehab. Maybe she's crazy like a fox. Two deaths, and two houses cheap."

"Hawkeye's murder is the one that doesn't fit," I said. "What do you know about the house with the troublesome kids? Caroline warned him about those kids pulling dangerous pranks."

"The kids are a nuisance," Margie said. "A lot of bikes have disappeared and cars have been broken into since they moved in, but we've never actually caught them at it. I did see the thirteen-year-old waving a gun in the gangway between the houses and I called the police. They took him into custody, but he was back the next day. Nobody likes those kids. I'm not going to defend them. But Caroline is the only one who's seen their so-called dangerous pranks."

"Something else I can't figure out," I said. "I talked with the medical examiner. Hawkeye's—I mean Johnny's—death was staged to look like an accident. The killer strung a wire across the alley to stun him. But why set it up in that alley? If a car came down there, it would pull down the wire. There would be lots of morning traffic, with the neighbors going to work."

"But that's just it," Margie said. "The people on the

upper half of the block drive out the other end of the alley. On this end, Mr. Henderson leaves for work at six A.M. Old Mrs. Meyer doesn't have a car. Dina leaves at eight o'clock on the mornings she goes downtown, but she told us that she'd be staying home the rest of the week. Dale drives Kathy into work and they take their car, which is parked out front. Caroline and I work at home, and unless I'm picking, I don't leave before ten. So if you live here, you'd know that no cars go down that alley after six o'clock for about four hours. Everyone knew Hawkeye turned into that alley at eight-oh-five. You could set your watch by him.

"Here's another reason why I think Caroline did it. Johnny Hawkeye's murder wasn't an ordinary mugging or shooting. This was a murder made to look like an accident. Caroline wouldn't want a murder to sully her street's reputation. It would be bad for property values. An accident would be regrettable but soon forgotten. Nobody would think twice if a jogger tripped and fell in an alley around North Dakota Place."

"But I still don't know why Johnny Hawkeye was murdered," I said. "I don't think even Caroline would be crazy enough to kill him for running on the grass."

"I do," Margie said. "That woman would do anything to protect her precious street."

We finished our drinks and went back to plaster bashing. I kept thinking about what Margie said. Margie had seemed a little wacky herself, swinging her pipe wrench at the wall and screaming "Take that, Caroline" until she was hoarse. Rehabbers literally sweated and bled to save these old houses. If the neighborhood went bad, they'd lose everything. Maybe they'd lose their minds, too. Maybe Caroline had killed Hawkeye. Talking to Margie only strengthened my belief that Caroline killed Otto and Scorpion Smith. It was time to talk with Mayhew. I checked my watch—

nine o'clock. I might still catch him at Uncle Bob's, if I was lucky.

I showered at Margie's house and changed into my suit, a sleek Donna Karan white-on-white stripe. "You look terrific," Margie said. "Let me walk you down to the door."

She unlocked her heavy oak and beveled glass front door. I walked out and saw two police officers on the sidewalk at the young rehabbers' house. "What are the police doing at Kathy and Dale's?" I said, pointing. We looked at each other and, without a word, started running toward their house. The police officers were just getting into their car and leaving.

Kathy was standing on the front porch, looking white-faced and woebegone. "Someone stole our gutters and downspouts," she said.

"The bastards!" Margie cried.

"Why would anyone steal gutters?" I asked.

"They're copper," Margie rasped. "Worth a fortune as scrap. On these old houses, you can yank the downspouts off in a few minutes. Most people who still have copper gutters paint them so the thieves won't get them."

But Kathy and Dale hadn't gotten around to painting their porch. Or their gutters. Margie's words hung there like an unspoken accusation. I started talking, to fill in the awkward silence. "Oh, yeah, I've heard about them. Copper thieves are bold. They stole the gutters off a house on Michigan while an eighty-year-old woman was inside. They stole a copper garage roof in Compton Heights. They climbed a slippery slate roof to take the copper cupola off the old City Hospital. And they stole yours in broad daylight, Kathy."

"I saw them, too," Kathy said. "They were pulling away in a rusted red pickup just as I walked up. Two men in khaki work clothes. I thought they were working on someone's house. I didn't pay much attention to them. Then, when I got to our front door, I realized something was wrong with our house. The bracket that holds the downspout alongside the porch was hanging halfway off. I looked at it and realized our gutters were gone. They took the downspouts, too. Do you think our homeowner's insurance will cover this?"

I bit the inside of my cheek to keep from laughing. Kathy and Dale with their chocolate-syrup eyes and caramel hair and their gingerbread house were so cute. Even their problems were cute. How do you get wallpaper off a bathtub? What do you do when your sander flies through the staircase? Were stolen downspouts covered by homeowner's insurance?

"Too bad you didn't come home half an hour earlier. You could have caught them," Margie said.

"Too bad I wasn't downsized quicker," Kathy said. "But it takes longer than you'd think to be told you're let go." Her lower lip wobbled and her eyes filled with tears, but she didn't cry.

"Oh, baby, you were fired?" Margie said, full of motherly sympathy. She took Kathy in her arms and patted her back. "I am so sorry. When did it happen?"

"Eight o'clock this morning, as soon as I got into work. I had this note to report to the human resources department. I had no idea the company was in trouble, or I would have never taken a job with them. They downsized sixteen of us. I haven't told Dale yet. I just took the bus home. What are we going to do, Margie? We're spending so much rehabbing the house, we can barely make the house payments with two salaries. And now Caroline is pressuring us to paint the porch." Two big tears escaped from her pretty brown eyes, then her face crumpled and she was crying in earnest. Suddenly Kathy's problems didn't seem so cute.

I guess I was already in a bad mood, but it didn't get any better at Uncle Bob's. For one thing, I didn't see

Mayhew, and I needed to talk to him. There's never a cop around when you need one. Marlene said Mayhew hadn't been in yet. She delivered my one egg scrambled, peppered with her usual sarcastic remarks, poured me enough decaf to drown three customers, and sat down with me at break time. Good. Maybe Marlene could help. The bar and restaurant world is a small one, and she might know Johnny Hawkeye, the dead jogger.

"I don't know him, but I'd heard of him," she said. "I knew some of the people who worked with him, and they didn't have a lot of good things to say about him. Johnny was one of those bartenders who put on a show for the customers but fudged on the tip-outs. He was supposed to tip fifteen percent to the staff who carry out the liquor, ice, glasses—the bar back—but Johnny stiffed them and only tipped ten percent. He also didn't do his clean-up. He expected the day shift to pick up after him. In other words, Johnny was all show and no substance. I didn't know him personally. Wet T-shirt and Shake Your Booty contests at the Meet Rack are not my scene."

"Is it a bad place? Drugs? Selling booze to minors? Other problems?"

"I didn't hear anything bad about the place," Marlene said, "unless you think selling Jell-O shots ought to be illegal. Sorry, can't help you any more than that."

"Then maybe you know something about Erwin, the man with the angel mother." I showed Marlene Erwin's spiky-print postcards.

"This guy is definitely one brick short of a load," she said, and shook her head. "Hope he doesn't come in here."

"All that talk about his angel mother gives me the willies," I said. "Sounds like Norman Bates in *Psycho*. I bet Erwin's got Mom stuffed and sitting in a rocking chair. Or buried in the basement."

Marlene stared at me. Uh-oh. She was warming up for a lecture. Sometimes she could sound remarkably like my mentor Georgia. "Francesca," she said severely, "please don't tell me you're planning to dig up this guy's basement looking for her body."

"There's something wrong with Erwin," I said.

"Oh, I agree. But you have this habit of going off half cocked." She sighed. "This guy lives in your neighborhood. Why don't you ask someone about him?"

"Pam Klein," I said. "She would know. She knows everybody. I'll call her later today."

"That's better," Marlene said. "It would be pretty embarrassing if you showed up with a shovel to dig up his basement and his mother answered the door."

I was saved from having to have a snappy comeback when Mayhew walked in the door. I waved him over to my table. It was a pleasure just to watch that man move. He was a one-man fashion show. He had a beautifully tailored tan jacket, the color of a golden retriever puppy, black pants, and black shoes. Nice choirboy face and a wicked grin. Nice wife and two kids. We were friends now, but we had a little history between us that I wasn't particularly proud of. On the other hand, I did know what was under that exquisite tailoring. But from what I heard, that wasn't a well-kept secret. Nobody ever called Mayhew Old Faithful.

Mayhew interrupted these thoughts with "Why the frown, Francesca? Things not going right?" Marlene came by to pour him coffee, and he said he'd order in a minute.

"I'm worried about my neighborhood. Folks are dropping like flies," I said. "Cutup Katie told me the jogger was murdered."

"He was. Have you solved the crime yet, Nancy Drew?"

I didn't like his tone. "No," I said. "But I know who did it."

"Oh, do you now? Let's hear the great detective's theory."

"It's Caroline," I said. "It has to be. She fought with all three victims and, a day or so later, they turned up dead."

"Do you have any proof she killed them?"

"Proof?" I said.

"Yeah, proof. Evidence. Hairs and fibers. Fingerprints. Witnesses. Little things like that. The courts are picky. They won't let me arrest people because the neighbors don't like them."

"I have a witness. Dina saw Caroline working late the night of the drug dealer's murder."

"I already know that," Mayhew said. "But from what I heard, it would be suspicious if Caroline *wasn't* out late at night. Did Dina see Caroline waving a gasoline can and carrying a book of matches?" He was sounding increasingly sarcastic. And my suspicions were sounding pretty lame, even to me.

"No, but Caroline argued with all three victims."

"Francesca, she argued with everyone on that street, and they're still alive. She's a real pain in the ass, I'll grant you that, but the neighbors think she's a hero when she harasses the city government. When she starts harassing them, that's different. Then she's a murderer. Some of those same thoughts about Caroline occurred to me, too, but when the victims are a drug dealer and crooked City Hall clerk, there are a few other suspects. Unlike you, I can't just jump to conclusions."

I'd had enough of his condescending tone. "You especially wouldn't want to jump to conclusions when the suspect is a major contributor to the mayor's re-election campaign," I said.

Mayhew slammed his cup down and slopped coffee into the saucer. Hah. I'd hit a nerve. "Yes, she is," he said slowly. He always spoke slowly when he was angry. "Caroline is also a respected citizen who's done a lot of good for the neighborhood."

"I didn't expect to hear you take up the local mantra. 'Caroline's done a lot of good for the neighborhood,'" I said in a singsong voice.

"This isn't a game, Francesca."

Furious blood rushed to my face. "Well, if you'd been doing your job last time, you would have figured out who the murderer was before I was attacked."

"If you'd stayed out of it like you were supposed to, nothing would have happened. We figured it out, but we had to go a little slower, because we couldn't take all those nice, illegal short cuts."

"Maybe if you'd spent less time chasing skirts, you'd solve this case quicker," I shot back, and wished I hadn't. Mayhew grinned, but it was not his nice little-boy smile. I tried to think of something to wipe that smirk off his face, but before I could answer, Marlene materialized with a plastic pitcher of ice water, which I thought she was going to throw on both of us.

"Are you ready to order?" she asked Mayhew.

"Sorry, Marlene, I lost my appetite," he said. He threw some money down on the table and left.

"I can see that went real well," Marlene said, pouring me ice water. "But maybe I can help out. I've been thinking about your bartender."

"You know him after all?" I said hopefully.

"No. I just have a question. The guy lives in the Central West End and works at a bar on the Landing, right?" Marlene said.

I nodded.

"So what's he doing jogging in your neighborhood?"

Trust Marlene to figure it out. Hawkeye—I still had trouble thinking of him as Johnny—lived in the Central West End. So why would he drive fifteen or twenty minutes to the South Side to jog when he had all of

Forest Park practically on his doorstep? It didn't make sense. His West End apartment was in a grimy red brick building with a bright-blue awning and a narrow entrance hall. A hand-lettered sign said MANAGER IN BASE-MENT APARTMENT. RING BELL. I did, and a heavyset woman came out, moving slowly with the help of a cane. She wore jeans, a loose smock top, dangling Indian silver earrings, and long straight gray hair, parted in the center. She said her name was Judith. An old hippie, for sure. I told her who I was and why I was here. Judith invited me in and settled herself into a well-worn easy chair, with two bed pillows piled on the seat cushion. A large orange tabby curled up in her lap. I took the couch, covered with a tie-dyed throw, and moved several fat candles aside on the coffee table to make room for my briefcase. Judith said Johnny had had an apartment there for four years.

"Wasn't he a hunk?" Judith said. "Until he opened his mouth. Then you saw what a calculating hunk of shit Johnny was, especially if he wanted something, and he usually did. There was a man who got through life on his looks. Lived off women—discreetly, of course—and his tips from bartending. Liked the plain ones. Didn't want competition, I suspect, and he knew women who weren't pretty would be easier to impress."

I thought of poor Patricia, her stringy looks transformed into real beauty by some attention from Johnny Hawkeye.

"Did he have any close friends?"

"Johnny?" She snorted. "The man was too much on the make to have friends. He brought a lot of women up to his room, but they all disappeared fairly soon. There was one guy he hung out with—another bartender at the Meet Rack. Name's Vinnie. Vinnie's another beautiful hunk with an ugly interior. Two of a kind, they were. Vinnie is a piece of work. It's worth the trip to the Landing just to meet him. He might help you, too. If anyone knew Johnny, it was Vinnie."

I called the bar from Judith's. "Yeah, Vinnie's here, who wants to know?" a voice said. I told him who and why.

"Then that's me. Come on by, sweet lips, if you look as good as you sound," Vinnie said. Oh, boy, this was going to be fun. The Landing wasn't far from the Central West End, but the highways around it were torn up for a massive construction project, and there were long waits on dusty, car-clogged streets. Construction trucks spilling dirt and gravel pulled out of nowhere and left clouds of dust and cursing drivers in their wake. After a frustrating half-hour crawl, I paid five bucks and left Ralph in a parking lot two blocks from the Meet Rack.

The Landing was right on the Mississippi River, literally in the shadow of the Gateway Arch. It was one of the oldest sections of St. Louis, set at the base of the steel and stone Eads Bridge. The streets were paved with cobblestones, which looked quaint but were murder on high heels. The handsome nineteenth-century brick and iron-fronted buildings were once warehouses that outfitted the wagons going west. Now they housed bars and restaurants for tourists and the young, moneyed downtown business crowd.

The Meet Rack seemed to be made entirely of neon and steel and black laminate, and there was a large inlaid dance floor. It looked like the kind of place where you could meet the *Saturday Night Fever* John Travolta. But at three-thirty in the afternoon you weren't likely to meet anyone but the beer delivery man. The place was deserted, and Vinnie was getting ready for happy hour, slicing limes and lemons. Vinnie wore skin-tight jeans and a muscle shirt, and the man had muscles to show. He should have been running with Johnny Hawkeye, though. Vinnie was starting to get a substantial beer gut above those tight jeans. Must be taking his work home.

"Whadda ya have?" he said, in a real "deese, dem, and dose" accent.

"Club soda with lime," I said.

"Oh, come on. Have a real drink. On me. How about some Hot Sex?" he said with a big grin, and held out a bottle. Good thing I read the label before I decked him. Hot Sex was the name of the liqueur. It looked brownish, like Bailey's Irish Cream.

"Don't know you well enough for Hot Sex," I said. "How about a Bud?"

"Cute," he said. "Beer. That's better." Vinnie opened a bottle and put it down in front of me with a cold glass. I didn't have to drink it, just order it, to make Vinnie happy. He was one of those men who felt threatened if he couldn't control a woman. Getting me to order booze when I didn't want it was his way of taking charge. Vinnie put the sliced fruit into plastic cups on the bar and set about polishing glasses. I watched him work. He was a scuzzy human but a good bartender.

"What do you know about Johnny's death?" I asked.

"Nothin'," he said. "I was real bummed out. Him and me, we had plans. Now I got nothin'."

"What kind of plans?"

"We was going to open a bar like this in South St. Louis. Had the name and everything. Pudknocker's. Cute, huh?"

"Cute doesn't begin to describe it," I said. He thought that was a compliment.

"This lady friend of Johnny's was gonna bankroll him with some money she got from her ex-husband. Man, she was hot for Johnny. She was about sixty, but not bad looking for an old lady. He had the place all picked out, too, near this real nice street, North Dakota Place. Thought we'd get us a classy clientele that way and do the neighborhood a favor. Liven the place up. We'd have your hot bod contest, your wet T-shirt contest, your Harley leather night, your shake your booty night, your karaoke and disco nights—something different every night. There's nothing like that there now. We didn't see nothing but gook and spic restaurants, and you can't eat in those places, unless you like eatin' cat, know what I mean?"

Vinnie took my stunned silence for approval and kept talking.

"You'd think those people would welcome a white man. Well, some of them did, and the rent was real cheap on this building, but then this nosy old bitch killed any chance of us gettin' a liquor license. No liquor. No bar."

"What was her name?" As if I couldn't guess. For once, I agreed with Caroline.

Vinnie taxed his tiny brain. "What was it? Karla? Catherine? Caroline! That's it, Caroline. Always wore cutoffs and T-shirts. Looked like a dyke to me. Spread a lot of stories about us running a biker bar."

Harley night. I made the connection. "You were the motorcycle bar she stopped from getting a liquor license."

"She was a liar," Vinnie said hotly. "All we had was one Harley night once a week, and she told everybody we were a Hell's Angels' hangout. It was just a bunch of yuppies who liked to wear leather. There weren't no bikers in our bar. Look around. You see any bikers here?"

I didn't see anyone, period. "This second time, Johnny was smarter. He found an even better place, a storefront right down from the entrance to North Dakota Place on Grand Avenue, but he kept real quiet about it. The building was owned by some gook."

I couldn't take it any more. "If the man was Vietnamese, say so," I said.

"Huh?" Vinnie said. "I don't know what he was. Vietnamese, Korean, who gives a shit?"

"Listen, Vinnie, just call him Asian, okay?"

He looked at me suspiciously. "Whatever. This Aaa-sian," he said, dragging the word out, "couldn't talk so good, so he wouldn't be telling anybody our plans. He just wanted his money in cash. This time Johnny was careful. Johnny was slick. He could work people around to his way of thinking, especially the ladies. He started runnin' around North Dakota Place every morning, wearin' those little short-shorts of his, showin' his glutes and gettin' them old maids around there all hot and bothered. That way they'd be on his side at liquor license time. Johnny knew running every morning with his butt hanging out was turning a lot of cranks."

Including mine. I thought of myself staring at him. Served me right.

"Johnny's ace in the hole was this homely, skinny broad, the dyke's best friend. He'd talk recycling and shit to her by the hour and she loved it. He figured if things got ugly, she'd side with him. I mean, he had a real dick, and her dyke friend didn't, and if he had to, he'd screw her. Johnny was already humping the old broad for the bar money, so what was one more lonely lady? Along with feeling out lonesome ladies, heh-heh, he was feeling out the neighbors. Took him ten seconds to figure out a lot of them didn't like Caroline the Dyke. He didn't say anything to them because the time wasn't right, but he thought they'd be in his corner just because she wasn't. Meanwhile, the more the neighbors saw him running, the more they'd know he wasn't a biker, if Caroline started spreading her lies again. Caroline was helping him, too. She was ticking people off right and left. Every time Johnny heard she had another fight he'd say 'That's one more for my side.' He even ran on her grass. He knew it would make her nuts and get him more supporters."

"Wasn't he afraid she'd make trouble for him?"

"What could she do to Johnny?"

Kill him. And for better reasons than he wouldn't keep off the grass. Caroline must have known what Johnny was up to. She knew everything in that neighborhood, and she knew he'd tried to start a bar before. When he dumped Caroline's wheelbarrow into the fountain, and we laughed at her, he was demonstrating his power. This time he just might have enough neighborhood support to get his liquor license. Even her faithful friend Patricia found him attractive. Why did Caroline keep her mouth shut about who Johnny Hawkeye really was? Maybe because she was planning something even more devious than he was.

Now it made sense. Now I had a motive for Caroline, and it was a lot better than running on her grass. The barbarians were at her gates, bringing wet T-shirt contests within the very sight of her angels.

All I had to do was prove it.

Well, actually, I had to write a column first. And check in at the office. And call Lyle. Ralph purred his Jaguar purr all the way back to the *Gazette* and didn't even get too unhappy when we sat for fifteen minutes in another downtown traffic jam. All around us cars were dying in the ferocious heat, and drivers were turning off their air conditioning to keep their cars running, but not Ralph. Ralph was cool. You could keep ice cream in Ralph.

For once things were quiet at the office. No new memos. No new gossip. No sign of Charlie or Nails. No messages from anyone, not even Lyle. I called his office and he wasn't there. The department secretary said she thought he was gone for the day. I called his home and no one answered. I wondered if Lyle was working late again, and if so, why he wasn't at his office. I thought about my father telling my mother he had to work late, when he was really screwing around. Charlie and the guys at the *Gazette* used the same excuse. Some wives tried to track their husbands down by calling them at the Last Word, but the bartender was wise to that trick. He'd yell real loud, "Is Charlie here?" and Charlie would know that was the your-wife's-on-the-phone signal and shake his head no. The wife wouldn't hear anything but the question.

But Lyle wouldn't do that. He loved me. He wanted to marry me. Of course, Charlie and his bed-hopping buddies were married, and so was my father. If I married Lyle, I wondered if I'd be calling the bars in a few years, another desperate wife with a cheating husband. It was an unworthy idea, and if Lyle had called me right back, he might have nipped it in the bud. But he didn't, and my suspicions blossomed into something ugly, and I couldn't get its roots out of my heart.

I think because I was so upset over Lyle, I didn't remember to call Pam Klein about the mother-loving Erwin. I stayed at work way too long, waiting in case Lyle called. He could call me at home, too, but I wanted to hear from him now. I kept putting off leaving. When the phone rang at seven-thirty, I pounced on it. But it wasn't Lyle. It was Margie, and she was laughing. I'd never heard her sound so genuinely happy.

"You gotta see my lawn," she said, her rasp softened into a burr. "I've been flocked."

"Forked?" I said. "I've already seen a forked lawn, thanks."

"Not forked, flocked. This is done with flamingos. You gotta see it."

It was déjà vu all over again, but I told Margie I'd come look at her lawn. What the heck. Lyle wasn't going to call.

Margie's lawn was a riot of hot pink, striped with

black evening shadows. There must have been a hundred plastic flamingos in her yard. Some were set up in rows and flocks and others were stuck in the ground at random. One flamingo peered out of the yew bushes, as if it had been flushed from its cover. Against the summer-green lawn, the plastic flamingos looked silly, stylish, and ridiculous.

"I did it." Dina giggled. "I gave her the bird. We needed a laugh, so I had Margie flocked. My church does it for a fund raiser. The women's club puts the flamingos on the lawn, and then you have to pay to have them removed."

"Church-approved blackmail?" I asked.

"It's a donation," Dina said. "Even if you don't give us any money, we'll take them away the next day. It's our most successful moneymaker. People consider it an honor to be flocked. It's like T.P.'ing for grown-ups."

That's what Margie reminded me of—a high school girl who had just discovered that her yard and all the trees and shrubs were covered with loops of toilet paper. Now she knew she was popular. "I love it!" she said. She picked up a flamingo and danced with it, then held it overhead like a trophy, while Dina took her picture. Then Dina photographed her with the flock. Dale and Kathy came over, arms around each other, looking chipper despite Kathy's recent downsizing. Even poor Patricia, lean and unloved in her "Walk for Wildlife" T-shirt, managed a pale smile.

"These are genuine Featherstone flamingos, designed by Don Featherstone, the inventor of the pink plastic flamingo," Dina said. "You can tell by the bright color. The other ones are Pepto-Bismol pink. Plus Featherstone flamingos are signed on their butts." She upended one, and we checked the signature.

"Tasteful," I said.

"That's what it's all about," Dina said. "I saw Featherstone on TV. He bragged that before he came along, only the rich had lawn ornaments. 'I brought poor taste to poor people,' he said." We considered Featherstone a St. Louisian not only in spirit but also by marriage. His wife, Nancy, was a St. Louis girl, even though she and her husband now lived in Massachusetts.

"This is so South Side," Margie said, and she was right. It played to the South Side obsession to decorate lawns with rubber and plastic. Along with buying countless plastic ducks, deer, swans, and donkey carts, we had the first known program for recycling truck tires. We made them into planters by turning the tires inside-out. Then we cut the edges into triangular flaps and painted the tires white. A yuppie hosta would die of shame if you put it in a tire planter. They require sturdier breeds like geraniums and petunias, which flourish in my neighborhood.

Tire planters, alas, would not be allowed on upscale North Dakota Place.

"How long are those tacky things going to be in your yard?" a voice demanded, and I didn't have to turn around to see who it was. I knew it was Caroline. She was wheeling her barrow down the sidewalk, and she looked like an escapee from the loony bin. The sweat was coming off her in sheets, and her eyes were wild and angry.

"They'll stay for as long as I want," Margie said, defiantly.

"You have to get them out of there," Caroline said, and I could hear the desperation in her voice. "They're bad for the neighborhood. They'll give the wrong image. People will think—they'll think you are gay."

"If you want, I can have my boyfriend fuck me on the front lawn, so everyone will know I'm straight," Margie said. "But if I was gay, what's it to you?"

"It's not what you are," Caroline said. "It's what the

West County real estate agents will see. It will look bad. I'm trying to sell that house at two hundred, and I'm bringing in a van-load tomorrow. You have to remove those tacky things." Her voice was somewhere between a command and a plea.

"I don't have to do anything. This is my property," Margie said, and her rasp sounded like a wasp on steroids. Her face was beet red with purple tinges, and veins stood out on her neck. Caroline was about the same shade, so furious she was having trouble talking. Their rage was so hot, I expected them to burst into flames. They flung insults across the lawn like Viking goddesses hurling thunderbolts. The rest of us stood ineffectually on the sidelines. Dina made a halfhearted attempt to explain that the flamingos would be removed tomorrow, but Margie shooed her away like a fly.

"Those flamingos will be gone by morning," Caroline said imperiously.

"Over my dead body," Margie screamed. "Better yet, over *your* dead body. Everyone hear me? Touch one flamingo, Caroline, and you're a dead woman."

Caroline picked up her wheelbarrow and rolled it toward her yard.

Dina burst into tears. "I only wanted us to have fun," she said.

"This is North Dakota Place," Margie snapped. "We can't have fun. It wouldn't look right."

I was dazed by the swift viciousness of the fight. I wondered if I'd see Margie alive tomorrow.

8

Caroline was screaming at Margie. Her sturdy face was distorted with rage. Her eyes burned with crazy anger. Her mouth was a black cave, filled with hate. Out of it came a scream as loud as a siren. It was a siren . . . several sirens . . . sirens. That's what woke me up. What time was it? I glanced groggily at my bedside alarm clock. Six-oh-six in the morning. Why were the sirens screaming again? I looked out the window and saw a howling parade of police cars. I didn't wait for the EMS ambulance, but I knew it would follow. They were all heading toward North Dakota Place.

Not again. Not . . . oh, no. This time it would be Margie. She was dead. I knew it. I knew that argument Margie had with Caroline last night would send the woman over the edge. I tried to put on some clothes, but I kept dropping things. I dropped my jeans. I got my arm tangled in my T-shirt. I couldn't find my sandals. I looked under the bed for them and hit my head. I did not want to see Margie's body, but I couldn't stay away.

I ran all the way to North Dakota Place, but I seemed to move in slow motion, like one of those bad dreams where you run and run and get nowhere. Police cars and emergency vehicles were parked crazily up and down the street from Dale and Kathy's all the way to Margie's house, but the activity seemed to be centered around Caroline's side yard.

I saw the neighbors huddled in a small, shrunken cluster. There was blond Dina, barefoot and lost in baggy shorts and and an inside-out T-shirt. Dale and Kathy were once again sharing pajama parts. Tall, lean Patricia looked scrawny and washed out. Even her startling blue eyes seemed dull and pale today.

I didn't want to look at Margie. I was glad I couldn't get near her body. The scene was blocked off with yellow tape and crawling with cops, some in uniform and some plainclothes. But I could see a woman lying on the grass, and she wasn't moving. The medics weren't making any effort to revive her. Even from where I stood I could see her skin was flat and gray-green, and I could see thick, dark blood on her head and chest. I remembered Margie yesterday, laughing and dancing with her pink plastic flamingos. Now one was stuck right in her body. Whoa! Was that right? I looked again. The skinny metal legs were planted in her chest. The flamingo implant swayed slightly in the breeze, looking horrible and harmless at the same time. My stomach gave a heave, and I almost lost it right on the lawn.

"She was killed by a pink flamingo?" I said.

"Flamingos don't kill people. People kill people," Dina blurted in a parody of the gun lobby slogan, and collapsed into shrill laughter. She laughed until tears ran down her face. Finally she wiped her eyes and got control of herself. "I found the body when I went out for my *New York Times* this morning. Sorry, Francesca."

Why was she apologizing to me for finding the body? Wait, she wasn't. Dina was apologizing for subscribing to the *Times* instead of the *Gazette*. Join the crowd, Dina.

"She wasn't killed by a flamingo," Dina said.

"There's something wrong with her head. It's all bloody and squashy on one side." Her teeth were chattering, even in the warm morning air. Shock must be setting in.

Kathy paled and buried her head in Dale's shoulder, although he didn't exactly look like a tower of strength. He wrapped his arms around her, mostly to keep himself upright.

"What the hell is going on here?" said a croaking rasp, and there was Margie, standing before us in her lumpy pink bathrobe, looking like the walking dead. Her eyes were sunken. Her skin was flabby and loose. But she was definitely walking and talking. I gave a startled yelp, then realized Margie wasn't dead, just so hung over she probably wished she was. But if Margie was alive, who was the dead woman on the lawn?

"It's Caroline," Dina said, shocking Margie into silence. "She was hit on the head with a big pipe wrench. It's right next to her. I think that's what killed her. Then someone stuck the flamingo in her body. Pushed it right in her chest. It was horrible." Dina was wide-eyed, teeth still chattering, and she was shivering now, too, as if she'd been pulled from an icy stream.

"Someone?" Patricia said, turning toward Margie with an accusing stare. "We know who it was."

"Not me," said Margie. She was trembling, but I didn't know if it was from the awful news or the hangover. "You've got to believe me. It wasn't me. You're my friends."

Patricia looked at her contemptuously. "Friends," she sneered. "I heard how you took the plaster off your walls, friend. You hit it with a pipe wrench and screamed 'Take that, Caroline.' You were practicing until you could swing at the real Caroline. We heard you screaming at her last night. You said you'd kill her, and you did. You killed my friend," she hissed. "I'm glad this is a death-penalty state. I hope you'll fry."

"Uh, I think she'll get stuck," Dina said, teeth clicking like castanets.

"Huh?" said Patricia, spoiling her dramatic moment.

"I don't think Missouri has the electric chair," Dina said. "I think we have lethal injection. Margie will get a lethal injection. Sort of like when the vet puts your dog to sleep."

"Oh, for chrissakes," Margie rasped. "I'm not going to do either one. I didn't like the woman, but I didn't kill her. Do you think I'd be dumb enough to kill someone after I *said* I'd kill her?"

We all stared at Margie. Patricia turned on her heel and stalked toward her home. Dina looked uneasy. Kathy and Dale hung onto each other like they were drowning. I had goose bumps. I remembered Margie pounding the wall with a pipe wrench and screaming, crazy with hate, "Take that, Caroline. And that, and that." Of course, I also remembered myself hitting the same wall and pretending it was Charlie. Would I kill him? In a minute, if I thought I could get away with it. But I'm the kind who always gets caught.

Finally Margie's rasp sawed through our thick silence. "I'm going to make some coffee and clean up," she said. "If anyone wants to arrest me, I'm in my kitchen. Dina, you want some coffee? You look cold." Dina obediently pattered behind Margie. They didn't get very far. A uniformed officer stopped them. Dina had already been questioned by the police, but the officer was definitely interested in talking with Margie.

I heard the officer ask, "What is your business here? Where do you live?" She must have invited him back to her house, because they were heading toward her steps. The woman was desperate for coffee.

I was, too. But it would be a while before I got a cup. Another officer had the same questions for me. The street was swarming with officers, uniformed and plainclothes, knocking on doors or questioning neighbors standing on the sidewalk. Police were also videotaping the crowd. Police photographers, in between photographing Caroline's body, also took pictures of the crowd. Mayhew had told me before that the killer often liked to return when the body was discovered. I looked at the neighbors in pajamas, hastily pulled-on shorts, and inside-out T-shirts, and wondered which one was the killer.

Finally I'd answered the cop's questions to his satisfaction, and I was free to go. I needed coffee, and lots of it. I walked home, found a blouse that had all the buttons and a suit with no visible stains, grabbed my briefcase, car keys, and purse, and slipped away before Mrs. Indelicato in the confectionary downstairs quizzed me. I'd been avoiding her, and she knew it. When she finally caught me, I'd be grilled like a ham steak.

At Uncle Bob's Marlene didn't greet me with any snappy remarks. She showed so much concern it was unnerving. I must really look bad. "You look like death on toast," Marlene said, confirming my suspicions. "What happened now?"

"There's been another death on North Dakota Place, and nobody made this one look like an accident," I said. I told Marlene about Caroline's bizarre death.

"I think this calls for real coffee instead of that unleaded stuff you drink," she said.

"No, give me decaf. My body's easily fooled, just like the rest of me." I was wrong about Caroline, but I couldn't see how. I had everything: motive, means, and opportunity. Except my killer turned out to be a victim. I tried to eat my eggs, but when I stuck the metal fork tines into the eggs, I thought of those metal flamingo legs pushed into Caroline's chest. I put the fork back down. I really wasn't hungry. Maybe I'd stick with coffee.

"This dead woman is the one you and Mayhew were arguing about?" Marlene asked.

I nodded. "Yeah. I told Mayhew she was a murderer. I said she'd killed Otto, the drug dealer, and Johnny Hawkeye the jogger. Now she turns up dead in her own yard."

"But if she's dead," Marlene said, "who killed them? And who killed Caroline? And why?"

Those were the questions I couldn't answer.

All the way downtown Marlene's questions went round and round in my mind, spinning uselessly, like a car wheel stuck in a mudhole. I got nowhere. Worse than nowhere. I got to the *Gazette*. The newsroom was restless, and there was a constant low buzz, like flies on dead meat. It was the office rumor mill, grinding away. There was going to be "an important staff announcement" tomorrow, according to the memo waiting at my desk.

I saw a radiant Nails sitting at her new desk in the All Business department, surrounded by enough flowers for Princess Di's funeral. She was wearing a triumphant smile, a very loose jumper, and a blouse with a pussycat bow. I had a feeling the next Reign of Terror was about to begin at the *Gazette*, and I knew I was one of the first names on Nails's list. Oh, well, too late to do anything about it now. I spent most of the day trying to write a column. About five P.M., I finally gave up and went through my mail. Press releases. Jokes. Story ideas. Funny letters from readers. And wouldn't you know it, there was another bizarre postcard from Erwin. "My Mother is gone and she shouldn't be," he wrote. "You are here, but you shouldn't be. You don't care."

Erwin was getting weirder. I figured I couldn't put off calling Pam Klein any longer. She knew immediately who I was talking about.

"Erwin," she said, "is definitely a strange one. He's

about forty. He lives with his mother, and he doesn't date. He's not unattractive, he's just very, very odd. He's sort of lumpy-looking, with narrow shoulders and a thick waist, like he shoplifted a pillow. He wears baggy pants and those clingy knit shirts that make him look like he needs a bra. I've never seen him go anywhere without his mother. He drives her Buick everywhere. I don't think he has his own car."

"What's he do for a living?" I said.

"He's a high school science teacher," Pam said. "Don't get me wrong. He's not a bad teacher. He's just different. And very close to his mother."

His mother. That's another reason why I was making this call. To see if this psycho was Norman Bates. "His mother is okay?"

"I guess so," Pam said. "I haven't seen her all summer. She's visiting her sister in New Jersey."

I could hear alarm bells ringing. "Did she tell you that?"

"No," Pam said, "Erwin did. It was sometime in May, I think. I know I hadn't seen his mother in a week or so and asked him if she was okay, and Erwin said she was in New Jersey, visiting her sister Gail."

"You didn't see Erwin's mother off to the airport? You haven't talked with her on the phone since she left?"

"Why would I do that?" Pam asked. "We aren't close friends."

"Would anyone do that?"

"No," Pam said. "I don't think so. She's a very nice woman, but she's not friendly with anyone in particular. Kind of keeps to herself. It's just her and Erwin."

"It may be just Erwin," I said. "Listen, I've been getting some very bizarre postcards from Erwin, and I'm kind of concerned."

"Oh, Erwin's harmless," Pam said. "He always writes weird letters, mostly to the Letters to the Editor column. He thinks the Kennedy assassination was a conspiracy between the state of Mississippi and the Mafia."

Great. That didn't make me feel any better.

"Can I ask one more question?" I said. "Has Erwin been doing any digging in the basement? Have you noticed any unusual activity around his house?"

"You really think Erwin's gone bonkers, don't you?" Pam said. "Look, if it will make you feel any better, Erwin has *not* been digging in the basement. Or mixing small batches of concrete. He hasn't bought an ax, a power saw, or a wood chipper. He's spent all summer in plain view in his backyard, working on his new vegetable garden."

"He dug a garden after his mother left?" I said, my suspicions rising.

"No, he started one a few weeks before," Pam said. "It's a nice big one for such a small yard."

She said goodbye so cheerfully, I felt cold. Nearly as cold as Erwin's mom. He *was* Norman Bates, after all. He'd buried his mother under the broccoli. I just had to prove it. I certainly couldn't go to Mayhew with my suspicions. He didn't believe me about Caroline—and with good reason, as it turned out. I'd just have to find the body myself. The question was, how? Maybe I'd go over to Erwin's house and snoop around a little today. I wondered if he was home now.

The telephone rang. It was a terrified Margie. "You've got to help me, Francesca," she said, rasping plaintively, like a lovesick cicada. "The police think I did it. They talked to me for hours. They asked about my fight with Caroline. They took my fingerprints. They said my fingerprints were on the flamingo in her chest."

"Of course they were," I interrupted. "You touched most of the flamingos. You picked them up and danced with them."

"I said that, but it didn't make any difference," Margie said. "They read me my rights. I asked if I was a suspect and they said everyone was a suspect right now. They asked if I wanted a lawyer to be present."

"Did you call your lawyer?" I said.

"No," Margie said. "I thought it would make me look guilty. And it would cost money. As it is, after they talked to me I was so scared I got a lawyer, anyway, and she said I was dumb to talk to the police without her. They haven't arrested me, but they did tell me not to leave town. I'm scared, Francesca. I'm really, really scared. You have to do something."

"What does your lawyer advise you to do now?" I asked.

"Shut up and don't say anything," Margie said.

"Then why are you talking to me?" I said. "I'm a newspaper columnist."

"You know I didn't do it. You've got to help me, Francesca. You've solved other murders."

"No, I didn't," I said. "I just blundered around. I've been wrong every time. I do think you're innocent, Margie, but with my track record, that's probably a bad sign. Look, was the police detective who questioned you named Mayhew?"

"I think so."

"He's a good detective," I said. "He won't railroad you."

"Then why is he treating me like I killed Caroline?" Margie wailed. "He says I have the perfect motive since Caroline broke up my marriage."

"She did?" This was a new one. How could the unlovely Caroline break up Margie's marriage?

"Why don't we meet somewhere to talk, and you can tell me about it," I said. "You can also tell me about anyone else who has a good reason to kill Caroline."

"Hah," Margie said. "You got all night? Listen, I

don't feel like going out anywhere. Everyone's pointing and staring at me. And don't say it's all in my head. I went to the supermarket this afternoon, and the neighbors were staring. Mrs. Rhodemeier, over on Iowa, snubbed me in front of the canned tuna, and she never even liked Caroline. I have lots of food. Come over and I'll barbecue some pork steaks for dinner."

Was I supposed to have dinner with Lyle tonight? We'd been canceling and rescheduling so much, I couldn't remember anymore. "Let me make a phone call and I'll get right back to you," I said.

Lyle was in his office and he answered his own phone. "Are we having dinner tonight?" I asked.

"I don't think so," he said. "I'm working late again." He sounded rushed and eager to get me off the phone. "Why don't we make it tomorrow night?" he said. "I really miss you."

"If you really miss me, why don't you want to see me tonight?"

"Francesca," he said, "don't be that way."

"What way? You mean, don't be angry because it upsets you. How should I be? Happy that you can't see me? Do you want to marry me—or do you want a Stepford wife who will do whatever you want?"

"You haven't so far," he said. "Please, Francesca, let's not fight on the phone. Let's have dinner tomorrow night. You know I love you."

Did I? Maybe he really did have someone else. Maybe I'd been spending so much time at North Dakota Place, I didn't even notice the signs that he was straying. Ever since I set foot on that street nothing had gone right in my life. So naturally I made plans to spend more time there. I called Margie and said, "Put the pork steaks on the grill, I'm on my way over. What can I bring?"

"Just yourself," she said.

I brought myself and a German chocolate cake from

Mrs. Indelicato's, which I got for ten percent off, with a free load of guilt. Mrs. I didn't mention that I'd been deliberately going down the back steps to avoid her. She didn't reproach me at all, which only made it worse. She's crafty that way.

It was after five when I got to Margie's. I knocked on the door and no one answered, so I went around back and opened the gate to the privacy fence. Margie was in the backyard, brushing barbecue sauce on four thick pork steaks sizzling on the gas grill. An umbrella table was set with two places. I put the cake down there.

"What are you using for barbecue sauce?" I asked. In St. Louis, barbecue sauce is a hotly debated topic. I hoped she wasn't one of those Worcestershire-and-butter purists. It made the meat too dry. Or worse, a dieter who marinated everything in low-cal lemon juice.

"I used a bottle of Maull's tangy sauce doctored with a splash of Budweiser and Worcestershire sauce," she said. She held up her almost-empty beer bottle, and I figured she drank what didn't go in the sauce.

"You got it," I said. "You've mastered the official St. Louis recipe. Some people add a little brown sugar, but I think that makes it too sweet. You've caught on well for an outsider. Where are you from?"

"Hartford, Connecticut," she said. "My dad worked for an insurance company and my mom was a housewife. But my ex-husband and I lived in Manhattan for so long, we considered ourselves New Yorkers. You know, I never saw a pork steak until I moved here."

"You won't," I said. "St. Louis is the pork steak capital of the world. Pork steaks are a cheap and tasty meat, cut from the shoulder end of the loin."

"You can barbecue them in about one six-pack," Margie said. "But I don't understand why they're so popular here."

"That's easy. We like barbecue sauce. Now, barbecue sauce is best on ribs, but ribs are messy and waste-ful. After all that work, marinating and barbecuing, you wind up eating a mouthful of meat and wearing a gallon of sauce. St. Louisans are too neat and practical to put up with that. Pork steaks taste like ribs, but they have more meat. They're also easy to eat, without slop-ping sauce."

"I get it," Margie said. "They're the seedless grapes of barbecue."

We sat down to juicy pork steaks, baked beans, Ger-man potato salad, and fresh sliced tomatoes. The per-fect summer meal. I drank ice water, but Margie had another beer, which I figured would loosen her lips a bit. By the time she cut us both thick slabs of German chocolate cake, she was ready to talk.

"So how did Caroline break up your marriage?" I said.

"She refused to refinance a loan," Margie rasped, stabbing her cake with her fork. She made the act seem angry and efficient. I hoped she didn't have to eat before a jury of her peers.

"And your husband left you for that?"

"You have to understand, it was the last straw. Bill and I bought this house from Caroline. I was crazy for this old house. We moved here because he got a job at McDonnell-Douglas. I'd been working for a PR firm in Manhattan. In New York we were living in a one-bed-room apartment about the size of my entrance hall, and when I saw this house with the stained glass, the four fireplaces, and all that space, I had to have it. After New York the price seemed ridiculously cheap. We got a deal on it, or so I thought, because it was only partly rehabbed. Caroline redid the kitchen, the bath-rooms, the plumbing, and the wiring, and repaired the slate roof. Then she sold it to us at what I thought was a good price, because I was too dumb to know I was being skinned. Back then I still thought all midwesterners were simple, honest folks who didn't understand money." We both took bites of chocolate cake and chewed on that for a while.

"Caroline wanted three hundred thousand dollars for a house that would cost two million anywhere around Manhattan. I did wonder when we couldn't get the whole amount financed by the bank. Do you know what comps are?"

I shook my head. "I didn't, either, back then," Margie said. "If I had, I wouldn't be in this fix. They're comparable prices. The bank looks at the prices of similar houses nearby and bases its loan on what they sold for.

"The neighborhood wasn't doing quite so well back then. Three blocks away fire-gutted shells of drug houses were going for ten thousand dollars. Fine old two-story brick homes were selling for sixty thousand. The bank laughed at Caroline's asking price of three hundred thousand. They wouldn't loan us more than two hundred fifty thousand and said we were lucky to get that. Caroline refused to come down on the price. She said it would be bad for us and bad for the neighborhood. She said the banks were prejudiced against the city, and house prices had to stay high for us all to survive. And I swallowed that load," she said, swallowing a huge forkful of cake.

"She offered us all sorts of perks to buy the house. I can't remember them all, but they included a new oven, microwave and dishwasher for the kitchen, a new marble floor in the guest bathroom, complete tuckpointing of the house and garage, free repair of the fireplaces, and free cleaning and maintenance on the fireplaces for five years.

"She also offered to lend us the other fifty thousand dollars. The terms were a little steeper than the bank loan. This was the mid-eighties, remember, when interest rates were ten and twelve percent. And while our bank home loan was for twenty years, her loan was for fifteen. My husband Bill said not to worry, we would refinance the loan in a year or two, and that would get the payments down. Then we could use the extra money to finish rehabbing the house."

"Sounds like a good plan," I said.

"It was, but nothing worked out the way we hoped. At the end of two years Bill was laid off at Mac, along with hundreds of others. This house needs two salaries to run it properly. Bill did get the bank to give him a new loan rate—three points lower. We were so excited. We would have a couple hundred a month extra. When we refinanced Caroline's loan, we'd have even more money. But it wasn't that easy."

Margie grew angrier as she talked. She stabbed the air with her fork to make her points.

"First, the mortgage company said they would refinance the loan for thirty years, but they only gave us one hundred twenty thousand dollars, not one-sixty like we'd hoped. Second"—another stab with the fork—"Caroline refused to refinance her share for thirty years. It had to be fifteen years, she said, or she wouldn't let us refinance at all."

"She could do that?" I said. I couldn't believe Caroline was powerful enough to block a bank deal.

"She could and she did. We checked the loan papers. It was right there, in print we never bothered to read—or have a lawyer read—because we trusted Caroline. She was an honest, wholesome midwesterner, and we were a couple of East Coast slicks. Yes, indeed, Caroline could block the bank loan unless she got her way. So she got a double income on her loan payment, and we had no financial relief—we didn't get lower monthly payments.

"That was the end for us. My husband Bill never really liked St. Louis, not the way I did. I guess we were drifting apart, anyway. I couldn't leave this house, so he left me, and moved to California. I wanted the house and I got it. Now it's a millstone around my neck, dragging me down. I can't afford to fix it up. If I sell it half rehabbed like it is now, I'll lose my shirt. So I'm trapped. I rehab a little here and there. I pick for a living and hope to make a big score in the antique business, but I might as well try to win the lottery. You heard me yelling at Caroline about my boyfriend screwing me on the front lawn. But the truth is, I'm not seeing anyone. This house is my life.

"After Bill left, Caroline offered to buy the house for half what we paid. Half! After all those lectures about property values. I refused to sell to her. I could have killed her when she made that miserable offer."

Margie stopped, realizing what she'd said.

"But I didn't kill her," she said. "So now I'm stuck with this house forever. Caroline owns me."

"Not anymore," I said. "You're free." Jeez, no wonder Mayhew thought the woman had a motive for murder. "Are you the only person Caroline used like that?"

"Nope, there are a lot of us in Caroline's sucker club," Margie said. "I'd say at least fifteen that I know about are part of her private loan scheme, and there may be more. I'm sure she took the money she got from us and lent it to some other poor sap.

"Then there's the Widow Ainslee. When her husband died, she flat out refused to sell to Caroline, because she hated her so much. Instead, she sold it to a nice young couple for a much lower price than Caroline offered her. Then it turned out the nice young couple were friends of Caroline's, acting as a straw party. Caroline wound up with the Widow Ainslee's house after all."

"Would the Widow Ainslee murder her?"

"If she could. But she's eighty years old, had a stroke, and is in a nursing home. Her children let me pick her house because I'd been good to their old mother. She had some nice things, too. Dina had a similar version of my story, but Caroline only lent her thirty thousand, and Dina has a little family money. She's not as trapped as I am."

"And Patricia?"

"Patricia never bought her house from Caroline. That's probably why they're such good friends."

"What about Dale and Kathy? Were they the sweet young couple who helped trick Mrs. Ainslee?"

Margie looked surprised. "Those two? No, they bought their house from Mrs. Fulton, and she really was a nice older woman. They're good kids, even though Caroline had them half crazy with worry with her demands. If Caroline hadn't died, they'd have had to paint that porch, and I don't know where they'd get the money, especially with Kathy out of work."

"Do you think they killed Caroline?"

"How?" Margie said. "They can't even sand a floor. How could they get away with murder?"

But I thought of that pretty bedroom, so carefully refinished and decorated, and those love-rumpled sheets. They were good at some things. How far would they go to protect that pleasant life?

"You can't believe Dale and Kathy would murder anyone!" Margie said. "Be serious." But I'd known sweet people who committed murder, and pillars of the community, too, if they were pushed far enough. And Caroline had pushed those kids to the very brink.

"Caroline was heartless with Dale and Kathy," Margie said. "I think she was jealous of their happiness. You can see how much they love each other. But Kathy and Dale were not heartless. They wouldn't kill her, no matter how hard she pushed them."

"Someone killed Caroline," I said.

"She had more enemies than I have unpaid bills," Margie rasped. "If you go up and down this block and the other streets around here, you'll find people just like me who were cheated by Caroline. Except one of them was angry enough to murder Caroline—and smart enough not to fight with her in public."

"Doesn't anyone ever get the better of Caroline?"

"Only one couple that I know of, George and Amanda. They bought a house at Caroline's inflated price, with all the perks and the private loans, just like Bill and me. Then George got transferred to Arizona and they had to sell, fast. That's when they learned the sorry truth—nobody was going to pay that kind of money for a house in an iffy city neighborhood, no matter how beautiful it was. They stood to lose fifty thousand, minimum, more if they sold fast. The only possible purchaser was Caroline, who once again offered them half what they paid her. But George and Amanda were clever. They knew Caroline's weakness: She hates children. Amanda had a lot of family here, and it was a big, noisy family with plenty of kids. She invited them over for a party. She let the little kids run through the gardens and the teenagers play touch football in the parkway and softball on her front lawn. One nine-year-old broke a basement window with a ball, and a toddler pulled all the flowers off an ornamental shrub. The front yard looked like a bad golfer had been carving divots in the grass. The bigger boys lounged on the front porch, playing loud rap music and looking scary. Caroline was beside herself. She finally called the police, but the party was breaking up anyway.

"The next day Caroline marched over to give George and Amanda a piece of her mind. Amanda told her, 'Why don't you take it up with the family who was here? I think they're going to buy the house, and they're going to pay my asking price, too. I'm so thrilled. They need a big house for their eleven children. You don't see families like that anymore. Don't you think a house like this cries out for children, Caroline? The mother, Maybelle, is a leader in the home schooling movement. She likes to have her children around all the time.'

"Caroline had a contract on that house the next day, and when the loans cleared, George and Amanda were out of there. I don't think Caroline ever found out there was no other purchaser."

It was a little after seven when I left Margie's. The angels looked as glorious as ever in their rainbow fountain, but I no longer thought North Dakota Place was heaven on earth. Those weren't angels. They were sirens. They'd trapped Margie with a beautiful white elephant and driven Caroline crazy.

I needed to get away from this place. I wanted to see Lyle. I wanted my suspicions to go away. I knew he wasn't a rat like Charlie. I knew he didn't cheat like my father. If I surprised him at the university, I'd know for sure. By the time I got to Lyle's office, I'd convinced myself that I was there because I was eager to see him. Not because I didn't trust him, or any man, for that matter. My father was unfaithful, and it made my mother crazy, and deep down I was afraid Lyle would do the same to me someday. I was driving out to his office to check on him, and we weren't even married.

Lyle's building was all but deserted at eight o'clock. I could hear a janitor whistling and cleaning an empty first-floor classroom. I saw a student stretched out on the floor by the lobby Coke machine, using his backpack as a pillow. When I got to the fourth floor, Lyle's floor, I saw someone coming out of his office. I hurried down the corridor to get a better look, my heels betraying me with click-tapping noises on the tile. But I didn't move fast enough. I only caught a glimpse of long blond hair and blue jeans. I heard Lyle call out, "Good night, Pat."

I was right. He was seeing someone else. I was sure of it. Almost sure. Sort of sure. Not sure at all, but I knew anyway, as sure as I was standing there, that he was as unfaithful as my father and Charlie. Why else would he be seeing a long-haired blonde at this hour?

I knocked on Lyle's door. He opened it. His office was about the size of a closet, and lined with bookshelves. More books were piled on the floor, and cartoons torn out of newspapers and magazines were stuck on his shelves, around his desk lamp, and taped on the wall. His blue shirt was rumpled, and he was putting on his light-blue summer jacket. He looked handsome but tired. He was packing what looked like typed essays into his briefcase, clearly preparing to go home.

"Francesca," he said, "this is a surprise!"

"I bet," I said, with more acid in my voice than I wanted. But he didn't seem to notice as he gathered me into his arms. "Let's go out to dinner," he said, almost pushing me out of his office. Did he want me out of there because he was tired at the end of the day, or because he didn't want me to see something?

I wasn't hungry after that meal at Caroline's, but I wanted to be with Lyle. We went to a little Greek restaurant up the road, and I poked at the spinach pie with the flaky crust, while he had the cheese pie they set on fire, except the young waiter had trouble getting the fire going, and we laughed about that. I told Lyle about Caroline's awful death, which maybe wasn't a proper dinner topic, but he seemed fascinated.

"The flamingo was stuck right in her chest?" he asked.

"Yeah, and her head was bashed in, too."

"Someone really hated that woman," he said.

"Lots of people hated her," I said. "That's the problem. The police think Margie is the main suspect."

"Do you?" Lyle asked.

"Not really. But none of this makes sense. Why are

Caroline's three worst enemies dead? Who killed them, if Caroline didn't? And who killed Caroline?"

"There has to be some link between them," Lyle said.

"If there is, I can't find it," I said.

Finally we talked out that story. I didn't tell him about the Nails and Charlie rumor, or any other *Gazette* gossip. I was afraid I'd get a lecture about how I should leave that rag and work somewhere else.

Lyle started telling me about his current university project. If anyone saw us, they would think we were in love and eager to be with each other, but there was an uneasy edge to our conversation, as if this were a first date and we weren't sure what to say but we wanted to keep the conversation going.

I remembered all the times my father came home late from work, slightly drunk and whistling too casually, and my mother met him at the door, drink in hand, dressed a little too seductively, nervous and eager to please him, afraid she'd lose him for good. Later, after I'd been sent to bed a little too early, I'd hear their bed springs squeaking. I wondered if I'd have the same uneasy, too-eager-to-please relationship with Lyle. Already I was avoiding topics that might upset him.

No, I wouldn't. I wouldn't be crazy like my mother. No man was worth that. If I had proof Lyle was seeing someone else, I would break off this romance. I'd . . .

"Francesca," Lyle said. "Are you there?"

Just barely. "You were telling me about the special project you were working on at the university," I said. What you were telling me, I have no idea. I was only half listening. I couldn't concentrate. I went back to brooding. I wished I knew for sure that Lyle was cheating on me. I had to know. I couldn't live like this, but the next thing I heard myself say was "I love you. Come home with me."

I couldn't explain why I invited Lyle to my place that night. He looked as surprised as I felt. We made love with every weapon we had. He drove himself in me. I raked my nails across his back. We bit and scratched, like alley cats in heat, and god help me, I liked it. We did not spend the time afterward wrapped in each other's arms, falling gently into sleep, the way we usually did. He did not stay the night, either.

"Maybe that will convince you," Lyle said, as he got up to leave, but he didn't say what it would convince me of, and I realized I didn't know myself. As he turned away to put on his pants, I saw some of the scratches I'd carved in his back were bleeding. I wondered if this was passion, or if we were beginning to enjoy hurting each other. I thought about crying, but before I knew it I was asleep and dreaming about a faceless phantom I chased down a long hallway, and every time I was about to catch up, she disappeared around a hidden corner, leaving only a swish of blond hair that lingered in the air like the grin of a fairy-tale cat.

9

I had a hickey on my neck. Thirty-seven years old, and there I was with a bite mark the size and color of a purple plum, courtesy of last night with Lyle. Damn that man.

I rubbed some foundation on my neck. It didn't cover the hickey. In fact, it seemed to highlight it. I rummaged in my dresser drawer, found a long, filmy leopard-print scarf, and wrapped it around my neck. There. The chiffon looked rather chic with my beige summer suit. I stepped outside and blinked at the blinding summer sun. The sticky, humid air felt like warm soup, and the chiffon scarf felt like a wool muffler.

"Why are you wearing that scarf in this heat?" asked Marlene, as I took my favorite booth at Uncle Bob's.

"Uh, it's the style," I said. This sounded lame even to me, two quarts low on my morning coffee.

Marlene peered at me closely. "Hides that hickey fairly well," she said. "Lyle give you that?"

"Yeah, I feel like a high school kid," I said.

"Is he trying to mark his territory?" she said. How could that woman be right so early in the morning? I kept the scarf on anyway, figuring Marlene was smarter than 99 percent of the population. I wasn't worried about the *Gazette* staffers noticing anything. If I pranced through the newsroom naked, the only thing they'd do was make bitchy comments about whether I'd shaved my legs.

I got to the office in plenty of time for Charlie's big meeting. The staff straggled in, resentfully slouching on desks or stealing chairs from empty desks. Others, like me, leaned against walls and pillars. We could slip away easier. We hated this interruption. The editors would leave work at their usual time, but reporters with stories due would have to finish them, no matter how long management blabbered on.

Charlie was standing in front of his office, plump, proud, and expansive, like one of the pigs in suits on the *Animal Farm* paperback I read in high school. Nails looked like she was expanding, and rapidly. Today she was definitely wearing a maternity dress. To complete the maternity ensemble, she had a shiny new gold wedding band. Pregnancy seemed to make her more substantial. She had a lot more weight, and she wanted to throw it around.

Smiley Steve put on a big insincere smile, like a game-show host. He was a good courtier, who kept his shoulders hunched and head lowered respectfully round Charlie and Nails. Smiley Steve was curt and arrogant to his underlings, but he knew how to cringe before his betters. He had two serious contenders in the current cringing contest: Roberto, the city editor, eager to abase himself before anyone more powerful, and Babe, our gossip columnist. If Nails had worn a train, Babe would have held it. Instead, he fetched her bottled mineral water (impending mothers do not drink coffee), laughed at her jokes, and told lies about the sex lives of staffers she didn't like. I pulled up my hickey-hiding scarf. In my case, the truth was vivid enough.

Promptly at ten, Smiley Steve stepped forward and, speaking into the portable microphone brought out for these ceremonies, treated us to an earsplitting feedback shriek. "Good morning, Gazetteers," he said. "Before we hear from our managing editor, I want to offer him and Miss Noonin our congratulations on their marriage. Let's give them a big hand."

There was the sound of six hands clapping: Babe, Roberto, and Smiley Steve, plus a light pattering from people who thought clapping might advance their careers. The rest of the staff stood there sullenly. If the applause was small, the wedding gift was smaller. Smiley Steve beamed while the bride unwrapped a silver-paper package. Inside was a stingy silver bowl, about the size of a teacup. Smiley Steve couldn't have collected much more than my twenty and Georgia's for this useless present. Nails gave it an appraising look and dropped it contemptuously on the nearest desk, without so much as a thank you.

After the grand opening Charlie bounced to the microphone. He was so short, there was a delay while he lowered it considerably to talk. "Good morning, people," he said. "Thank you for your good wishes on my marriage to Nadia." Dimpletoes paused to throw Cupcake a little flirtatious smile. She threw it back. I nearly threw up.

"But along with this good news, I am sorry that we have bad news," he said. "We have hired the Frobisher Corporation, of Cambridge, Massachusetts, to conduct a series of focus groups, and the results have not been good."

The staff groaned. More consultants. In the past few years, the *Gazette* had spent millions on focus groups and consultants, sometimes hiring two sets of consultants at once. Each had different ideas about how to pull the *Gazette* out of its slump, so we'd been pulled in a dozen different directions. We needed to write short, light, uplifting stories, said one set of experts, and the front pages were infested with chirpy eighty-year-olds who went back for their college degrees and high school classes who raised four hundred fifty dollars for AIDS by washing cars. We needed more local news stories, said another set of consultants, and the front pages were overrun with car crashes, drug-related shootings, and six-column photos of downed trees after every storm. We needed stories that were "local but positive" said a third expert, and the shootings and accidents were pushed off the front page by unmarried mothers who graduated from college at age thirty-five in a double ceremony with their oldest child (These were always African Americans. White women were not unmarried teenage mothers in the *Gazette*) and car dealers who donated almost-new cars to worthy causes. The charitable dealers were always major advertisers and the donated cars looked shiny in the six-column photos.

What we needed was to kick out the consultants and put in editors who knew what they were doing. When the *Gazette* thrived, it scoured the city like a hard rain. We did stories about senators involved in swindles. We ferreted out corruption at City Hall, the police, and the school board. We did lighthearted but insightful features in far-flung suburbs from Florissant to Fenton, places most current *Gazette* reporters had never seen.

But real reporting cost millions, and the *Gazette* had already spent that money on consultants. It also took guts, and *Gazette* editors didn't even like to take phone calls from readers. Which is why the reporters were going to be stuck with the latest consultant scheme.

"Interviews with focus groups reveal that the *Gazette* staff is seen by readers as arrogant, distant, out of touch with St. Louis, and uninterested in the community or its welfare," Charlie said. This meant the public had a pretty accurate picture of the *Gazette*.

"Our consultants have a suggestion," he said, and

the silence was thick and despairing. Whatever it was, it would be more misery for us.

"We are instituting a new Meet Your Neighbor program. We want you to have more contact with our readers. We want readers to see that you are people like them, people who share their concerns, who pay the rent and shop at the supermarket, just like they do. That's why, effective immediately, all *Gazette* reporters will be required to knock on the doors of fifty homes within a two-block radius of their own residence and introduce themselves. We will be passing out sheets with addresses and names. You must get a signature beside every name to show that you have met your neighbors. You will have one month."

Scattered cries of "Fuck me," "What?" and "This is stupid" filled the newsroom, but it was hard to say who was speaking. Jasper's snarl broke through the confusion. "What do they think we are? A bunch of politicians?" Jasper hated everyone, but particularly readers. I was sure the people who met Jasper would not change their low opinion of the *Gazette*.

Then Nails jumped in, wearing the superior smile of the teacher's pet. "Even though I am an editor and therefore not required to participate in the Meet Your Neighbor program," she said, "I felt I should introduce myself in our neighborhood. I enjoyed the experience immensely. I signed up two families for home delivery of the *Gazette*. I helped an eighty-eight-year-old woman put away her groceries and learned that she was one of the first women accountants in St. Louis, a story suggestion I have given to the Family section. I talked to a gentleman who had a complaint about the stock market quotations, which I will be able to correct in my new post as the All Business editor, and I straightened out a problem for a reader whose paper was not properly delivered."

It was hard to hear all Nails's good deeds over the

noise of the reporters making fun of her. Naturally, I was one of them.

"As I was saying to Charlie in bed last night . . ." Nails said.

"Oh, for god's sake, Nails, we can all see you sleep with him," I said, right when there was an unfortunate and unexpected silence. Everyone heard my comment.

Nails swung my way, and we squared off like a couple of gunfighters at high noon. Showdown. Nails was so calm and deliberate, I knew she must be seething. She was still smiling her superior smile. "One of the things I did *not* add," she said, carefully choosing each word, "is how many people did not like your column, Francesca. They think it's trivial. They would like to see women writing serious stories."

"Did you tell Charlie that in bed, too?" I said. "Is that where you think serious women discuss business? I save my discussions for the office. But then I have a different . . . position."

The blood drained from Nails's face. She said something, but I couldn't hear what it was. Smiley Steve grabbed the microphone, put on his game-show host grin, and said, "Thank you very much, Gazetteers. Please sign for your Meet Your Neighbor list at the city desk." The meeting broke up with bitter cheers and catcalls. Charlie and Nails stalked off toward his office. Nails didn't bother to take their wedding gift. Smiley Steve ran after the bridal couple and handed Nails the present.

"Way to go, Francesca," Jasper said, slapping me on the back. "Care to contribute to the Nails Is Nailed pool? We're taking bets on which day she'll whelp. It's a dollar per guess on the baby's arrival date, time, and birth weight."

"I'll take ten chances, Jasper," I said, fishing in my purse for a bill. I was eager to recoup the money I had lost on Charlie and Nails's wedding gift. As I filled out my ten entries, other staffers came over to congratulate me. Endora was first. Her rich girl's horse face looked pathetically eager to get this gossip to her society friends. Trashy, topheavy Scarlette, one of Charlie's minor squeezes, hated Nails for replacing her. She teetered over on her high heels and patted me on the back. She was followed by a flock of third-rate reporters and newsroom climbers who shook my hand or slapped my back. I looked at their ratlike smiles of congratulation. Tomorrow any one of them could turn on me and start fawning over Nails. I didn't respect them personally or professionally. How did I get to be a hero to these people?

Worst of all, O'Hara, the burned-out feature writer, came over to congratulate me. O'Hara was known to the older reporters as "Pants" because of how the copy desk once butchered his story. The desk was always making outrageous grammar rulings, such as deciding people said "feel" when they should say "believe." They also believed "like" must be corrected to "as though," with no exceptions. So one election night O'Hara interviewed a losing candidate who said "I feel like I've been kicked in the pants." What he said in the *Gazette*, thanks to the copy desk, was "I believe as though I've been kicked in the pants."

Pants O'Hara was the reason I fought the *Gazette* editors so hard. He started as a writer of great charm and talent. His fatal flaw was he always did what he was told. He covered every bad story, dutifully making sows' ears into silk purses. He interviewed charity horse show chairpersons who said, "I'm honored to help our city's finest hospital." He interviewed civic leaders who didn't even say that. If the story disappointed him, he had a little drink at the Last Word. O'Hara had a lot of disappointments and a lot of drinks.

Now my personal nightmare was shaking my hand.

I looked around in panic and saw my mentor, Georgia, the person I most respected at the *Gazette*. She saw me, but she turned away without a word and went into her office. I picked up my list of Meet Your Neighbor names and left. Actually, I don't know why I made such a big deal out of it. Now I had an excuse to meet all the neighbors and ask them about Caroline.

I started with the names on North Dakota Place. No one was at home at the first eight names. Number nine was answered by a wet, angry-looking woman who said, "It's bad enough the *Gazette* telephone salespeople interrupt me night after night while I'm at dinner. Now you get me out of the shower. I wouldn't subscribe to your rag if it was the last newspaper in the country. There isn't an ounce of news in it. That's why I take *The New York Times*!" She picked up the *Times* in a blue plastic wrapper from the hall table. For a minute I thought she was going to hit me with it. Instead, she slammed the door in my face. So much for making friends while meeting people.

No one was at home at Dina's, Kathy and Dale's, or Patricia's. Caroline's house was dark, and the porch was piled with yellowing newspapers. I passed it with a shiver.

At the fourteenth house, I got lucky. It belonged to a woman of about eighty who I'd seen around the neighborhood. She had neat, short white hair, a neat, short body, and clear skin. She wore a freshly ironed blue-flowered house dress that zipped up the front, white socks, and tennis shoes. "Come in, dear," she said. "I'm Theda Meyer. I know who you are. I love your column. So true to life. I've just made lemon bars and I have iced tea. Come in, come in, we'll have a nice visit out on the screened-in porch." The porch was shaded by a big old maple tree. It was a cool, comfortable place with old-fashioned plants in clay pots: red geraniums, parlor ferns, and angel-wing begonias. The brown wicker furniture was padded with flowered cushions. I helped carry in the tea and cookies. Mrs. Meyer turned on the ceiling fan. She took the wicker settee and I sat in the rocker. "This is nice," I said, and that's all I needed to prime Mrs. Meyer. She was a good talker. She also made a mean lemon bar, tangy without being sour. Sort of like her conversation.

It was easy to steer her toward Caroline's death. "I heard Caroline and her ex-husband the lawyer fighting the week before she died," Mrs. Meyer said. "Oh, it was a terrible fight. Just terrible. The things they said. I heard every word, you know. They argued with the windows open, and I happened to be weeding in the side garden. The ex-husband said he paid Caroline four-thousand-a-month maintenance and his law practice wasn't doing so well, and he wanted some financial relief. Caroline refused. She threatened to foreclose on his house in Clayton to get the maintenance he owed her. She said she'd take his BMW. He laughed and said, 'Good luck, baby. It's leased.' He was in a rage, screaming that she'd be sorry. She said she'd been sorry since the day she'd laid eyes on him. And then she made some derogatory remark about the size of his, of his . . ." She looked at me and I nodded to make it clear I knew which part of his anatomy was being discussed. "I swear, Francesca, I think he would have killed her on the spot, he was so angry, but by that time he was aware of me weeding under the window. Called me a nosy old . . . person. It was nasty, I tell you, very nasty. And coming so soon after that terrible scene Caroline had with Sally and her boyfriend."

We both fortified ourselves with lemon bars before Mrs. Meyer continued. "Is Sally the one who lost her boyfriend because Caroline wouldn't let him park his pickup on North Dakota Place?" I asked.

"Ah, you've heard about that," Mrs. Meyer said. "Personally, I think Caroline drove Darryl away because she didn't want a hoosier roosting on this street. I don't have to tell you what a hoosier is, do I?"

"Of course not," I said. In St. Louis, a hoosier is not a person from Indiana. A hoosier was an uneducated lowlife. A hoosier thought Bondo was a car color and a pickup was incomplete without a gun rack.

"Sometimes I think a hoosier is any ill-bred person we don't like," Mrs. Meyer said. "What's your definition, Francesca?"

"A guy who goes to a family reunion for a date," I said.

Mrs. Meyer nearly spit out her iced tea. "Very good, dear. Caroline simply did not want one on the block, and Sally's interest in this man seemed to be increasing. She's such a nice young woman, with a responsible job as an accountant, and this Darryl—that's his name, Darryl—was so unsuitable for her. He was practically living at her house. His disreputable pickup was parked out there almost every night, and it was covered with the rudest pictures and bumper stickers."

"Was that the truck that had the bumper sticker, 'Don't like my driving? Dial 1-800-EAT . . .'"

"Ah, yes," Mrs. Meyer said, interrupting me. "And it had this picture on the back window of a little boy urinating on a Ford logo."

I bit into a lemon bar to hide my smile, but Mrs. Meyer was too sharp. She caught me. "I know you think I'm an old prude, but some things should not be for public display."

"I was laughing at your delicate description," I said. "That truck would never win any neighborhood beautification award."

"After Darryl changed his oil in front of Sally's house, Caroline was determined to get him out of there," Mrs. Meyer said. "She said Darryl was bad for property values." That was the ultimate South Side condemnation. A real hoosier like Darryl could make

Otto look like Martha Stewart. Soon Sally's lawn would be sporting a couple of junked cars, and the lawn furniture would be replaced with an old car seat. Screens would fall off the windows, and curtains would start flapping outside. Domestic disturbances and police cars would be next. No wonder Caroline wanted him off the street.

"Darryl got into a tremendous fight with Sally after he got that ticket for parking in front of her house. They were in Sally's backyard, which had several of his truck parts in it, and I happened to be going for a stroll in the alley, and I heard them. I'd have to be deaf not to. I will spare you Darryl's exact language, but you've seen his pickup, so you can imagine. Darryl wanted Sally to pay his parking ticket. He was quite adamant. She refused. She said she'd picked up the last tab for Darryl, and it was time he got off his behind and went to work. I think Darryl's request for money opened her eyes. It was the end of their relationship. Darryl blamed Caroline for the breakup. He threatened her, right in my presence. I happened to be weeding again, when he rang Caroline's doorbell. She wouldn't let him in, of course. They had their disagreement right on her front porch, and I could hear everything without straining. Darryl was quite drunk, on beer, I think. He carried a six-pack of Busch, minus the one in his hand, and he belched often. He was disgusting in an inebriated state.

"Darryl swore he'd get even with Caroline, but I just thought it was the beer talking. He drank a lot of beer, you know, and he wasn't really the sort of man Sally should have been dating. I'm so glad that now she's seeing that nice accountant she met at work. After the scene on Caroline's porch, I saw Darryl around Caroline's house once or twice, as if he were stalking her. He'd park his pickup right in front of Caroline's house. I think she even called the police once more and he got another ticket. I guess that's why I thought Darryl was the one who killed Caroline at first. That pink flamingo was his kind of touch. He'd know Caroline would be mortified to be associated with something so tacky."

And what did Sally know about her ex-boyfriend? Had he told her about his plans to get even with Caroline? How did she feel about the breakup? Did she blame Caroline? Or was she relieved he was gone for good? I'd have to ask Sally. Suddenly there seemed to be all sorts of candidates for Caroline's killer. Darryl the stalker, blaming Caroline for the loss of his meal ticket. The ex-husband, pleading in vain for financial relief. Plus Dale and Kathy, the sweet little rehabbers Caroline was hounding into financial ruin. Four people who had excellent reasons for wanting Caroline dead. Might as well try for five or more.

"Caroline thought the kids in that rundown house pulled a prank that could have killed that jogger in the alley," I said. "Do you think that's possible?"

"Oh, my, yes. They were up to all sorts of mischief in that alley: setting trash fires, torturing a stray cat, selling drugs and guns and god knows what else. There are at least four of them living in the trouble house. That's what we call it—the trouble house. The youngest is eleven and the oldest and meanest is almost eighteen. He looks quite capable of anything. I can see their backyard and part of their house out my back window upstairs, if I hold the blinds just right. I saw more than enough of their illegal comings and goings, including drug and gun deals. When I complained to the police about their antics, they broke all my garage windows. Of course, I couldn't prove it was them, but I knew it was those children just the same. It didn't do any good to talk to their parents. There wasn't any father, and the mother was hardly ever home. Those children do as they please. People are afraid of them.

Caroline was after them constantly. It wouldn't surprise me if they killed her and the jogger, too."

And maybe Scorpion Smith, the drug dealer, over some kind of business deal. That would take care of three of the four murders. Otto could have been done in by someone he stiffed at City Hall.

Four more suspects, and these could neatly wrap up most of the murders on North Dakota Place. This was going incredibly well. I couldn't believe my luck. Then Mrs. Meyer said, "Although I still think Margie probably killed Caroline. She has quite a temper, you know. She drinks a little, too. And she didn't get along with Caroline at all. Margie tried to cheat my friend Mrs. Grumbacher, offering a ridiculous price for her grandmother's silver. I don't trust that Margie person."

I couldn't see how lowballing led to murder, but I didn't say that to Mrs. Meyer. She'd been a tremendous help. She didn't know the last names of Sally's boyfriend and Caroline's ex, but I could find those out from other sources. I thanked her and left. I really didn't feel like hitting any more houses. I'd had so much iced tea I sloshed, and when I went to put on some lipstick, my face was sprinkled with powdered sugar from all those lemon bars. Anyway, I wanted to digest all that information. On the way back to my car, I stopped by Margie's house, just for the heck of it, and to get her signature on my Meet Your Neighbor list. This time Margie was home. I stayed long enough for her to give me the name and address of Caroline's ex-husband. She didn't know Darryl's last name, but she did know he hung out most days at a bar called the Big House. I knew the place. The name had nothing to do with the size of the building. It was an inside joke. A lot of ex-cons drank there. Ironically, it was located near the old Lynch Street police station. I decided I might as well see if I could find Darryl. The Big House would be an interesting contrast to Mrs. Meyer's begonias and lemon bars.

The Big House had bars on the windows and doors, which must have made the clientele feel right at home. Inside, the place was dingy and dirty, and smelled of old grease, Lysol, and stale cigarette smoke. Charlie Daniels was singing in a flat, nasty voice about leaving this long-haired country boy alone. I sat at the bar and ordered Bud in a bottle. The bartender, a balding guy wearing a gray apron that used to be white, brought it and a glass that had orange lipstick on the rim. I poured the beer, but I didn't plan to drink it. I knew the bartender wouldn't talk to anyone who ordered a club soda with lime. I asked the bartender if Darryl was there and he said, "Which one?" I realized half the clientele must be named Darryl. Mentioning that this Darryl drove a beat-up pickup with a 1-800-EAT-SHIT bumper sticker wouldn't narrow it down. "Used to date a classy lady named Sally," I said. "If he brought her in here, you'd remember her."

Because she'd stick out like a sore thumb, I didn't add.

"Oh, that Darryl. I could see what he saw in her, but I never understood what she saw in him. But then I guess I never do. He's down there at the end of the bar, eating boneless chicken for breakfast." Boneless chicken was bar slang for pickled eggs. There was a jar on the bar, next to a rack of Beef Jerky. A man who could eat pickled eggs for breakfast, even when breakfast was at two-thirty in the afternoon, had a cast-iron stomach.

Darryl was so skinny the elastic on his underwear stuck out over his jeans. His spaghetti arms barely had room for a panther tattoo. His hair needed an oil change and his eyes were flat and yellow, like a goat's. He was wearing a too-short, stained black T-shirt with an American flag. "Try burning this flag, asshole," the

T-shirt said. A real patriot, Darryl. He sat ready to defend his country's flag wrapped in a beer fog. The bottle of Busch in front of him was definitely not his first. I introduced myself, and Darryl said, "A newspaper lady. Well, ain't you cute. What brings you here? The fine cuisine?" He pronounced it coo-ZINE, and blew enough beer fumes my way to get me high. "Or do you want to do a story on me, Newspaper Lady? I know all kinds of interesting things." He showed a lot of yellow teeth and gave me what he thought was a knowing, sexy grin.

"I'm trying to get some information on Caroline," I said.

"Don't know no Caroline," he said. "I know a Sandy, a Dee-Anne, and a Wanda, and I left them all satisfied ladies. But a Caroline? I don't think I ever had the pleasure of filling her hole." He seemed to think that disgusting euphemism was the height of gallantry.

"No, you didn't," I said. "You got in a fight with her, several fights, in fact—on North Dakota Place."

Darryl went from amorous to angry in two seconds flat. "What kind of shit are you trying to start?" he said, his goat's eyes narrowing. "You trying to pin that on me, because I done some time? The cops already talked to me. I don't have to talk to you, period. Get the hell out of here, bitch, before I punch your lying mouth."

"Hey," the bartender said, suddenly showing up at our end. "That's enough of that talk, Darryl. I warned you before to watch your mouth. Can I get you anything else, ma'am?" he said to me, which is bartenderese for asking me to move on.

"Ah, no thanks. I've got to get going," I said.

"I'm just getting started," Darryl said, hiccuping. "I'll have another Busch."

"You've had all you're gonna have, Darryl," the bartender said, and pulled out a length of lead pipe wrapped in duct tape from under the bar. "If you don't leave now, I'll have to throw you out, and it will be permanent. You'll be eighty-sixed." Eighty-six was the bar code for eternal banishment. Darryl must have believed the bartender, because he pushed back his barstool, dropped some money on the bar, and mumbled, "I don't have to take this shit."

I was almost out the door by then. Darryl followed me down the street, cursing and muttering to himself. I pulled out my car keys, the way the instructor told me to when I interviewed her for a women and self-defense story. Right now, the rubber-topped key didn't look like much of a defense. I wondered if I could really jab it into Darryl's eye, or neck, if I had to. Wasn't that the other way to fend off an attacker—a key in the neck? Did I shove it in his Adam's apple or the hollow at the base? I couldn't remember. Fortunately, Darryl's pickup was parked closer to the bar than my car, and he decided to get in it. He slammed the door loudly, still cursing. I noticed, besides the decorations Mrs. Meyer mentioned, the rusty truck had duct tape over the missing gas cap.

I climbed gratefully into Ralph, locked the doors, and roared out of there, desperate to get away from Darryl. By the time I was on the highway, heading for Clayton, I didn't see any sign of his rusty pickup. People like Darryl weren't supposed to go to Clayton, but I had the feeling he was familiar with my next stop, or some place similar. The Clayton law offices of Caroline's ex were a little classier than the Big House, but not much. James Graftan was a criminal lawyer who catered to the lowest of the low—rapists, murderers, and child molesters. Clayton is the county government center, and it's supposed to be rich and modern and infinitely superior to the city. I'm always surprised how many Clayton office buildings put up a nice front but have slummy interiors. Graftan's law office looked like the inside of a cheap trailer. The reception room had a water-spotted dropped ceiling with tiles missing, plywood paneling, orange shag carpet, and a particleboard desk for the brunette receptionist. She looked cheap, too. Her ruffled blouse was cut low to reveal outsized breasts. Her hair was long and curly, her makeup thick, and when she walked to the file cabinet, she wobbled on red spike heels. She wore a short skirt that was bunched with wrinkles at the back and an ankle bracelet with a gold heart. Dress for success. A brass plate on her desk announced that her name was LaVyrle. Two clients sat on hard orange plastic molded chairs and stared at LaVyrle's boobs or her butt, depending on whether she was sitting or filing. The two men looked like Darryl's degenerate cousins. One of them winked and grinned at me. I noticed he was missing several teeth.

"I'm sorry, but Mr. Graftan is not seeing clients without an appointment," the receptionist said crisply.

"I'm not a client, I'm a newspaper reporter," I said. "I wanted to ask him some questions about his former wife."

"He still can't see you without an appointment," she said firmly.

"You could ask him and make sure," I said.

"She doesn't have to," Graftan said, emerging from his office. Caroline's ex was short, always a bad sign in a lawyer. He had mean eyes, a tight, ungenerous mouth, and an impatient manner. He was wearing a sharkskin suit. I wondered if it made his ostrich boots nervous. The boots added two inches to his height, but he still only came up to my shoulder. He was also irrationally angry. "I don't want to talk to you and I don't have to. Get out," he said. "Now. Before I call the police. Don't call and don't come here again. LaVyrle has orders to hang up on you, if you call again."

"Okay," I said. "If you're sure you won't change your

mind." He turned on his high heels and stomped back into his office, slamming the door.

LaVyrle glared at me and said, "You better go. No telling what he'll do when he's this mad."

I suppose I should have been honored to be thrown out of Graftan's office, considering who he let in. But I still felt lousy. Two ugly encounters in one day. I wasn't ready for a third. I thought I'd tackle the dangerous kids at the trouble house another day. I would spend tonight with Lyle. I'd pick up some wine and cheese and a baked chicken from the supermarket, and we could meet for dinner by the lily ponds at Tower Grove Park. It was one of the most romantic spots I knew, with the evening shadows slanting over the pale, pointed blue flowers and the giant leathery green pads. We could watch the college students playing Frisbee with their big dogs and the lovers kissing near the fake Roman ruins. We could relax and talk and forget why we ever argued.

But before I stopped at the supermarket, maybe I should swing by the mother-loving Erwin's house. It was only three-thirty in the afternoon. I parked a block up from Erwin's address on Utah Street. He lived in a single-family reddish brick bungalow of preternatural neatness. His neighbors on one side weren't home. On the other side, they were deep into a TV show. I heard music and canned laughter.

South Siders were famous for their cleaning, but even among world-class neat freaks, Erwin's place was outstanding. The white painted trim looked fresh. The gutters were done in regulation forest green, and the concrete steps were painted battleship gray. The birdbath planted precisely in the middle of the front yard was also painted white, and so was the concrete Madonna sitting in the middle of the birdbath. On the porch were two white-painted concrete pots, each holding one scrawny red geranium. I went up on the porch and knocked on the door, pretending I was a legit visitor. No one answered, so I peeked in the blinds. Yep, this was a South Side house, all right. We favored the layered look. The wall-to-wall carpet was covered with throw rugs, and the throw rugs were covered with plastic runners. The sofa had two sets of slip covers, good and every day. The actual sofa would only be seen once, at the estate sale, where it would be in perfect condition. The lamps still had on their plastic shade covers. The end tables gleamed with polish. The windows were washed. Everything had been scrubbed and dusted within an inch of its life. It was clear no one was home, but I thought I'd better check the garage, just to make sure, so I walked around the block to the alley. Like all good citizens, the Shermann family put their address on the back gate. I couldn't see into the garage windows because they were covered with starched white curtains, but I peeked in the little portholes on the metal garage door and saw there was no Buick. So I let myself in the back gate. The backyard was the size of a door mat, and most of it was taken up by an enormous garden, about six feet long and four feet wide. Crammed into that space were rows of cucumbers, bell peppers, tomatoes, and zucchini. Why would anyone grow zucchini? Did you ever know anyone to get a craving for a fresh zucchini? There was also a row of yellow-orange marigolds, which South Siders plant to ward off garden pests, although I never saw a marigold yet that did its job.

I studied the garden. The ground was oddly mounded near the marigolds, as if it had been recently disturbed. I looked closer. The soil there was looser and looked freshly turned, unlike the rest of the garden. I remembered Pam saying Erwin had worked all summer on his garden. She also said his mother went to visit her sister in New Jersey, although Pam hadn't actually seen Mom leave, suitcase in hand. In fact, nobody had seen Erwin's mother since mid-May, and now it was July. That was a long time to savor the delights of New Jersey. I thought I should investigate that suspicious garden mound, but I didn't have a shovel with me. I wondered if Erwin kept his garden tools in the garage. The side door to the garage was unlocked. I opened it. Inside, the garage was neater than my apartment. Besides the starched curtains, the concrete floor had been waxed, and newspapers put down to catch oil drips from the car. The tools were hanging in rows, shiny-clean and dust-free. The work-bench had been dusted, too, and the baby-food jars of nails and screws had been washed.

I saw the shovel hanging on the garage wall be-tween the rake and the edger. It was the only tool that wasn't cleaned. The clumps of dried dirt on it would look normal anywhere else, but here in this scrubbed and dustless garage, they were shocking—and to me, proof that Erwin's angel mother was no longer on this earth. Otherwise, she would have cleaned the shovel. What had Erwin written me? "She understands, but she's no longer with me." And "My Mother is gone, and she shouldn't be."

And why shouldn't she, Erwin? Because you went nuts one night and killed her? And ever since you've been working hard in your garden, digging and dig-ging. It's a very lush garden. I bet I know what you use for fertilizer.

What did Pam tell me—"Erwin is definitely a strange one"? Of course he was strange, growing up with Mrs. Clean. I wondered if Erwin's dad left, or if she just cleaned him out. I had to find out if Old Weird Erwin had buried Mom in the garden. I could hear Georgia and Lyle and Marlene and Mayhew all advis-ing caution and saying I should wait and go through the proper channels. But if Erwin suspected anything, he would move the body before officialdom found it.

Far better if I did a little checking now. If I didn't find anything under the marigolds, I could quietly hang up the shovel and go home. No one would know if I was mistaken. Erwin would not be embarrassed and neither would I. This was really the most cautious and sensible way to handle it, I told myself, as I reached for Erwin's shovel and started toward his garden.

I kicked off my heels, took off my jacket, rolled up my sleeves, and started digging. The ground around the marigolds came away easily. Three big scoops, and I was deep into a predug hole. Then my shovel hit something. A rock? No. It didn't feel like a rock. It felt . . . padded somehow. I carefully removed a small scoop. Nothing there but dirt and a bit of green bottle glass. I tried a second scoop, even smaller. This time I didn't take enough dirt to fill a coffee mug. Still nothing. On the third scoop, I saw something. It looked like a hunk of gray hair. I hunched down and carefully brushed more dirt away. I saw a mass of gray hair and rotting, mangled tissue. I screamed and screamed and screamed.

10

"You dug up a dead *cat*?" Marlene said the next morning at Uncle Bob's.

I shook my head yes. I still had trouble talking about the whole ugly episode. The nightmare vision of gray hair and bloody flesh turned out to be a twelve-pound medium-hair gray tomcat. I took a huge gulp of coffee, but it didn't wash away the memory. Marlene poured coffee for two people at the next table and then came back to mine to continue her questioning.

"So that weirdo Erwin was torturing animals and burying them in the backyard?" she said indignantly.

"No," I said. My voice sounded like a croak from a tomb. "No, Erwin buried the animal as an act of kindness. The gray cat was a stray that the older people in the neighborhood fed. The cat didn't belong to anyone, but he went from house to house bumming table scraps. Last week a couple of kids driving their mom's red Miata took the corner too fast and nailed the cat. The old people couldn't bear to throw the cat in the Dumpster, so Erwin said he'd bury it in the garden. Told them he'd put it by the marigolds so it would always have flowers on its grave."

"Hoo-boy," Marlene said. "So how much trouble are you in?"

"Lots," I said. "The neighbors heard me screaming bloody murder when I saw the gray hair and blood.

THE PINK FLAMINGO MURDERS

They called the police, who came over and laughed their asses off. I might have gotten away with it, except Erwin pulled up then and went ballistic. He had me arrested for trespassing. They issued a summons right there and then released me."

"You're kidding," Marlene said. She looked slightly dazed. She poured herself a cup of coffee and added about a quarter-cup of sugar. The spoon could stand upright in the cup.

"He tried to make it breaking and entering, but the garage door was open, and even he admitted nothing was missing inside. I used his shovel to dig up the cat, but I claimed the shovel was outside in the yard."

"Thank god for small favors," Marlene said. "He must have his mother stashed somewhere else."

"New Jersey," I said. "Mom is alive and well and living with her sister in Atlantic City. The police called and talked with her. She refused to come home. Said she was three-hundred-sixty dollars ahead playing bingo and the slot machines, and she was staying with her sister through July. Then she told the cops to remind Erwin to paste-wax the dining room table and keep the blinds closed in the morning so the sun wouldn't fade the carpet."

"The woman shows no mercy." Marlene took another gulp of her coffee. I just stared at mine.

"Neither does her son," I said. "Now he says he's going to sue me for defamation of character. He says a teacher's reputation is his only possession, and I've damaged his, and he's calling Jasper Crullen."

"The lawyer who advertises on TV?"

"Yeah, him. The one who says 'Don't be pushed around by the big guys. Let Jasper Crullen, the fighting lawyer, put them in their place.'"

"But you're not a big guy," Marlene said. "I mean, you're a tall woman, but you don't have any money."

"But the *Gazette* does," I said. "I said I was there

working on a story. If Erwin sues the newspaper, you can just bury me and my career. We're both dead."

"The newspaper must have insurance for lawsuits," she said.

"It doesn't make any difference. Charlie has been looking for ways to get me for years, and now I've handed him this opportunity. With Nails egging him on, he won't stop. And even if he does, when that lawsuit is filed, I'll be a laughingstock in journalism. I can see the headlines now: 'Reporter Accused of (Cat) Grave Robbing.' And the cat puns. Copy editors love cat puns. The stories will have headlines like: 'Reporter Digs for Story; Finds Cat-tastrophe.' Not to mention: 'Teacher Sues *Gazette* Over Catty Remarks' and 'Grave Situation Causes Bad Felines.' I'll never live it down. I'll be a bad joke."

"No, you won't," she said firmly. But right on cue, Mayhew walked in and meowed when he saw me.

He sat down at my table and said, "I hear you don't pussyfoot around when it comes to investigations."

Marlene bopped him on the head with the teaspoon she used to stir her coffee and said, "This isn't funny, Mayhew. She's in big trouble over that stupid cat. That weirdo has been writing Francesca threatening letters for a month. I saw them, and they scared me. See what you can do to help her."

Mayhew looked contrite. He really was a nice guy. "Sure. Do you have the letters?"

"They're postcards," I said. "They were so weird I kept them." I pulled the postcards out of my briefcase.

Mayhew read them and shook his head. "This character is very careful how he phrases things. The letters can sound threatening if you read them one way, but if you read them another, they're just warnings for your safety."

"Terrific," I said. "I'm going to sound like the nut."

"I didn't say that. But some of these paranoid types

are very smart. They know just how far they can go before they bring the law down on themselves. Erwin wrote some strange letters, but unfortunately there's nothing we can do about that—and he probably knows that. I can do some checking and see if there have been other complaints about his letter writing."

"He's guilty of something," Marlene said. "I just don't know what it is."

I was sick of talking about it, and I knew I'd have to talk about it a lot more at the *Gazette*, and no one there would want to help me. If I was going to get any breakfast down, I'd better change the subject. "Speaking of guilty," I said to Mayhew, "do you still think Margie is a suspect in Caroline's murder?"

"You know I can't talk about an ongoing case," he said, turning suddenly stuffy.

"So you do think she's guilty."

"I didn't say that," he said.

"Might as well, when you use that tone of voice."

"That's what I like about you, Francesca, your subtle technique. Why don't you say what you want straight out?"

"Okay, I've talked with Margie and some other people on North Dakota Place and I don't think Margie did it. I don't think she'd be dumb enough to kill Caroline after having a loud public fight with her and then plant a pink flamingo in the body. It's just too obvious."

Mayhew's eyes narrowed. "Let me get this straight," he said. "A few days ago you wanted me to arrest Caroline for murdering three people because she had loud public fights with them. Now you want me to *not* arrest Margie because she had a loud public fight with Caroline. Why was Caroline guilty because she had the fights and Margie innocent?"

"It would be too obvious for Margie to kill Caroline," I said. Even *he* should be able to see that.

"It's almost always obvious," Mayhew said. "When a wife dies, we look at the husband. When a husband dies, we look at the wife. When a pregnant nurse dies, we check out her married doctor boyfriend. You know what? Nine times out of ten, they did it."

"This is the tenth time," I said. "I'm convinced of it."

"You were also convinced Erwin's mother was buried in the garden," he said. I winced. "I'm sorry, Francesca. I didn't mean to hurt your feelings. You're one hell of a writer. But I don't try to write your columns, and you shouldn't try to do my job, either. You are not a homicide detective and I am not a newspaper columnist."

I wasn't going to be a newspaper columnist much longer, either. Not if Erwin sued. I gave up trying to eat anything and went to the *Gazette* to get my butt chewed out. I didn't even make it to my desk before I got the summons. "Charlie's looking for you," said my editor, Wendy the Whiner. She was wearing a wrinkled white suit of some weird loose weave that looked like old place mats. Her no-color hair was frowsy and badly cut. Her thick white heels were scuffed. Wendy didn't bother hiding her smirk. "He wants you in his office as soon as possible. He's very upset with you." She was almost vibrating with suppressed glee.

I walked across the newsroom in a thick and absolute silence. Reporters pretended to type, but they watched my slow progress through slitted eyes. Editors didn't even pretend to be busy. They just stared at the condemned columnist. Nails was talking on the phone, but she put it down and watched me with a little smile. I waved at her. Georgia, my mentor, the one person I wanted and needed at the *Gazette*, was nowhere around.

Charlie put on a good-old-boy front, but I thought his office revealed his true personality. It was black and cold and empty. Space was a luxury at the *Gazette*, and he flaunted it. Miniblinds hid the unimpressive view of the *Gazette* parking lot. The desk was slippery, shiny black, and could have seated twelve. Rumor said his black leather chair was specially built to make him look taller. When I walked in the room, Charlie did not greet me. I retaliated by not sitting down. He hated that I towered over him. The only thing on his desk, except for a telephone, was one sheet of white paper. "This is a letter from Jasper Crullen, delivered by courier this morning, informing me of his plans to sue the *Gazette* for your actions at the home of his client yesterday," he said in a cold, angry voice.

"Why doesn't he sue me instead of the paper?" I said, even though I already knew the answer.

"Because you told the police you were on assignment, although your editor had no idea what you were working on when I questioned her. But Crullen claims you were acting as an agent for the *Gazette* and therefore we are responsible for your actions."

"Has he filed suit yet?"

"He's giving us a chance to settle first. I've talked to our attorneys. They want to research the situation, but they have advised me that they will probably recommend that we accept his offer."

"Those cowards!" I said. I couldn't help it. The words just escaped. The *Gazette* lawyers always recommended settling. They were terrified of a jury trial, because the jury would be made up of people who had been sneered at and hung up on by *Gazette* editors and had their names misspelled by *Gazette* reporters.

"Do you know who Jasper Crullen is?" Charlie asked, and I caught the hysteria in his voice.

"Sure," I said. "He's the sleaze with the TV ads."

"He's the attorney who won the half-million-dollar judgment in the Ladue Card Shark Lawsuit."

Oh. I forgot that. For a while, that story was all over the media. You couldn't turn on the radio or TV without hearing about it. The jokes from the morning show jocks were endless. The situation was irresistible. A card-playing grande dame in the wealthy suburb of Ladue was forced out of her regular Wednesday bridge game by gossip from another dowager. The woman claimed the grande dame cheated at cards and, even worse, played for money—because she needed it. Stuck at home watching the soaps on her regular bridge afternoon, she saw Jasper Crullen in his TV ad, promising to fight for her for no money down. She made the call. Jasper got her half a million bucks and an apology.

"But the gossip was true," I said. "She *was* a card cheat, and her creditors were swarming around her. The only check that didn't bounce was the one she wrote to the country club. She won because the defendant was such a snob. The jury punished the gossiper for looking down her nose at them."

And how would a city jury react to the *Gazette* lawyers, those sleek, well-fed, and extremely condescending suburbanites who held their noses every time they were forced to step into the city? I knew that answer.

"Juries are idiots," Charlie said. "You can't predict what those ignorant slobs will do. If we settle now, it will be two hundred fifty thousand. If we go to court, Crullen will ask for five hundred thousand dollars."

"Half a million dollars for digging up a dead cat? What for?" I said. I had trouble taking this all in.

"He says you slandered his client and falsely accused him of murdering his mother. Who, unfortunately for us, is still alive."

Probably unfortunately for Erwin, too, but I didn't say that.

"In addition to the defamation, you trespassed on his property and caused Erwin extreme emotional distress and mental suffering upon seeing his beloved pet exhumed."

"His pet?" I shrieked. "That cat was a stray. All the older people in the neighborhood fed it."

"Then keep your mouth shut before every old geezer on the block files for emotional distress," Charlie said, his voice rising and his face turning red. Even his bald spot was red. "We have one week before this lawsuit is filed. You may continue your regular duties for now. If we are forced to settle for a substantial sum, or if the suit goes to court and we lose, you will be reassigned to city desk, where you can be retrained in the principles of serious reporting." Charlie could not keep the satisfaction out of his voice. It oozed out like liquid from a rotten fruit.

Retrained? I'd be destroyed, and he knew it. I'd be thrown into the snake pit, at the mercy of the ambitious incompetents who ran city desk. I'd never have a decent story again, and if I did, the copy desk would go at it like Lizzie Borden went after her stepmom and dad. Charlie's anger had reached its peak. He was pounding the desk for emphasis as he said, "In the meantime, *[pound]*, you must tell your editor *[pound]* where you are going *[pound]* when you leave the building *[pound]*. The lawyers may want to talk to you *[pound]*. I want to know where you are *[pound]* at all times *[pound, pound, pound]*."

He already knew where I was. I was in deep yogurt. There was no way I could get out of this. The best I could hope for was a jury trial, which would prolong the agony long enough so maybe I could get a job somewhere else—like the Mexico, Missouri, *Ledger*. Well, I wasn't going to hang around the office and watch everyone dance on my almost-dug grave. I had to get out of there—if I could find my editor, Wendy the Whiner. Just tracking Wendy down would add to my workload.

Like most *Gazette* editors, she wasted little time dealing with reporters. She spent the day in meetings with other editors and consultants, then went to meetings about the meetings, then wrote memos about the meetings. If you wanted a good story, you found your own ideas. Wendy's stories came straight from the pile of press releases that she received by mail and fax. This morning Wendy was at her desk for a change, and I took great satisfaction in letting her know exactly where I was going.

"I'll be at the morgue," I said. "I need to get the autopsy report for the story tentatively called 'Death of a Neighborhood Activist.' I'll be at the funeral, too. This autopsy should be interesting. Caroline's head was bashed in pretty bad, blood and brains all over the grass, and then the killer stuck a pink flamingo in her chest. I imagine the killer leaned on it, and then pop, those little metal legs went right in between her ribs and . . ."

"Eeewww," Wendy said, looking revolted. The press releases she got her story ideas from were always upbeat and completely sanitized. "Don't tell me any more. I don't want to know." Good. A few more days of disgustingly detailed reports and Wendy wouldn't care where I went.

Unfortunately, Lyle didn't seem to care where I went, either. My plans for an impromptu romantic picnic in the park last night were buried when I dug up the dead cat. Lyle still didn't know about that embarrassing episode, and there was no way I'd leave him a message trying to explain what happened. Now, before I went to see Cutup Katie, I deliberately took time to call him, using a pay phone on the *Gazette* backstairs for privacy. But Lyle wasn't at the university or at home, and he hadn't left any messages for me. I couldn't help but take that as a bad sign.

I'd lost the swagger I'd had around Wendy by the time I got to Cutup Katie's office. Katie was wearing a semiclean lab coat with only a few light-brown stains that I told myself were coffee. I was in no mood to make morbid jokes. I asked her straight out how Caroline died.

"The police found a large pipe wrench next to the victim," Katie said, "and the injuries are consistent with that. She was hit just above the ear, on the temporal lobe. The skull is thin there and easy to smash. She was hit hard, and often, by someone who was very angry. The bone was indented inward and there were extensive brain contusions. The scalp was ripped, exposing bone, blood, and brain gook. The victim was hit so hard her eye socket and cheek bone caved in."

Oh, man. I wasn't feeling so chipper. The details I delighted telling Wendy the Whiner made me queasy when Katie said them.

"What an awful way to die, killed by a pipe wrench," I said.

"Technically, she was killed by the pink flamingo," Katie said. "She was still alive after the attack, although probably not for long. I found more than a liter of blood in the chest cavity. The killer thrust those metal flamingo legs in the chest between the ribs. The legs pierced the heart and vena cava, and that's what actually killed her."

Poor Caroline. All flesh was grass, but hers was a low-rent lawn. Murder made her into a joke. "She would have died of shame," I said. "She thought pink flamingos were tacky."

Katie shrugged. "That's a matter of opinion. This is the first time they were terminally tacky. You usually don't die of bad taste."

I thanked Katie and left the morgue, still brooding about this latest death. I knew Caroline. I didn't like her, but I liked some of the things she did. Caroline was fierce, strong, and energetic—not this helpless, battered creature. Who did this? A lot of people wanted Caroline out of the way, but could they actually kill her so brutally?

I decided to head back to North Dakota Place for some answers. The street was starting to look bedraggled. The parkway grass was shaggy and dotted with beer cans and other litter, and a *Gazette* was floating in the angel fountain. Caroline was not there to care, and no one on the street was taking over her duties. I saw Dina out on her porch, bringing in her mail. I asked when there was going to be a funeral for Caroline. "I thought Caroline's ex-husband was taking care of the arrangements," she said, "but I'd like to know, too. I'll call him and find out."

I went to work on my Meet Your Neighbor list again. I started knocking on doors. Three were slammed in my face when I said, "Hi, I'm from the *Gazette*." So much for community relations. Four doors never opened, and from the unlighted silence, I guessed no one was home. At the eighth house I hit pay dirt—or rather dust. The front door was opened by a skinny, sandy-haired guy with a beginning gut—a training gut, if you will. He was covered with a fine layer of plaster dust, like flour. Hanging around his neck was a paper filter mask. He said his name was Ron. He didn't have to tell me he was a rehabber. Ron wore paint-spattered cutoffs and an Imo's pizza cap. His stained and sweaty T-shirt celebrated the St. Louis Brews, a beer-making club. "Give a man a beer and he wastes an hour. Teach a man to brew and he wastes a lifetime," the shirt said.

Ron invited me along to White Castle for lunch, and I was so relieved to see a friendly face I offered to pick up the tab, on the *Gazette*, of course. I figured even they could afford forty-cent hamburgers. And the nice thing about White Castle was that no one would look twice at a woman in a suit lunching with a guy covered in plaster dust. It had seen stranger combinations. My blue Jaguar followed his blue Chevy pickup to the parking lot—friendly feelings aside, I wasn't about to get into a pickup with a man I didn't know. We ordered, I paid, and we sat at a table, wolfing down oniony sliders, salty, fat-soaked fries, and large orange sodas. Yum. Not an ounce of fiber in the whole meal, unless we ate the paper bag. While we ate, Ron talked about Caroline. He seemed grateful for the opportunity, as if he wanted to sort out what he thought of her.

"Caroline didn't just fix up an old house," he said. "She loved those old houses. She appreciated their beauty and their irreplaceable craftsmanship. She had real passion, you know what I mean? She cared for that street like it was her child. I liked that about her. What I didn't like was the way she did business. She was cutthroat, man. She tricked me once and bought a house I'd been negotiating for right from under me. I thought I had the deal sewed up until she wormed her way in, and I lost money big time. I guess she didn't do anything worse than any businessman, and maybe if she'd been a man, she'd be admired as somebody who cut a hard deal. But people expect women to be different. More caring and sensitive, you know what I mean?"

I knew Caroline had the sensitivity of a hammerhead shark.

"She might have gotten away with being a tough businessperson if she hadn't tried to run North Dakota Place like a reform school. She never understood that people move to the city because they want freedom. They weren't interested in living in some tight little suburban planned community. All her rules about where to park and what flowers to plant pissed people off. They weren't going to stand for it, no matter how much good she did. Caroline couldn't let people be. She wanted perfection. So the neighbors rebelled and didn't appreciate her work. To make it worse, she was always dragging West County real estate people down here, trying to sell them on North Dakota Place as some kind of a luxury community. It wasn't going to work. This area is too diverse for those white-bread types, you know what I mean? But none of them had the guts to say that. So they kept making cockamamie suggestions about flowers and fountain grass. And Caroline never caught on. After the real estate people left, she'd buy more flowers and fix whatever they said should be fixed, and then she'd show them the street again, and the West County real estate people would find more things wrong. She never understood she was getting the runaround, you know what I mean?"

I did. We dumped our trash. Ron went back to work on his house, and I decided I'd been sufficiently fortified by belly bombers to tackle the dreaded trouble house. If the drug-dealing, gun-selling kids threatened me, all I had to do was burp. I parked my car two blocks away and walked toward the place. It did look threatening. It was also rundown. The porch sagged and the paint was peeling. Bed sheets were tacked over the front windows. The screen door bulged out. There were two kids sitting outside on the porch steps, but I couldn't tell their ages. They were big as grown men and muscular as prizefighters. They wore baggy gang clothes and the black silk skullcaps known as do-rags. Some kids. The biggest one said something vile to me, and I quit thinking, or feeling, anything except angry. Maybe I was reacting to Erwin, or Charlie, or maybe I just don't take well to ugly offers of oral sex from strangers, but I turned on him, gave him my deadliest glare, and said, "Watch. Your. Mouth."

He looked surprised and amused. "You talking to me, cunt?" he said slowly.

"Shut up!" I said. "Just shut up." What was the matter with me? I could get shot for talking back to young hoods like these. But right now, I didn't care. Both kids stood up, smirked, and blocked my way up to the porch.

"Get out of my way," I said. They didn't move. What was I going to do next—kneecap them with my briefcase? I wondered if they were armed and when they were going to pull a gun on me. Now I was scared—after I'd opened my big mouth. Too smart, too late. As usual.

I could see out of the corner of my eye that blinds were being lifted in nearby houses. The neighbors were watching. A door opened at one house, and an old man with gray shorts and fishbelly white legs came out with a video camera. He started taping us. A second neighbor, a gray-haired woman in a pink polyester pantsuit, charged out of a second house with her video camera running. The scary kids saw them, turned, smiled menacingly, and walked inside, slamming the door after them. That was it. They were gone. The confrontation was over. Suddenly I was shaky and short of breath. I thanked my rescuers. They introduced themselves as Herman and Dolores.

"We're two members of the vigilante committee," Herman said.

"We've had enough," Dolores said, looking tougher than I thought possible in pink polyester. "For a while they were running a drug supermarket, with curb service even. People would pull right up in front and buy. We put a stop to that."

"We started taping everything they do," Herman said. "A car pulls up and we tape the license plates, and guess what? There's no drug buy. Those young thugs start threatening you and we tape it and guess what? They disappear inside. We figure a few more weeks of this, and they'll be gone. They'll move where the neighbors don't watch them so much."

"Where did you get the idea?" I said.

"From TV," Dolores said. "We tried everything else. We called the police, but by the time they got here, whatever we called about—the drug sale, the fist fight—would be over. We complained to the landlord, but he just took his phone off the hook. He lives in Chesterfield. All he cares about is the rent money. He doesn't care what his rental house does to our neighborhood."

"Videotaping has been done in other neighborhoods," Herman said. "It works. We always tape in pairs, and we use as many different people as possible, so if they take one of us out, there are others to witness what goes on." Herman must have gotten his language from the TV, too. But I was touched and proud of my neighborhood. They'd found an ingenious way to reclaim their street. I hoped it worked. I thanked Dolores and Herman again, and my two rescuers insisted on seeing me to my car. They waited until I locked the door. I waved good-bye and wondered where I was going. It looked like I wasn't going to get the signatures of anyone at the trouble house for my Meet Your Neighbor sign-up sheets. Maybe I'd try some of the houses on North Dakota Place where nobody had been at home. I also wanted to talk to Sally, the former lover of the despicable Darryl. She hadn't been home when I knocked on her door before. When I parked my car, Dina came out of her house and ran over. This woman was not the funny, fluffy, cat-loving Dina I knew. She was furious. "That scumbag!" she said.

"Which one?" I said.

"Caroline's ex-husband, James Graftan. Do you know what he did? He told us he'd handle the funeral arrangements. He handled them all right. He had Caroline cremated and dumped her ashes in the parking lot at the Galleria. Like she was a full ashtray. He said it was where she spent her happiest hours—and all of his money. The miserable bastard. It's unfair."

"Untrue, too," I said. "Judging by her wardrobe, Caroline never spent a nickel shopping there."

"Graftan said there would be no memorial service, that her work was memorial enough," Dina said. "He's just too lazy or too mean to honor her memory. He's not getting away with that. We'll hold a memorial for Caroline right here at the angel fountain. She deserves better. I'm going to get Patricia, and we'll get to work on a service for her."

"Why isn't Caroline's family handling her funeral?" I said.

"She doesn't have any family. Her parents have been dead for years. She doesn't have any close friends, except for Patricia, Margie, and me."

Some friends, I thought. The police thought Caroline's good friend Margie may have killed her. Caroline's good friend Dina hardly had a good word to say about her. Even her good friend Patricia had only lukewarm praise for Caroline. It was a sorry mess all around. No funeral, no family to mourn her, and nobody knew who killed her, although there seemed to me to be more suspects than I knew what to do with. I counted them off: Margie; Dale and Kathy; Sally's boyfriend, Darryl; and the four scary kids. I wondered if I should add Ron the Rehabber to the list. I'd like to know just how angry he was over her slick business deal. Of course I had no proof that any of them killed her. But right now Caroline's ex-husband was acting the most despicably, so he was my chief suspect. Poor Caroline. I never thought of her as someone to be pitied, but it was sad that a man Caroline didn't like was put in charge of her body. It was sadder still that he treated it with such contempt.

I wondered if Caroline had been killed as part of a series, and if so, what was her connection to Johnny Hawkeye, Scorpion Smith, and Otto. None of these deaths made sense. They didn't fit into any pattern.

Well, if I couldn't solve the murder, maybe I could meet my neighbors. I knocked on more doors, but no one was at home. I really wanted to talk to Sally. After Caroline's ex-husband, she struck me as someone who might have a key to unlock this mystery. Maybe Sally was relieved that Caroline had driven off her awful boyfriend. Maybe she was still holding a grudge. Maybe she knew just how angry at Caroline Darryl really was. I had to know if Sally knew anything. I wished I knew where she worked. I'd stop by Sally's house tonight, when there was a better chance she'd be home. Besides, I was too discouraged to continue. I didn't want to go home, but I needed a phone to check my messages. I was probably the last person in America who didn't have a cell phone. I hated how they invaded everything. I'd go to a meeting, and everybody's briefcases would be ringing. At restaurants, people were talking on their cell phones instead of talking to their dinner partner. They had a phone in their ear when they walked down the street. I even saw a guy talking on the phone at the pool. I refused to be tied to a phone that way, which meant the local drug dealers and I were in a constant search for an unvandalized pay phone. So, of course, I headed for Uncle Bob's. Maybe I needed Marlene's smart sympathy, too. I pulled into the parking lot and knocked on the kitchen window, so the cook wouldn't start my "usual." Uncle Bob's had a good late lunch crowd of local car salesmen, businesspeople, and hospital workers. Marlene was still working. "Hi," she said. "Just coffee?"

"Yeah, I already have a belly full of belly bombers," I said.

Marlene grimaced. "Has your day gotten any better?" she said.

"Nope," I said. "It's gone downhill. Erwin did get Crullen as his lawyer, and Crullen is demanding two hundred fifty thousand to settle. If the *Gazette* doesn't settle right away, and Crullen files suit, he wants half a million for Erwin's distress and damage to his reputation."

"What reputation? He's a letter-writing weirdo," Marlene said.

"When Crullen finishes with him, he'll be Mr. Chips," I said gloomily. "Crullen has already made the stray cat into a treasured pet. Oh, and to top it off, we have the *Gazette* consultant's latest halfwit idea, the Meet Your Neighbor list. I need fifty signatures and I have about three. I've been threatened, insulted, ignored, and had doors slammed in my face. I don't want to meet any more neighbors. It's been traumatic enough already. I'd forge the signatures, but I need so many, and I'm not sure I can fake them all."

"So what are you going to do?" she said.

I shrugged. "I'll think of something. Meanwhile, I'll make some phone calls." I took my coffee cup, notepad, and a pile of change to the little phone alcove near the cash register and started dialing. First, I checked in at the *Gazette*. No one was looking for me, thank goodness. Then I checked the messages on my office answering machine. I had one from Lyle and one from Pam Klein. I called Pam first, so I could spend time with Lyle.

"Are you okay?" Pam asked. She'd been on the edge of the crowd at Erwin's house and seen the whole debacle.

"No," I said. "I'm a mess. Erwin is suing."

"*What!*" she said. "What for?"

I told her the story. "That little creep," she said. "I know he's guilty of something. I'll find out what it is."

I dialed Lyle's number at the office, but it was busy, so I went back to the table. Marlene handed me the stack of Meet Your Neighbor sheets. All fifty spaces were signed and filled out in different handwriting. There was a huge smile on her rosy Irish face.

"What's this?" I said. "How did you do this?"

"Meet your neighbors," Marlene said, and threw her arms out to the tables at Uncle Bob's. I saw business-people in suits, men and women in hospital white, college students, mothers with toddlers, tired older shoppers getting a bite to eat. They saw me and ap-plauded. I bowed and applauded them back. I looked at the filled-out sheets. For the first time that day I felt some hope. I'd been saved by my readers.

"I took the sheets around from table to table and told everyone what was going on," Marlene said. "They were glad to sign the sheets. You're finished. Now, take the rest of the day off. And tomorrow, too. It's Fourth of July, a holiday that should not be missed in St. Louis."

"I'm allergic to crowds," I said. "I refuse to go to the Fair St. Louis downtown and stand in the sun with a million people."

"So don't go." Marlene shrugged. "Come along with us for the fireworks at night. I get a group of friends together every year. We don't go all the way downtown into the crowds. We have an undiscovered place where we can see everything. You can't miss the fireworks. Bring Lyle, too."

"Sure," I said. "Sounds like fun." That's what we needed—something simple and all-American. Fire-works on the Fourth of July, fried chicken and lemon-ade. Well, okay, beer for Lyle. I couldn't quite see him swilling lemonade. Before I left Uncle Bob's, I called Lyle's office again. This time he was in. He was all sympathy when I told him of my harrowing last two days.

"I'm so sorry, baby," he said. "Maybe you need a lawyer. Your own lawyer, not one of those *Gazette* clowns." He named some names and we talked some more, and I felt better. My life was reasserting itself. My readers had helped me, and Lyle was so comforting. We made plans to meet for the fireworks tomorrow.

"I know we didn't plan it, but I'd really like to see you tonight, too," I said.

There was an awkward silence. Then Lyle said, "I'm working late tonight, but I could see you after nine. It will take me that long to get back to the Central West End. We could meet at my place."

"You don't sound too enthusiastic," I said.

"I always want to see you," he said. "I want to marry you, remember? But my workload has been doubled because of that project. These long days are getting to me."

"I'll see you after nine," I said, but when I hung up the phone the doubts set in, eating into my brain like acid. Lyle working late at a university the night before a holiday? Not likely. Universities weren't corporations, or even newspapers, where the work had to be done no matter what. They were still civilized enough that people could take time off. So why was Lyle working so many hours? So he could be with the blond Pat? Is that why he put me off? I had to find out. I'd stop by Lyle's office that night and find out just who he was working with. But how would I explain my visit? I had a book Lyle borrowed for me from the university library. I could say I had to return it to the university library before the holiday. The excuse sounded pretty flimsy even to me, but it was all I had to cover myself.

I went home and paced until it was time to go. At seven forty-five at night the university parking lot was almost deserted, except for two cars at the campus radio station and a few more scattered about. The campus was green and shaded by big, old trees, a perfect spot for strolling lovers. I would have enjoyed the walk, except for the ice in the pit of my stomach. What if I found Lyle in a clinch in his office with that Pat person? Then I'd know, wouldn't I? It was better to know. I'd rather be alone than be a fool like my mother, living with a man who lied to her. I opened the door to Lyle's building. Inside, it was dim, cool, and shadowy. My footsteps echoed down the empty hall. I didn't take the elevator. It would make too much noise. Instead, I walked up the back stairs to the fourth floor. I was puffing slightly when I got to the top. I could hear the voices coming from Lyle's office, but I couldn't tell what they were saying until I got a little closer. I paused and picked out the following sentences.

"I just don't see that sex should be taken that seriously," said a light, young voice. "I mean, like, if you screw around, it shouldn't ruin your whole life. It's just, you know, a little fun."

"Is that all you see sex as, a little fun?" Lyle said, seriously.

I didn't stop to hear the rest. I almost ran down the hall to his office. His door was partly open, but any halfway smart instructor did that. Lyle wouldn't want to risk a complaint from a student that he attacked her behind closed doors. I peeked in. I saw Lyle talking intently to someone sitting in a chair, back to the door, someone young and slight with blond hair curling down past narrow shoulders, crisp white shirt, plain jeans. Ah, the innocent look. What man could resist that?

I threw open the door all the way and walked in without knocking. "Hi," said Lyle, not looking at all surprised. "Let me introduce you to Pat—Patrick Sullican, who needs some quick journalism credits to transfer to Mizzou. We're reading and discussing Tom Wolfe's essay on the campus sexual revolution in the early seventies. But I'm afraid Pat has a low opinion of ancient history. We're just finishing up. I'll see you after the holiday, Pat."

Patrick shrugged, said good night, gathered up his books, and left.

Lyle was furious. "Are you happy now, Francesca, that you didn't catch me with another woman? Or, since Pat turned out to be Patrick, are you convinced I'm gay and that's how I'm cheating on you?"

"How? What? How?" I said. It's all I could manage. Lyle had plenty to say.

"How did I know? I can read your face. You walked in here looking for trouble. You were stunned when Pat turned out to be a boy. You've been suspicious since the other night, when you heard me say good night to Pat. No, I take that back. You've been suspicious for weeks, but after Pat, you had something to pin those suspicions on. You don't trust me, Francesca."

"I do," I said. "Lyle, this is so unfair. I've had a terrible day. Please don't fight with me. Let's talk about this at a better time."

"What better time, Francesca? You always have a terrible day, because you work at a terrible place. I've asked you again and again to leave the *Gazette*. I'll go anywhere, if you'll leave. I'll relocate to another city. I don't care. I just want you out of there."

"You may get your wish," I said. "I may be fired."

"No, they won't fire you. You're too much fun to kick around." I must have looked shocked because he reached out and took my hand. "Francesca, I want to live my whole life with you—but not with this chaos. They're just a big unhappy family substitute for your small unhappy family. Leave there, before it's too late. I'm begging you. Marry me."

"I want to marry you, Lyle. But I need time."

"We've been dating three years," he said. "How

much more time do you need? The love and trust we have is slowly dying. I can feel it.

"When we went out the other night, I tried to tell you what I was working on and why I was staying at the office so late, but you were so wrapped up in your own problems, you didn't even hear me. Do you remember any of what I said? I told you about the advisor who had been giving bad advice to students for at least two semesters. She was diagnosed with a brain tumor. Now some of the faculty are trying to pick up the slack and help these kids graduate or transfer with the proper credits by giving them reading courses. They're time consuming, but they're the best solution we can come up with. Patrick won't be able to transfer to the University of Missouri at Columbia next semester, unless I give him this reading class.

"But you thought I was cheating on you. Why do you suspect me, Francesca? Because you can't see any man as anything but a rat like your father. He played around, so I will, too. Since the day we met, you've been waiting for me to be like him. Francesca, I'm asking one more time: Set a date to marry me."

"I want to marry you, Lyle. I love you, but . . ."

He let go of my hand, or maybe I took it back. I wasn't sure. "But you won't, will you, Francesca? No matter how much I beg and plead, you won't marry me, ever." I saw that his blond hair was mussed, and he had a cute curl on his forehead. I longed to touch it, but I stood there, frozen. He began shoving papers into a briefcase.

"What are you going to do?" I said.

"I'm going to leave, while I can. Because I don't want to star in your little psychodrama, Francesca. I'm not your father, but if we keep going on this way, I will be."

"Wait," I said. "You don't understand. I love you. I just don't want to marry you."

"Because if you married me, and it worked, you'd have a future," he snapped. "But you'd rather cling to the old, dead past than start a new life, wouldn't you? You'd rather live with the dead."

He stopped at the door, and now he looked more sad than angry. "Good-bye, Francesca, I'm sorry. So very sorry. Call me if you change your mind, but I don't think you will."

He grabbed his jacket and walked out. I followed him out of the room. He slammed and locked his office door, then walked down the hall. I stood there watching him, but I didn't cry. Not one single tear. I wouldn't cry for a man who refused to understand.

11

At eleven o'clock that night the phone rang. I grabbed it, hoping it was Lyle calling. "It's me, Pam," an urgent voice said. "Get over here quick."

"What for?" I said. I'd been dozing in my grandmother's recliner in a sad, restless sleep that left me tired. I didn't want to go out again. But Pam insisted.

"It's Erwin. He's in his backyard, digging in his garden."

"Maybe it's legit," I said.

"At this hour?" Pam said scornfully. "With no light? Do you want to catch him or not? Get over here. I'll meet you at the top of his street. And hurry."

I slipped on my shoes, grabbed my house keys, and ran down the steps. I didn't stop running the three blocks to Erwin's street. Even at eleven o'clock at night, it was hot. The heat added a velvety quality to the darkness. The blue-black sky had a scattering of stars, but no one was outside to enjoy them. Most of my neighbors were in bed, with their lights out. I noticed there were no lights on at Sally's house. I still wanted to talk to her, but I didn't stop at her place after my fight with Lyle. I was too upset to talk to anyone then. But I was convinced Sally knew something useful. The more she eluded me, the more I wanted to talk to her.

I met Pam at the top of Erwin's street, and we ran

half a block to the alley entrance. "How did you spot him digging?" I said, talking in whispers. We were getting close to Erwin's and I didn't want to scare him off.

"I can see his backyard from my deck," she whispered back. "I let the dog out and saw Erwin digging by the light of the streetlight. It looked fishy to me, so I called you."

"I sure hope he's up to no good," I said. "Otherwise, he'll add stalking and harassment to his other complaints against me."

"He's guilty of something," she said firmly. "I saw his face the night the police were at his place. I haven't been a mom all these years not to recognize that guilty look." She put a finger to her lips for quiet. We were two houses away. We tiptoed up to Erwin's, and Pam eased open his back gate. There was enough light that we could see Erwin standing in front of a shallow hole, pulling out something the size of a small suitcase. It looked like it was made of hard plastic. He had just opened the box when Pam cried, "Okay, Erwin, drop it."

Erwin let out a frightened yelp.

"What's in there?" she said.

"It's mine," he said, shutting the lid quickly. "It's perfectly legal."

"Then why did you bury it?" I said. His face swung toward me, and that gave Pam enough time to open the red-orange plastic watertight box.

"My, my," she said. "It's packed with porn. Just look at these magazines: *Bad Girls of Dicks High*. Here's a good one, *Perky Peterville Pom-Pom Girls*. Ugh, look what those women are doing with that Pekingese. Erwin, you are absolutely disgusting."

Pekingese? I thought that was a hairy pom-pom. At least Erwin wasn't into underage porn. These women hadn't seen high school since around 1965. They looked really dissipated in their super-short Catholic school girl uniforms. Those hard faces weren't made for Peter Pan collars and plaid jumpers. At least they didn't wear those outfits for very long. The pom-pom girls were particularly athletic performers in the pictures.

"And you're a high school teacher, too," Pam said, her voice oozing disgust. "What would your students' parents say if they knew the slop you read? What about the school administration? And your mother?"

For the first time Erwin showed real fear. "Don't tell my mother," he pleaded. "Please don't. I'll do anything you say." Erwin was afraid of his mother. That was interesting.

"You've got some nerve claiming Francesca damaged your reputation," Pam said. "Why are you burying this scummy stuff? Are you too ashamed to keep it in the house?"

"I tried," Erwin whined. "Mother always finds it. She cleans everything. She vacuums between my mattress and the box springs. She goes through all my closets and drawers. There's no place she won't clean. I even tried hiding the magazines in the furnace ducts. She found them there. Mother dusted the furnace ducts."

The angel mother was a cleaning fiend. "What about the garage?" I suggested helpfully.

"Have you seen the inside of that garage?" he said.

I had, but I wasn't going to admit it. "There are curtains on the windows," I said truthfully.

"She dusts my workbench, waxes the garage floor, and puts down newspapers so the car doesn't drip oil on the waxed concrete," he said bleakly.

"And I thought *I* was a cleaning fanatic," Pam said.

"The garden is the only place she won't clean," Erwin said. "She has no interest in that kind of dirt. So when I get the urge, which isn't often, I dig up my books. This is your fault, Francesca. I hadn't needed them for months and months, and then you got me all upset, and I had to relieve the tension."

Jeez. Now I was accused of breaking and entering and beating off.

"You made me," he whined. "Now is a bad time to dig. I could hurt my cucumbers."

"Is that what you call them?" I said.

"The cucumbers in my garden," Erwin said, shocked. "You have a filthy mind."

"*I* have a filthy mind? I'm not reading this trash. These books exploit women. Get yourself a girlfriend."

"I tried," Erwin said. "Mother doesn't approve of the women I bring home. She has very high standards."

"What would she think of these?" I said, grabbing the *Bad Girls of Dicks High*.

"Or these?" Pam said, picking up *Perky Peterville Pom-Pom Girls*.

"You won't tell her?" He whimpered in terror.

"We will," we said together.

"No!" Erwin said. "You can't. You don't understand. The last time she found them, she said I'd go to hell if I touched those magazines again. I promised her I'd never, never touch them."

"We're telling her unless you drop the lawsuit and the trespassing charges," Pam said.

"I can't," he said. "You can't."

"We can," I said. "We will."

"You can't prove it," Erwin said, sounding desperate.

"I'll have these magazines dusted for your fingerprints and then I'll tell your mother," I said. I sounded ridiculous.

"I'll tell her I saw them, too," Pam said. "She'll believe me. We go to the same church. We were on the bake-sale committee together. I gave her my recipe for peanut butter brownies." She sounded convincing, and not just to me. Erwin bowed his head and accepted his fate.

"I want your letter at the *Gazette* by ten o'clock tomorrow morning," I said.

"Tomorrow is the Fourth of July," he said.

"July fifth, then," I said. "Ten A.M. I want the trespassing charges dropped, too, or this goes to your mother." I brandished the *Bad Girls of Dicks High*.

"And we want an apology," Pam said sternly, waving the perky pom-pom girls. We slammed the gate on the way out for emphasis and didn't say one word in the alley. When we got to the street corner, we couldn't hold it any longer. We burst into wild laughter that subsided into helpless fits of giggles.

"I almost feel sorry for Erwin, stuck with his cleaning angel mother," I said, still laughing and wiping the tears from my eyes.

"Don't waste too much sympathy on him," Pam said. "He sideswiped your career and nearly totaled it. Now I have to go home. It's late for me." I gave her a hug and started back home, feeling lighthearted again. Saved. I was saved. The suit would be dropped, and the charges, too, and I wouldn't be sent to the *Gazette*'s seventh circle, the city desk. Charlie wouldn't get me this time, and he'd be madder than hell. I couldn't wait to tell Lyle my good news. Lyle . . . Lyle was gone. He'd walked out on me. I couldn't tell him anything ever again. He wouldn't listen to me. My good mood went crashing through the floor. I spent a restless, sleepless night, twisting the sheets and pounding the pillows. Finally I gave up about three, got up and cleaned the house. I wasn't a fanatic cleaner like Erwin's mom, but I saved insomniac nights for boring chores like cleaning. Why waste a fine Saturday afternoon mopping the floor, when you could do it in the unwanted hours of the night? I finished about fivethirty and fell into bed. I slept until ten o'clock and woke up feeling more tired than when I went to bed. My eyes were red and puffy, as if I'd been crying, but I hadn't. I wouldn't waste a tear on that man.

I called Marlene to tell her Lyle wouldn't be at the fireworks picnic. I didn't want her asking me awkward questions in front of her friends. "You had a fight, didn't you?" she said.

"We've broken up," I said. The sooner I got it out, the better.

"I'm sorry," she said, and sounded like she meant it. "What happened?"

"He wants to get married and I don't."

"I don't understand," she said. "How did the only man in America who's not afraid to commit find the one woman who doesn't want to?"

"I don't know," I said. I could feel my voice wobble. I was *not* going to cry. Time for a change in tone. "If I could figure out how men think I wouldn't be a newspaper columnist, I'd be a millionaire."

"You said it, sister, and I'd be the first to pay for that information," Marlene said. "See you this evening about seven."

It was a long time until seven o'clock, and I had to do something besides pace the freshly vacuumed floor. I tried to locate the mysterious Sally, but no one answered her doorbell. I checked her porch for signs that the house was deserted. There was no mail collecting in the box, no circulars stuck in the screen door, no yellowing newspapers piled on the porch. The lawn was mowed and the flower beds weeded. Sally was living there. I just wasn't catching her at home.

Patricia was in her front yard, weeding her hosta bed. She waved to me, and I walked over. As I approached, I saw again how pale and sad she looked. Her brilliant blue eyes were dull and watery, as if she'd cried them out. She'd lost weight, and her bare arms looked like sticks in her "Wildlife Rescue" T-shirt. Poor

Patricia. She must be taking her friend's death hard. But she still gave me a smile, even though it was an effort. "Hi, Francesca, what are you doing?"

"Trying to find Sally," I said. "I need to talk to her."

"For a story?" Patricia asked.

"Eventually," I said. "I'm looking into who killed Caroline, and I wanted to ask Sally some questions."

"I saw her car leave about eight this morning, and she hasn't been back since," Patricia said. "But when I see her again, I'll tell her that you're looking for her."

I thanked her and went back home. I wanted to get another one of Mrs. Indelicato's German chocolate cakes to take to Marlene's fireworks picnic. But it would be tricky. I wasn't sure I could hide my sorry state from the shrewd Mrs. I. She took a keen interest in my love life and was extremely partial to Lyle. She took over the store after my grandparents died and appointed herself my guardian. Her goal was to see me married, and Lyle was her chosen candidate. If she found out we'd broken up, I was in for one heck of a lecture. Fortunately, Mrs. I's store was usually packed on a holiday. My strategy was to wait until there was a big crowd, so Mrs. Indelicato would be too busy to talk. Both the 15-MINUTE PARKING, TOW-AWAY ZONE spots in front of her shop were taken, and I counted at least six customers through the plate-glass window. Good. That should keep her busy. But the minute I walked in the door, everyone rushed out. You'd have thought I yelled "Fire!" By the time I'd grabbed a cake off the bakery shelf and headed for the cash register, the place was empty. Armed guards must be barring the door, too. No one walked in.

The widowed Mrs. I was probably in her early sixties, but she was not a young, swinging sixty. She had iron in her hair, steel in her spine, and starch in her shirtwaist. She also had a warm heart, but she was unbending on the subject of marriage. She did not believe a woman without a man was like a fish without a bicycle—she was a fish out of water. I dreaded the next few minutes and prayed a customer would rescue me.

"Is this cake for Lyle?" she said, ringing it up and tying string around the box for easier carrying.

"It's for a picnic," I said. "We're watching the fireworks tonight." I was using the royal we, but she didn't have to know it.

Mrs. I was not fooled. "So when do I see him again?"

"Uh, he's busy," I said. Being a jerk.

"Tell me when he'll be in again, and I'll make him my special anise cookies," she pressed.

"You only make them for me at Christmas," I said, but she would not be distracted. The woman was relentless.

"Did you have a fight?" she asked.

"Yes. No. Sort of."

"What about?" she said.

"Marriage," I said.

"Ah, you want him to marry you, and he won't. Men are like that. I don't mean to criticize. I know things are different with young people today, but what is his incentive? Why buy a cow . . ."

"But he wanted the cow," I interrupted before she finished that horrible old saw. "I mean, he wanted me. I just don't want to marry him."

Mrs. I was shocked into silence, but not for long. Soon the words poured out in a torrent. "You turned that fine man down. That good provider. That—"

"I can provide for myself," I said.

"Not a respectable home!" she said. "He would make you an honest married woman. Francesca, what would your grandmother say?"

I could imagine. My grandmother married at sixteen and stayed married to the same man for fifty-two years, for better or worse, until death parted them. But

I was saved from answering when a crush of customers poured through the door. I grabbed my cake and ran. Then I sat and brooded for the rest of the day. Lyle was a fine man, except that he insisted on marriage. Things were different from my grandparents' day. They would understand, if they were alive. . . . . This had to stop. It was over. Period. Time to get a life. Time to catch a murderer. I'd love to prove that smug Mayhew wrong. He was another man who thought he knew everything. I was convinced Sally could help unravel Caroline's murder. I had to talk to her. I went to Sally's house twice more that day, but she wasn't at home.

At seven that night I met Marlene at the entrance to a hotel parking garage off Market Street. Marlene had her daughter and about six friends and their kids. It was a noisy, funny crowd. We all paid to park and drove to the top level. The garage was an open concrete area on a hill, a full twenty blocks from the worst of the Fair St. Louis crowds. It was our own private viewing stand for the Fourth of July fireworks. Marlene and her friends brought coolers of beer and soda, fried chicken, ham sandwiches, and more salads, chips, and snacks than I could count. The kids ran around and played, and the adults pulled out folding chairs or sat on car bumpers and talked. After dark, we watched the fireworks. Then the conversation never got much past "Oooh" and "Aaaah." That was fine with me.

It was the Arch that made fireworks so gorgeous in St. Louis. The six-hundred-thirty-foot silver structure was a huge mirror, reflecting the bursts of color, dramatically doubling the spectacle. I lingered until the grand finale turned the night sky into showers of pure color: red, white, green, gold. Then I thanked Marlene for insisting that I see the fireworks and headed for my car to try to beat the traffic home.

I could see small fireworks celebrations going on in backyards along the route home. Kids were playing with sparklers while their parents watched. Cherry bombs and other illegal fireworks were exploding with loud pops and crackles. There was not a city dog or cat in sight—they must be hiding from the incessant noise.

I didn't want to go home to my empty apartment. Instead, I made a slight detour to North Dakota Place. For years I'd hardly noticed the street, and now I couldn't get away from it. There were no celebrations, large or small, on this street. It had a forlorn look. Caroline's and Otto's houses were dark. There were lights on at Margie's and Dina's houses, but no people were visible. Ditto for Patricia, and Dale and Kathy. Mrs. Meyer was up late, too. It even looked like someone was home at Sally's, but it was too late for me to knock on her door. I could hear overtaxed window air conditioners rattling up and down the block. I turned down the alley behind Dina's house to see what—if anything—was going on at the trouble house. Trouble, of course. The inmates were playing booming music and setting off loud, illegal explosions. It sounded like a small war in that backyard.

My car Ralph and I rolled down the alley past the trouble house, but no one took any notice of us. A few houses down, I saw a small chest of drawers sitting next to the battered city Dumpster. It looked in good condition. Alley scavenging was a citywide habit, and I had it. I once found a perfectly good vacuum cleaner in an alley. The only thing wrong was the suction tube was blocked with paper. I got out of the car to examine the chest more closely. It had a few scratches, but those could be hidden by Old English Scratch Cover, the rehabber's friend. The chest looked like it even had the original carved wood handles. Were the drawers broken? The top drawer looked fine, but the bottom drawer was suspiciously crooked. I heard some pops but ignored them. More firecrackers from the trouble house, probably. As I bent down to examine the bottom drawer, there was another pop close to my ear. Actually, it was more like a hammer hitting concrete—an odd sound for a firecracker. What were those kids shooting off? These firecrackers were dangerously close. One hit the concrete wall by the Dumpster and missed my head by inches. I went over to look at what hit the alley bricks.

It was not a firecracker. It was a bullet casing lying on the ground. Someone was shooting at me. *Pop. Pop.* More shots. I heard echo-y running footsteps in the gangway between two houses, but which homes, I couldn't tell for sure. Then I heard a car engine starting up. I ran for Ralph, yanked open his door, started him up, and floored him. One thing a Jag loves to do is go fast. Ralph got to the end of the block in no time. I saw a car with no headlights driving crazily the wrong way down the divided boulevard, but I couldn't identify the make in the dark. I heard the honking blare of another car's horn, as it encountered the crazy car. At the stop sign, the renegade car crossed over, so it was now driving in the correct lane. I knew what it was rushing to do: Cut me off at the end of the next block. I'd be trapped in the alley, unable to turn around. And the crazy driver had a gun.

But this was a long alley. Halfway down, it opened into another alley to form a T. Salvation was just around that corner. I made a quick left into the branch, driving through the alley at sixty miles an hour. I ran over a fallen mattress, squashed several trash bags in my path, and sideswiped an old couch. I didn't slow down until I stopped right in front of a cop car—and a hated cop at that. We'd met before. He and his younger partner did nothing when Ralph was beaten with a cinder block. But he was ready for action now.

"Well, well, well," he said, getting out of his car and coming over to mine. "Look who we have speeding in an alley. Unlike some members of the force, I don't believe in favoritism for certain reporters." He was talking about Mayhew, who'd helped me out more than once. "I believe they should be treated like any irresponsible speeding citizen."

"I was speeding for a good reason," I started to say.

He interrupted with "Everyone has a good reason. I'm ticketing you for speeding, careless and reckless driving, exceeding the speed limit in an alleyway, flat speeding, driving across a sidewalk . . ."

"Driving across a sidewalk!" I yelped. "Where did you get that one?"

"You have to cross a sidewalk to get into any alley in the city," he said. "And I just noticed you're not wearing your seat belt."

"I didn't have time to put on my seat belt when someone was shooting at me."

He didn't look like he believed me. "Let's go see the site of this famous shooting," he said. I drove at a sedate pace back to the chest of drawers, and he followed. The alley was empty and quiet. There was a scar in the concrete, but the casings were gone. The tickets, however, were definitely there. He wrote out a separate one for each charge.

"Be grateful," he said. "I could have charged you with careless and reckless driving. Then I'd have to book you."

"You're damned lucky, Francesca," Charlie said. He sounded disappointed. Erwin had dropped the trespassing charges and threats of a lawsuit. The letter was on Charlie's desk by ten o'clock, and it included a handsome apology. I'd escaped. But, of course, it wasn't that easy. Not at the *Gazette*.

Charlie fixed his little beady snake eyes on me. "I still believe you should sharpen your skills by doing some serious reporting," he said. "I've received complaints that your columns are too frivolous." I knew who those complaints were from. Nails was no doubt bending his ear nightly.

"In addition to your other duties, I expect you to write an article for our special recycling issue." He could barely suppress a smile, the sawed-off slime. He knew what a thankless chore that section was. Every year we recycled the same old, obvious information. The *Gazette* wasn't interested in printing anything that would really change anyone's attitudes and habits. That might upset our major advertisers, who were often major polluters. We'd print the usual pablum: a list of recycling centers and some toothless articles. Or, in Charlie's words, "We will be doing a pullout section that will offer a total recycling package."

Including where to throw away that issue, I thought. But I said, "Charlie, I have columns to write. You won't pay me overtime for the extra work. I don't have time for this."

"You had time to dig up people's yards, Francesca," he said. "You can find time to dig up a few recycling facts. I want thirty inches on recycling advances and opportunities. You have no choice. This is a direct order."

If I refused, I could be fired under our union contract. It wasn't worth the fight. But I felt like I was contributing to the problem. All those trees, dying in vain for our recycling section.

I was in a bad mood, anyway, and it didn't improve when I picked up the *Gazette*. I'd been looking forward to seeing my story on Miriam Smithell, the unknown South St. Louis artist who was about to make it big in

New York. The *Gazette* arts reviewer had scornfully turned her down as a nut case when she called with her story, but Miriam wasn't crazy. She was a sixty-one-year-old sculptor who used found objects—mostly car parts—to make sculptures of the female body. I'd particularly liked one called "Breastworks," which used the front bumper of a 1956 Chevy. Miriam couldn't get a St. Louis gallery to carry her work, but tonight her show was opening in Soho. My column would break the news in St. Louis. It had terrific pictures of her sculptures. I'd seen them. But I hadn't seen the headline. It said, "Junkyard Granny Cleans Up with Old Cars." Granny? The woman was a serious artist of sixty-one. Why did the copy editor use such a condescending term? I stormed over to the copy desk. "Who wrote this ridiculous headline?"

"I did, and I don't appreciate your tone," Cruella snipped. Her long black hair was pulled into a French roll. Her sausagelike figure was encased in a red silk dress that threatened to split its seams. Between the French roll and tight red dress, she looked like a hotdog on a bun.

"Why did you call this woman artist 'granny'?" I demanded. "I never used that word."

"Because your story says she has two grandchildren," she said.

"So does the mayor. But you don't call him 'Grandpa Politician.' She's an artist who happens to also be a grandmother. What you've done to her is sexist and ageist."

"It's accurate, Francesca," Cruella said. "You're just looking for excuses to complain."

I had more reasons when I glanced through the paper. Nails had written another column on the Eichelberg sex discrimination case. "We deplore the fact that the company president promoted his lover over the woman originally groomed for the job," Nails wrote. "That candidate was qualified, and we believe the courts will find her suit has merit. Adam Eichelberg's actions are a disgrace to the St. Louis business community. Our businesswomen have enough of a struggle advancing in corporations without this setback."

Amazing. Nails could not see the parallels with her own situation. Did she really delude herself that she was promoted on merit? If Charlie hadn't bedded her, she'd still be another anonymous assistant city desk editor, with a failed special project. Sadly, more stories about corporate sex discrimination needed to be written. Too many old, inbred companies got away with it. But our business editor had no business delivering that lecture—and too many people in St. Louis knew it.

I couldn't take another moment in this hypocritical place. Work was the cure. I needed to get out and start pounding the pavement on Caroline's murder. That was a real story. The recycling section could wait. I'd throw my story together at the last minute, like everyone else assigned to it. I slipped out of the office and headed for home. I needed someplace quiet to make sense of things. First, I had to find out who killed Caroline. Then maybe I could figure out who killed the others and why. Right now, I thought Caroline's sleazy lawyer ex-husband had the best shot of winning the killer prize. James Graftan desperately wanted relief from his four-thousand-a-month maintenance payment and had a huge fight with Caroline right before her death. Was he in St. Louis the night of Caroline's killing? I'd never get into his law offices again to ask him. His secretary, LaVyrle, wouldn't even talk to me on the phone. But I had a way around it. I called his office. LaVyrle didn't pick up until the tenth ring. "Yeah, Graftan law offices," she said. Real professional.

"Hello," I said. "I'm from Visa internal security. I have a report that charges were put on Mr. Graftan's credit card that are inconsistent with his normal charging procedures. Was he in Tampa, Florida, in June?" I gave the date of Caroline's death.

"No," LaVyrle squawked. "He was right here in St. Louis that whole week with me. At the office, I mean."

"Very good," I said. "We'll remove the charges from his card. Let me give you a special case number, and if those charges show up, you can call our billing office and recite that number. Ready: 2028667–3D. That's D as in dog." LaVyrle must have dutifully taken down the numbers. She repeated them back to me. Really, I was getting a mean streak in my old age.

I hung up, but my triumph was short-lived. I'd established that Caroline's ex-husband was in St. Louis the night of the murder, but so what? Even if Graftan wasn't in town, what did that prove? With his clientele, he knew dozens of independent contractors who could remove his ex-wife. Heck, maybe Darryl was even one of them. I had to talk to Sally. She might know something about the violent Darryl and his plans. I'd walk over there right now. On the way over I thought about the questions I'd ask her: Was she home the night Caroline died? Did she see anything unusual on her street? When was the last time she saw Darryl on North Dakota Place? Was Darryl planning some kind of revenge?

But Sally wasn't home, or at least she wasn't answering her doorbell and her car wasn't parked out front. The street looked so peaceful with its sun-gilded leaves and mellow brick—and no Caroline to bedevil anyone with her demands. Did some beleaguered homeowner want release from Caroline's harsh loan terms? Was that person Margie?

No, it couldn't be. I still thought the ex-husband was the most likely suspect, but I needed more than suspicion. I needed solid rumor. It was time to see my friend Jinny Peterson, information-gatherer extraordinaire.

"Oh, do come over," she said, when I called. "I was just making popcorn. We can sit outside and talk."

Jinny lived in the suburb of Kirkwood, a place I found hopelessly calm and peaceful. I'd never had a normal life, and I was fascinated by hers. She had a white two-story house with black shutters and a picket fence. Red-haired Jinny opened the red-painted front door with the shiny brass knocker. Her perfection extended to the fine art of popcorn making. None of that hot-buttered Styrofoam from a microwave for Jinny. She put oil in a pot and popped real corn, drizzled a stick of butter on top, and served it in mixing bowls, not those dinky little serving dishes.

We munched happily by her backyard fish pond until we got down to crunching the last unpopped kernels. (We were too politically correct to call them old maids.) Then Jinny gave me the dirt on Caroline's sharkskin and cowboy-booted ex-husband.

"He is sleazy, even for a criminal lawyer," she said, "and there are definite rumors of money trouble. Caroline's four-thousand-a-month maintenance should be pocket change for that man. But I hear he gambles it away on the river boats. Loses thousands every week and is in hock up to his eyebrows. And he's making nice money with his disgusting clientele. The man represents the absolute scum of the earth."

"Yeah, I've interviewed him before," I said. "He told me things like 'Every American is entitled to the best defense. It's guaranteed in the Constitution. The same Constitution that protects Francesca Vierling's right to say what she wants in her column.' But I noticed he doesn't defend many poor people."

"You'd think if he really believed everyone was entitled to the best defense, he'd be a public defender,"

Jinny said. "But his clients always manage to come up with lots of money—beg, borrow, or steal. He makes them, or their mamas, mortgage the double-wide and the shiny new extended cab pickup and he takes it all and more. Sometimes he gets them off, and sometimes, thank heavens, that slime he defends gets put away."

"What did you know about Caroline's relationship with him?" I asked.

"Well, there were rumors that Caroline was gay," Jinny said. "But I don't believe them. You hear that about any strong, successful woman. You know, she can't be one-hundred-percent female and succeed in our world, she must be part man. But I never saw Caroline with another woman. In fact, I never saw her with another man. She always seemed to be by herself, even when she was married."

Jinny was right. I never saw Caroline with anything but her wheelbarrow. I didn't think she'd been killed for love. What about money?

"Alas, I don't know anything about Caroline's money, although god knows I tried to find out," Jinny said. "She may have inherited a nice nest egg from her elderly parents, but that's about all I know. I don't know where her money came from, but I do know where it's going, because I'm on the board. It's going to our Columbine House women's shelter, and the shelter would hardly kill another woman to get that bequest."

Follow the money was the old Watergate advice for reporters, and it's still good. Caroline's husband would have enormous financial relief now that Caroline was dead. Who else would benefit? I needed to understand her income, before I could figure out the out go. Ira, my accountant, was the best person I knew for figuring out finances with only fuzzy details. After all, he handled my finances. Every March I dropped two Schnucks' grocery bags of receipts on his desk, and he came up with an income tax return by April 15, and no cheating, either.

His offices were in an office tower in Olivette, which meant Ira must make good money straightening out other people's money. His eight zillion family pictures were framed in solid silver, and he sat behind a desk bigger than my backyard. An assistant brought me coffee in a bone china cup. I filched some candy out of the Waterford crystal dish on his desk, and figured between that and the popcorn I didn't have to worry about fixing dinner.

I told him what I knew about Caroline's finances and said, "So how much money could Caroline be making with her deals?" I popped a butterscotch into my mouth and crunched while he thought.

"Potentially," he said after a bit, "a lot. These are guesses, now, since I haven't seen her records. But she's probably making money several ways. First, she's buying those houses under market value through a straw party or other circumstances, so that gives her an extra profit edge."

Other circumstances. Like the deaths of Otto and the drug dealer.

"Second, she's making money selling those houses at above market value," Ira said. "If the bank lends, say, one hundred thousand on a house she's selling for one-twenty, then that twenty thousand is above the market price—and pure profit.

"Keep in mind she's already had a profit by buying the house cheap, and she would have made a decent profit selling it at market value, so now she's making an indecent profit. Don't get me wrong, that's what makes this country great.

"Third, she's making more profit by lending the money for the rest of the house price to the new buyer."

"But what if the home buyer defaults on the loan?" I

said. "Wouldn't she lose everything?" At least, I hoped that's what I'd said. I had a mouth full of butterscotch candy.

"She's not making an unsecured loan," Ira said. "She's probably taking a second position behind the bank. So if the person defaults and the bank forecloses, the bank would sell the place, take their share, and Caroline would get what's left, if anything. Then the bank would probably sell the house below market value to get rid of it."

"And guess who would buy it?" I said. It was fiendish—a perfect circle that trapped some poor home-buying sap.

"How many people was she lending money to?" Ira asked.

"I'm not sure," I said. "At least ten, maybe twenty or more."

The accountant whistled. "Very nice. They're probably each making payments of four hundred to nine hundred dollars a month. She gets a minimum of four thousand a month. Maximum eighteen thousand. Her private loans must look like a good deal to the home buyers, because they get a house for little or no money down. They might think if the loan is a little high, they can always refinance later."

That's what Margie's husband thought. Boy, did he get a rude awakening. So did Margie. Caroline killed Margie's marriage and crippled her financially.

"But they can't refinance, except on Caroline's terms," I said. "She demands her money, so there's no relief for them. Her private loans were arranged so that if the person had a thirty-year bank loan on the house, Caroline insisted on a twenty-year private loan. If the homeowner had a twenty-year loan, Caroline wanted her part paid off in fifteen years."

Ira said, "So Caroline's payments are higher, she's paid off quicker, and the poor devil who has the house isn't off the hook after all. And if the home buyer defaults, Caroline still comes out ahead."

"Bad business," I said.

"No, good business," Ira said. "Not illegal. Not even immoral. Just tough. I know lots of rehabbers who do some of this, on a one-house basis, but that's not enough to make any real money. It looks like Caroline combined several elements and made a huge profit. Smart woman."

"Dead smart," I said.

Hmm. Following the money wasn't such a good idea. The trail led right back to Margie. Then there were those ugly whispers about Margie's honesty. Just because she might—or might not—have lifted a silver cigarette case didn't mean she bashed in Caroline's head. But Margie seemed to travel in a cloud of suspicion. I needed more information. Ralph and I were both stuck in rush-hour traffic on Highway 40, his engine idling, my mind racing, both of us getting nowhere.

I was frustrated. I swung by North Dakota Place again, but Sally still wasn't home. I knew it was irrational, but I felt like she was hiding from me. The rest of the street was deserted, too. It was after seven when I pulled into the parking space behind my house and went up the shadowy back steps to my empty flat. I was worn out, empty, and sad. I missed Lyle. I didn't feel like fixing dinner, but I was mildly hungry. I rummaged in the cabinet and found an almost empty bag of broken pretzels. I dredged a handful of pretzel pieces through a jar of peanut butter. That would hold me till morning.

Then I checked my answering machine. Dina had left this message: "Francesca, the memorial service for Caroline will be tomorrow morning at ten o'clock at the angel fountain. Margie, Patricia, and I will give the eulogies. Then we will have a flower planting in Caro-

line's honor and a little reception at my house. Everyone on the street will be at the service, and, of course,
you're invited. We hope you'll be there. And uh, do you
want to contribute some money for the flowers?"
There was a little embarrassed pause. Then she said,
"You don't have to, but I thought you'd want to."

Yes, yes, yes, Dina, I thought. Thank you. I'd be glad
to contribute and attend the service, too. Everyone I
needed to see would be there. Caroline's memorial service would make a good column. Margie, the chief
murder suspect, was giving the eulogy. That was a
story, and I knew the *Gazette* would never cover it.
How could I forget Patricia, the premier recycler? She
was smart and enthusiastic. She'd do most of my work
for me. All I had to do was talk to her after the service.
And if everyone on the street was going to be there,
then the elusive Sally would show up for the memorial
service.

For once, the answering machine really did have
the answers.

12

"Who threw these beer cans in the angel fountain?" said an enraged, disembodied voice, and for a moment I thought that Caroline was alive. But it was only Margie, hot, damp, and irritated, pulling soggy trash out of the water on the other side of the fountain.

"Thoughtless slobs," she rasped, shoving the wet trash into a dark-green plastic bag. "Look at that. A trash can is standing there ten feet away, and they toss these in the fountain."

Margie had volunteered to clean up the area before the memorial service. It seemed strange that the woman who was supposed to be Caroline's killer wanted to help with her memorial service. Did this mean Margie was guilty, or innocent? I wanted her to be innocent, but I wondered if she was. Despite the rumors and warning from Jinny, I couldn't help liking straightforward raspy-voiced Margie. Maybe it was because Margie treated Caroline the way I would: She didn't compromise, or avoid her, or run from a confrontation. Margie stood up to Caroline. Now she was accused of Caroline's murder, just as I would have been. I hoped I didn't identify with Margie so much I didn't see what was going on. I'd been wrong before.

"Where is everybody?" I said. "And how did *you* get the yard work?"

"Just lucky," Margie said, pulling another *Gazette*

and a Big Gulp cup from under some bushes. "That and the fact I can't cook." She grinned. "They keep me out of the kitchen, and I like that just fine."

"Me, too," I said. There I went again, identifying with Margie. It was dangerous, but I couldn't stop it.

"The memorial service isn't for another hour yet," she said, pulling a plastic grocery bag off a low-hanging tree branch. "Dina and Patricia are busy setting up the buffet at Dina's house. After the memorial service everyone is going there for food. Dale and Kathy are baking bread and making mostaccioli."

"Mostaccioli, huh?" I said. "The kids are traditionalists. The newer South Siders are plumping for pasta con broccoli."

"Plumping is right. That broccoli junk is made with cream sauce. They wanted Caroline to have a real South Side sendoff. It's my job to spruce up the outside, but I'm nearly finished here, and I'm going to look like hell at the service if I don't clean myself up next."

I gave her a ten and said, "Here's a donation for the flowers."

"Thanks," Margie said, shoving it in her pocket. "I'll make sure Dina gets it. See what we've done? Doesn't it look good?"

She pointed to a new ring of red, white, and pink impatiens planted all the way around the tree-shaded fountain, except for one empty spot in front. There was a shovel with a white ribbon on the handle and a big plastic pot with one last plant. A microphone was set up on a stand nearby. Next to it was a stack of white paper that was probably homemade programs, weighted down with half a brick. A motley collection of lawn chairs and folding chairs were set up in rows on the grass.

"I wonder what Caroline would have thought of people sitting on her grass?" I said.

"Well, she ain't here to protest," Margie said sarcastically, and just for an instant I heard something ugly. It left me chilled on that hot summer morning. Then the bad feeling was gone, and so was Margie.

"Gotta get dressed," she said, waving good-bye and running toward her house. "See you in a bit."

And I was alone. In a way, Caroline's sleazoid ex-husband was right. The angel fountain was Caroline's final tribute, and she didn't need anything else. The angels looked like they were dancing in the rainbow-spangled water. The sun-dappled trees covered them with a lush, cool green canopy. Caroline had created a little bit of heaven on earth, and it would live on after her bad temper and sharp business practices were forgotten.

I hung around the area, talking to people as they arrived for the memorial service, hoping to learn something new. The only thing I picked up was Dale and Kathy's latest rehabbing disaster. They'd successfully woodstripped all the wallpaper off the flowered bathtub and finished the molding in the living room, Kathy told me.

"I have time to work on it, now that I'm out of a job," she said cheerfully. "And we don't have quite the money pressure we thought we would."

Now that Caroline was dead, I thought, and no longer around to blackmail you into an expensive rehab on your porch.

"When I finished the living room molding, I was so relieved," Kathy said. "I leaned against the wall with one hand, looked around, and said, 'You know, Dale, I think we're finally getting somewhere.' And with that, my arm went through the wall up to the elbow."

"Good lord," I said. "What happened?"

"The previous owner had patched the holes in the plaster with cardboard, then wallpapered over it," Dale said. "It looked fine, but when Kathy leaned on the papered-over cardboard, she caved in a four-by-six-foot hole in the wall. We started sounding the other walls throughout the house. That was the biggest hole, but there are others. But we'll get them." He kissed her lightly on the nose. Kathy smiled at him and kissed him back. I felt achingly lonely. Lyle and I used to look at each other like that. Dale and Kathy were so wrapped up in each other, they didn't notice when I moved away. I wanted to cry, but I didn't. Tears would have been out of place at this memorial service. It was more like a cross between a cocktail party and a neighborhood meeting. I was surprised by how many people were there, from old Mrs. Meyer in a dark-blue house dress to a cleaned-up Ron the Rehabber, plus city officials and neighborhood activists. The chairs had filled up, and now people were standing.

I was also surprised at who didn't show. Caroline's ex-husband, James Graftan, wasn't there. There was no sign of the elusive Sally. I didn't expect her former boyfriend, Darryl, to be at the memorial service, and I wasn't disappointed. Mayhew was not there, either, and he usually showed up at funerals. Maybe he didn't know about this one. Well, that put me ahead of him. Whatever I learned today was my exclusive information. Too bad it was nothing, so far.

The memorial service started about ten-ten. Margie had had time to dry her damp hair and put on a dark-brown pant suit. Dina, in a navy suit and beige blouse, served as master of ceremonies. She looked out on the crowd of maybe sixty people, some standing, some sitting uncomfortably on the leaning and sagging chairs, and thanked everyone for being there. All signs of fluffy, cat-loving Dina were gone. This woman was a smooth politician with a firm, clear speaking voice. "Caroline worked tirelessly to improve North Dakota Place," she said. "She was literally on the job night and day. I saw Caroline with her wheelbarrow at six in the morning, and at six at night. I even saw her working at three A.M. She was unstoppable."

Patricia began sniffling when Dina said that. She continued, "Caroline never thought of anything but the welfare of North Dakota Place."

Well, no one would argue with that.

"Now you see the results all around you. Caroline's good work has taken root, and it will continue to grow into a beautiful memorial for her."

That was tactful, I thought. Dina told the truth but put a nice spin on it. No wonder she did so well at City Hall. Patricia was next. As she walked to the microphone, I saw how awful the woman looked. Her hair was dirty, and her washed-out blue eyes were hidden behind an ugly pair of brown-rimmed glasses. She had gone from slender to gaunt. Her chest, which was always a billboard for some cause, looked naked with only a plain white blouse.

"Caroline did a lot for this neighborhood," Patricia said. "She made so many changes. . . ." Then Patricia started sobbing so hard, she couldn't go on. Dina had to lead her away from the microphone and back to her chair. Poor Patricia. I thought those were probably the only tears anyone would shed for Caroline, and I felt a howling loneliness.

Next Margie stepped up to the microphone. There was a little dissatisfied murmuring, but she quickly quelled it when she said, "As you know, Caroline and I had our differences." There was a long pause. "Caroline had differences with nearly everyone on North Dakota Place. She was hot-tempered. She'd do anything to make a buck. And she acted like she owned the whole street, instead of every other house on it. But however she got her results, I think there's one thing none of us can argue: Caroline did an outstanding job of bringing North Dakota Place back to life. Now it is up to us to make sure Caroline's work doesn't die with her. She gave us something, and now we can give it back to her."

Maybe it was an odd thing to say at a memorial service, reminding everyone of the deceased's faults. If she had asked me ahead of time, I would have tried to talk Margie out of that speech. But it was exactly right for this ceremony. It was what everyone was thinking. I saw many North Dakota Place residents nodding their approval, and a few even applauded, then stopped, embarrassed, as if applause didn't belong at a memorial service.

After Margie, the alderman put out his cigar and stepped up for the final ceremonies. He planted the last impatiens and then unveiled a plaque dedicating the angel fountain to Caroline. He gave a short talk about cooperation being the key to the city's revival but stopped short of a campaign speech. Dina thanked everyone and invited them back to her house for refreshments.

As a memorial service, it was better than nothing, but it left me curiously unsatisfied. I would have preferred that Caroline be sent off with candles and incense and music. Nothing beats the Catholics, my old church, for pure ritual. Then I saw Caroline's sturdy no-nonsense figure in my mind and realized she probably wouldn't have enjoyed that kind of funeral fuss. She'd want exactly the good-bye she'd had, as long as no one hurt her grass. Still, I felt vaguely depressed as I headed toward Dina's house. But this was a funeral, of sorts, so I was supposed to feel depressed. I was also hungry. Funerals did that to me.

Dina's house looked a lot like Margie's, except it was a little smaller and a lot better furnished. Stan the cat was nowhere to be seen. Dina met us at the door. I told her what a great job she did organizing the service. She thanked me and waved me toward the dining room before the next group arrived.

Dina had her dining room table covered with a real St. Louis spread: half a spiral-sliced ham, a platter of sliced turkey, cold cuts and cheeses, a basket of rye bread, white bread, and dollar rolls. There was another basket of warm corn bread, cranberry bread, and walnut bread, undoubtedly baked by Dale and Kathy. Little ornamental dishes that had to be somebody's wedding presents were filled with homemade relishes and pickles, jams and jellies, mustard, mayonnaise and ketchup. There was Sterno burning under a huge pot of mostaccioli, the all-purpose St. Louis noodle dish that feeds the multitudes cheap. If Christ were a South Sider, he would have skipped the loaves and fishes and brought out a big bowl of mostaccioli. There was three-bean salad, marinated mushroom salad, rice salad, corn salad, and a couple of other salads I couldn't identify. The air was perfumed by stainless steel urns of coffee, decaf and regular. There were jugs of cold white wine and tubs of iced beer. On the mahogany sideboard were cakes of every description: chocolate layer, coffee cake, split-lemon cake, and homemade carrot cake on an old-fashioned fancy flowered plate.

I fixed myself a ham sandwich, piled on the mostaccioli, skipped the salads, and cut a huge slab of carrot cake, so I'd get my vegetables. I made polite conversation with various people and then went looking for Patricia, so I could talk to her about the recycling section. I found her standing in the living room, staring straight ahead, with a nearly empty glass of white wine in one hand. The flush on her face and the unfocused look in her eyes indicated this wasn't the first glass of wine she'd downed, and it didn't look like she'd eaten anything. I'd better start sobering her up, if I was going to get any information out of her. I fixed her a plate of food, loading up on mostaccioli and bread, then added a turkey sandwich. Patricia wolfed it all down, as if she hadn't eaten in days. From the gaunt look of her, maybe she hadn't. After she cleaned up her plate, her eyes seemed a little clearer. I brought her some coffee. Then I cut her a slice of chocolate cake and carrot cake, too. She was thin enough to eat both.

"I made that," she said, taking a forkful of carrot cake. "It's not too bad," she decided.

"It was delicious," I said. I'd already cleaned up my piece, and if people hadn't been looking, I'd have cut myself another. But after the initial rush at her food, Patricia picked at the rest of the carrot cake and didn't eat any of the chocolate. She'd lost interest in food.

But she had plenty of interest in the recycling section. Patricia was eager to talk about it. Her eyes lit up with the fire of a fanatic about to make a conversion. "Let's go to my house right *now*," she said. "I can't wait to start. There's so much to talk about. I'll show you what can be done by the individual, then I'll give you some phone numbers of people who will have more information."

Fine with me. If Patricia wanted to do my work for me, I'd let her. I found Dina, said my good-byes and thank-yous, and went out the front door with Patricia. A taxicab was pulling up at Sally's house, and I saw a lumpy forty-something brown-haired woman in a beige suit get out. "Is that Sally?"

"It sure is," said Patricia. "She's almost never home during the day. I wonder if Sally's feeling bad?" I didn't know why she was home, but I was certainly glad to see her. That woman was harder to find than Jimmy Hoffa. As Sally turned to pay the driver, I got a good look at her face. She had dark bruises around her eyes, big white bandages on the sides of her face, and an Ace bandage wrapped over her head and neck.

"Look at Sally!" Patricia said. "She looks like she was in a car accident."

That was one possibility. Or she could have been

beaten up by her ex-boyfriend, Darryl. Whatever, she wasn't going anywhere in her current condition. She could hardly walk to her front door. This was getting more and more interesting. I couldn't wait to talk to Sally. Just as soon as I got this recycling interview out of the way, I'd knock on her door.

As I followed Patricia around to her backyard, she began tossing off little recycling facts. "Some of the things you can do to save energy are so simple," she said. "Don't leave the refrigerator door open when you pour yourself a glass of milk. That wastes enormous amounts of energy."

"Sure does," I said. "All those moms screaming at their kids to close the fridge door."

Patricia's look flash-froze my feeble joke. "Buy used whenever possible," she said, as if this command was on stone tablets. "Almost everything I own is refinished, reused, or renewed." When we passed the compost pile she said, "Did you know that composting can provide natural, nonchemical fertilizer and keep up to fifty percent of your household waste from using up valuable landfill space?"

"Amazing," I said, trying to scribble notes and step over a rusty garden tool. I thought Patricia kept a neater yard than this. Tools were lying in the grass and weeds were clogging the organic garden.

Patricia kept spouting recycling facts. "Did you know that by installing low-flow shower heads, you can save more than six thousand gallons of water a year?"

"Do they work any better than low-flush toilets?" I said. "I can't see how I save water when I flush three times instead of once."

Her voice went absolutely flat. "That kind of obstructionist thinking is destroying the planet," she said as she opened the back door to her beautiful kitchen. Except it didn't look so beautiful. The place was a mess. Dirty dishes were piled in the sink and all over the counter. Any space not covered with dishes was a jumble of food containers, crumbs, sticky knives, dirty spoons, and open jars. Milk had been spilled on the counter. It ran down the cabinet and onto the floor. The dishrag draped over the faucet was gray with dirt and smelled sour. I remembered that carrot cake I'd eaten so enthusiastically. It had been baked in this pigsty. I hoped the baking sterilized everything.

Patricia must be really depressed. Maybe I couldn't cook, but I could clean. The woman obviously needed help. "Why don't you sit down, Patricia, and I'll clean up while we talk," I said. "Do you have any paper towels?"

Wrong question. Patricia launched into an impassioned speech about how paper towels were environmentally destructive. It finally ended with "and besides that, paper towels take up valuable landfill space."

Speaking of landfills, her kitchen was beginning to resemble one. At least I could get some of those dishes out of there. "Then let me load these dishes into the dishwasher," I said. "Where is your dishwasher, by the way?"

Another mistake. Dishwashers were also environmentally incorrect. Patricia wouldn't have one in the house. She hand-washed her dishes, and she was careful not to let the water run needlessly when she rinsed. I listened to another lecture on water and energy waste. "More than eighty percent of a dishwasher's energy goes just to heat the water," she finished. Patricia was growing more agitated, pacing back and forth in her filthy kitchen, talking about how laziness and insensitivity were ruining Mother Earth. Mom was doing fine here. Patricia had enough dirt on the floor to start a small organic farm. I found a mop behind the door, hoping to wipe up the sour milk. But when I rinsed out the mop, it smelled so bad, I figured using it on the floor would only make the problem worse. I gave up on the idea of cleaning Patricia's kitchen. She was still pacing. She needed something soothing to calm her down. Judging by the way she reacted to the white wine, booze was not the answer.

"Do you have any herbal tea?" I asked. Patricia said yes, and found a canister of chamomile tea. That should be very soothing. I put some water on to boil in the teakettle and then followed Patricia into the butler's pantry. "There is no reason to throw out anything, ever," she said. "It can all be recycled or reused if you know how." I took notes while Patricia pointed out the proper storage and preparation for recyclables. She had quite an operation there—a can crusher, and shelves or bins for cardboard, newspapers, white paper, green and white glass, brown glass, and rags.

"Rags," I said. "My grandmother had a rag bag. She'd cut the buttons off old shirts, keep the collars, if they weren't frayed, and use the rest for dust rags."

"That generation understood recycling," Patricia said, smiling for the first time. "We've forgotten all their good habits. I bet your grandmother also washed and reused aluminum foil, glass jars, and plastic bags. She also cleaned her house with environmentally friendly cleaners like vinegar and water."

"Right again," I said. Patricia was calming down.

"And she cleaned everything without using a single paper towel," she said, a not-too-gentle jab at my ignorance. But at least she was smiling.

"True," I said. "But I'm not sure she would now. Grandma thought rags were a drag. They mildewed. They had to be washed and hung up. And they could be embarrassing. I remember getting in trouble as a kid because I went in her rag bag without permission and used her rags to make a kite tail. Unfortunately, I flew her old underwear in Sublette Park. I never heard the end of that one. But I love pawing through rag bags—I always have. You can see a person's life history in there. Let's see, what do you have?"

Mostly worn and faded T-shirts, which was no surprise. The memorial service was the only time I'd seen her out of uniform. One shirt looked newer than the others. I pulled out her "Walk for Wildlife" T-shirt. It had been washed but was splotched and spattered with blood. Lots of blood. Walk for Wildlife? The shirt looked like she'd been walking on wildlife.

"Jeez," I said. "What did you do, step on a possum?"

Patricia turned whiter than her funeral shirt. What a strange reaction. Why would Patricia go pale over an old T-shirt? Her eyes looked frightened—and almost as colorless as her skin. They used to be such a brilliant blue. What changed them? Why were Patricia's eyes so washed out? I stared at her. She was wearing glasses. But they were a recent addition. "Contact lenses!" I said. "That's why your eyes were so blue. You wear blue contact lenses."

"Gas-permeable contacts," Patricia said. "They take a week to ten days to replace. I dropped one down the sink the night . . . Caroline died."

The blood on the shirt. Patricia wore the "Walk for Wildlife" T-shirt the day of Caroline's death. Patricia looked frightened when I pulled out the bloody T-shirt. Patricia said she always borrowed Caroline's tools and Caroline always used her kitchen equipment. It was all falling into place for me. "And you didn't want to wait more than a week for a new contact lens. So you ran over to Caroline's to borrow her big pipe wrench, in case your lens was still lodged in the sink pipe."

"No," Patricia said. But she was shaking all over and edging back toward the pantry.

"Yes," I said. "You killed Caroline with the pipe wrench. You hit her with it and got her blood all over yourself. You wore that 'Walk for Wildlife' T-shirt the day she died. I remember it. So will Dina. Caroline killed those people, didn't she? You knew it. But you didn't care if she killed Otto or the drug dealer."

"I didn't know she killed Otto," Patricia said. "Not for sure."

"But you suspected, didn't you?"

Patricia said nothing and took another step backward. "She killed the dog. That bothered me," she said. "It was a nasty animal, but only because of the influence of its human companion. It wasn't right to send it to the shelter to die. But I never knew if Caroline killed Otto."

"But you suspected, didn't you?" I said. I felt frightened and queasy, but I couldn't stop talking, because suddenly I saw how it all came together. "Someone as handy as Caroline would have no trouble fixing Otto's Christmas lights so he was electrocuted. When did you find out for sure Caroline was a killer—when she murdered the drug dealer? That would have been her third death, if you counted the dog. She was getting careless by then."

Patricia seemed relieved to talk. "I figured it out when she came home so late that night. She was sweaty and dirty, and I saw her red gas can, the one she used for her lawn mower, in her wheelbarrow. She didn't bother hiding it. I knew she wasn't cutting grass at that hour. The next day I heard about the drug dealer being burned out, and I knew she did it."

"He wasn't burned out, Patricia. He was burned to death. Roasted alive. That's murder. And you said nothing."

"What about all the people he murdered with his drugs? No one cared about them. He was a human cockroach, and she stamped him out," she said defiantly.

"But maybe if you'd said something and stopped her then, Caroline wouldn't have killed the human hunk. That's what you discovered when you went looking for the pipe wrench—something that told you she'd killed Hawkeye the jogger."

Patricia's eyes began to fill with tears. "Don't call him that silly name. His name was Johnny," she said, "and he was a beautiful man, spiritually and physically. He believed in recycling and composting. Caroline killed Johnny. She didn't even care."

"Caroline had the same attitude as you did—Hawkeye was another pest, and she exterminated him."

"No, no," she wailed. "Johnny was different."

"Yeah, he was a white boy. A handsome white boy you found attractive. Caroline was truly without prejudice. A pest was a pest, regardless of race or muscular development."

"You're despicable," Patricia said.

"Yep. Now back away from that wooden block of kitchen knives you've been heading toward. Go stand over there by the microwave."

The only other thing I saw on the microwave cart was an electric blender. I wondered how someone with Patricia's environmental sensibilities could justify electric appliances and a microwave, but I'd ask that question later. I suspected I knew the answer, anyway. She had them because they were convenient for her. Just like it was convenient for her that Otto and the drug dealer died. She felt more remorse over the death of a dog than a human being.

"You found something that told you Caroline killed Johnny Hawkeye," I said. I was moving slowly backward across that endless kitchen to the wall phone by the door, so I could call 911. I didn't want to turn my back on her.

"I couldn't find the pipe wrench on the garage wall pegboard," Patricia said. "That's where Caroline usually hangs her bigger tools. So I started rummaging around in her tool box. I found the pipe wrench about the same time I found a spool of thin wire. I'd heard that the police thought a wire had been stretched across the alley to kill Johnny."

"So you killed Caroline for that? For wire that could be found in half the toolboxes in the city?"

"No," Patricia said sharply. "I killed her because she came into the garage right then and saw the wire. And when I asked her if she killed Johnny, she didn't bother denying it. She knew I'd figured out that she killed Otto and the drug dealer and I'd said nothing, so I guess she thought I approved of all her murders."

"You did."

"Not Johnny!" she screamed. "She said something so callous, so cruel. She said instead of ruining her grass, he was making himself useful pushing up daisies. Then she laughed. She laughed and walked away again. She was outside, standing on the grass between her place and mine. Her back was turned to me. I picked up the pipe wrench, walked up behind her, and swung without thinking." I stared at Patricia in fascination while she grabbed the heavy glass blender by the handle and swung. I started thinking and ducked. Now I understood how she killed Caroline. For a skinny woman, she had an arm like a stevedore. If she'd hit me in the head, I'd be pushing up daisies like Hawkeye. Instead, she cracked me on the left elbow. I shrieked, half blinded by the flash of pain. I slipped to one knee, then staggered to my feet, but I couldn't move my left arm at all. Good thing I was right-handed.

She ran for the kitchen cabinets, pulled a gun out of the silverware drawer, aimed at me, and fired. Damn! She hit the phone. There went my chance of getting help. The second shot went wild, too, and took out the glass in the side kitchen window. I hoped her next-door neighbor would hear the noise and call the police. Then I remembered the neighbor on that side was Caroline.

Patricia was furious. "That's the original glass," she said. "It's your fault." I was crawling toward the butler's pantry, when she closed in on me. The gun was only a few feet away from my head, and this time, I didn't think even Patricia could miss. She pulled the trigger. I waited for the sound, probably the last one I'd hear. There was nothing. The gun had jammed. She threw it at me and finally hit me. It hurt, too. But it got my brain working.

"You bought that gun from the kids in the trouble house," I blurted. "They were selling stolen weapons, and those don't come with money-back guarantees. You're the one who shot at me on the Fourth of July. You missed then, too."

"It's harder than you think to shoot someone," she whined. "Besides, my hands were shaking. I was going to kill you later. But then I had a long talk with Margie and found out you didn't know anything, so I quit worrying. I figured it was safer to let you blunder around. You were so far off, it wasn't funny."

She was right. I wasn't laughing. My elbow hurt too much. Patricia's voice turned scornful. "I heard you talked with Caroline's ex-husband and Sally's old boyfriend Darryl. How could you be so stupid? You weren't even close. And then today, you wanted to talk to Sally. You thought her redneck boyfriend beat her up, didn't you? All I had to do was make a couple of remarks, and you jumped to another wrong conclusion. Do you know why she was really wearing that bandage on her face? She had a face-lift. You were wrong again, Francesca. You couldn't . . . you couldn't find your ass with both hands."

It sounded funny when Patricia said it, because she wasn't used to cussing. Besides, I'd found the mop with one hand. My good hand, too. The one I could still move. I tried to keep her talking, so I could either hit her with the mop or rush past her and get out of

here. "Who told you that I'd been talking with Darryl?"
I demanded.

"Margie," she answered. "I took over a bottle of
bourbon one night and we talked until one A.M. Margie
didn't suspect me, either. She was just as dumb as you,
and she wanted someone to talk to. We . . ." She
grabbed the biggest knife out of the block, but I hit her
hand with the mop handle first. Even one-handed, I
must have got her good. She dropped it and screamed.

I picked up a big crock of sugar by the handle and
threw it at her, but my aim wasn't so hot. It caught her
on the shin and then skidded across the floor, scattering sugar everywhere. She went over backward in the
slippery stuff. This put her in range of a shelf full of
pots. She heaved a heavy Dutch oven at my knee. I slid
out of the way on the sticky, sugared floor, and began
throwing dirty dishes out of the sink at her. They only
slowed down Patricia slightly, but at least she wouldn't
have to wash them.

I had a nasty cut on my hand, probably from crawling in the broken china. She had a cast-iron frying pan
that looked positively lethal. I heard the tea kettle
whistling. So did she, but I was closer to the stove. I
picked it up and threw the boiling water at her. The
full kettle was too heavy for one hand. My aim was off,
but I managed to scald Patricia with boiling water on
her face and arms. Her eyes were protected by her
glasses, but her arms and face had red streaks and
splotches. She screamed in horror. So did I. I'd never
hurt anyone like that, not ever. The pain only seemed
to enrage her and make her stronger, while I felt sick
and weak. She charged me, and the tea kettle banged
to the floor. She had my hand in a grip I couldn't
budge. I tried to pry her fingers off it, but she dragged
me over to the butler's pantry, where she began forc-
ing my hand into the can crusher. "I'll be scarred,
Francesca," she said, "but I'll still be able to work.

You'll be out of a job. When this can crusher finishes mashing your hand, you won't be able to write another stupid word. You won't be able to write anything, anyway, because after I cripple you, I'm going to kill you. But you deserve to suffer first."

I didn't mention that she was trying to crush my left hand, and I was right-handed. Her eyes looked wild and crazy. The veins stood out on her neck. She was beyond reason, and I couldn't talk. Pain was shooting up my already injured left arm. I fought her off with my right, but I was getting weaker. I couldn't think. She had me backed against the bin of brown glass.

When I quit thinking, my South Side heritage reasserted itself. Brown glass. Beer bottles—the ultimate saloon defense weapon. In finest city style, I grabbed a brown glass beer bottle by the neck and hit it against the counter. Now I had the perfect weapon—nasty, jagged, and potentially lethal. And I wasn't afraid to use it. I rammed the jagged edges in her neck, as hard as I could.

Patricia made awful gurgling noises, and there was a bloody froth around her throat. Blood. There was lots of blood, and that horrible inhuman sound from her throat. She let go of my hand and clawed at her throat, smearing the blood. She was dying, right in front of me. I couldn't look. I was afraid I'd pass out.

"I'm a murderer, just like my mother," I thought.

Epilogue

"Patricia! It's me, Dina."

I could hear Dina knocking on the kitchen door. I stood there, woozy and stupid with horror, watching the blood bubble out of Patricia's throat. Her skin was gray, and she was clawing at her throat, smearing the blood on her neck and her white blouse. I never could stand the sight of blood, and now it was everywhere. The place looked like a bunch of hellish kindergartners had been playing with red fingerpaint. There were bloody handprints and gory splotches on the walls. Long drips of blood ran down the cabinets. There were more smears and handprints where Patricia had flopped around and tried to grab onto things.

I noticed weird little details: A single red blood spot on a black-and-white ceramic cow cookie jar looked quite decorative. A long bloody drip was lined up exactly under the numeral six on the round pantry clock. The floor was covered with splashes, spatters, and pools of blood. I saw my footprint in one red pool, grabbed onto a cabinet handle to keep upright, and left a bloody handprint on the handle and a long smear on the counter when I steadied myself. My hand was next to the broken beer bottle, its jagged edges bright with blood. The room started to close in black around me. Then the black pulled back from around the edges, and my head cleared.

Where had that footprint come from? I couldn't move my legs, much less take a step. I knew I should run to get help for Patricia, but my legs felt like a couple of concrete posts. I couldn't get them to move in time. Time. That was the problem. I wasn't inside time any more. The clock in the butler's pantry said it was noontime, but it seemed like days since I'd attended Caroline's memorial service and then cut carrot cake for a killer. Now the killer was going to die, too. She was still thrashing around on the floor. Her head hit something, the cabinet or the floor, hard, and she quit flopping around quite so much. But I could hear Patricia making a horrible sucking gurgle. I wished she would stop that nightmare noise, except when she did she'd be dead. I wondered how long she would keep trying to breathe.

"Patricia!" Dina's voice was louder and more insistent. She rattled the door handle. "Patricia. I just want to drop off your flowered plate. I know you wouldn't want it broken. I'll just leave it on the kitchen counter." I heard the back door open. Then Dina said, "Oh, my god," in a slow, shocked voice, and there was the sound of china hitting the floor and smashing to pieces. Patricia's precious plate had joined the other broken crockery in the kitchen.

Dina did a crunching run across the kitchen floor and found Patricia and me in the bloody butler's pantry. She didn't scream. She ran over to Patricia, disregarding her navy power suit, Ferragamo pumps, and ten-dollar panty hose, and knelt in the blood and glass to examine her wounds. Dina thought we'd fought off an intruder. "Who did this, Francesca?" she asked. "Who attacked you and Patricia?"

"We did this to each other," I told her. "Patricia killed Caroline and tried to kill me when I figured it out."

"Patricia?" Dina was stupefied. "But why?"

"Because Caroline killed Johnny Hawkeye. And the drug dealer and Otto, too, but Patricia didn't care about them."

Dina listened, her mouth hanging open. She kept saying "Patricia? I don't believe it. I just don't believe it." The more she repeated it, the more it sounded like some weird bird cry—the North Dakota loon, maybe.

Fortunately, the police believed it. The kitchen phone was shot through the heart, but Dina found a working phone in Patricia's living room, hit 911, and soon the house was swarming with EMS paramedics and police, including Mayhew. The police were very interested in the bloody "Walk for Wildlife" T-shirt and the jammed automatic with Patricia's fingerprints on it. They also took the wire out of Caroline's toolbox, although I wasn't sure what good that would do. Patricia was in no shape to make any statement. She was loaded on a stretcher and hauled off by ambulance to the emergency room. It left with its lights flashing and siren screaming, so the EMS crew must have believed Patricia was going to live long enough to try for the hospital.

The uniformed officers and Mayhew asked me what happened. Then they made me go to the hospital, too. I thought an ambulance was a little dramatic. I was able to walk and talk, even if I did look like an extra in *Friday the 13th*. But they insisted. Once inside the ambulance, I was scared. I'd killed a woman. The ambulance rocked and swayed and the siren shrieked and I craved a drink, really craved it, and begged the paramedics for a shot of bourbon. I guess I had my parents' alcoholic blood after all. The paramedics promised that the hospital would give me shots of something better than bourbon if I could hang on a little longer.

I calmed down once I got to the hospital. I wondered if I'd be charged with manslaughter—or womanslaughter. I didn't much care right now. My left elbow throbbed and I couldn't bend that arm. It was turning an ugly red-purple, too. I was "stabilized," which made me feel like a wobbly table with a matchbook shoved under the short leg, and given a shot of something that made me feel comfortably woozy. Then Mayhew came into the examination cubicle and questioned me. He made me tell my story again and again and again, but no matter how many times he asked the questions, I gave basically the same answers. I felt like I'd talked for hours, but I hadn't. I still didn't have a proper sense of time. Finally Mayhew said the physical evidence supported my version. I figured I didn't have to worry about Patricia horning in with her side of the story.

After four hours I was released, with my arm strapped uncomfortably to my chest. I had a broken elbow—the end of the ulna was snapped off, if you want to get technical—plus minor cuts and major bruises. I had some antibiotics and a bottle of pain pills. Later that night, when my arm was really hurting, I discovered the bottle had a child-proof cap, and I had to break it open with a hammer.

Dina had waited for me, and she drove me home from the emergency room. She kept saying "Patricia? I can't believe it. I just can't believe it."

I couldn't, either. I mean, everything added up. The evidence was there, although a lot of it would not be admissible in court. But I'd seen the way Patricia had looked at Johnny Hawkeye when he jogged down North Dakota Place. She worshiped that man. Maybe if she'd had a chance to spend more time with him she would have realized what a sleaze he was. Maybe if Johnny hadn't tried so hard to charm her, she would have seen the ugly little man inside that gorgeous Greek god exterior. But he didn't. Johnny had fatal charm, all right. It killed a woman.

He was Patricia's dream lover, and when she found out that Caroline had killed him, she lashed out at Caroline in fury and hit her with the pipe wrench. I wondered if Caroline knew what hit her—or why. If she was in any kind of afterlife, it must infuriate her to know she had to leave this world for someone like Johnny. All her grand plans for North Dakota Place and all her clever financial dealings were undone for a dumb guy with a good body. I wondered if knowing that was her own particular hell. I certainly didn't think she'd spend eternity dancing with the angels in showers of rainbows. Not after she killed three people and a dog.

Patricia wasn't dead, thank God. She wasn't even hurt too badly. The beer bottle didn't cut anything vital. She had a sore throat for a while and talked kind of raspy, so she almost sounded like Margie. But she healed up fine. For her court appearances, she wears high collars and scarves to cover my slash marks on her throat. There were no scald scars, so I don't have that guilt. Patricia had enough guilt for two. She was arrested in the hospital and she refused to deny that she'd killed Caroline, no matter how often her family's lawyer told her to shut up. She seemed relieved to have been caught.

I wondered why I didn't know Patricia was a murderer. I couldn't believe I'd eaten carrot cake with a hot-blooded killer. I sat there and talked with her and didn't have a clue. Some judge of character I am. My only consolation was that Mayhew didn't know, either. I felt better when he said "Damn, you got me that time, Francesca." We were back on our old friendly footing, but we weren't too friendly, either. Except for one period of temporary insanity, I avoid married men. Our relationship was professional. He no longer treated me like a bumbling civilian. Well, not too much.

Mayhew agreed that Caroline probably murdered Johnny Hawkeye, Otto, and Scorpion Smith, although

Otto's case remains officially open. There wasn't enough evidence to close it. Still, it gave me some satisfaction to know I was right about Caroline, even if all her murders would never be officially acknowledged.

I found out what happened to those missing casings, when Patricia fired at me in the alley. Mayhew told me one morning when I was eating my usual at Uncle Bob's. Scrambled eggs and toast may be boring, but I can get them down with one arm in a sling.

"Patricia said after she took those shots at you, she ran between the houses and got into her vehicle, which was parked on North Dakota Place, and drove after you in a careless and reckless manner," he said in copese.

"That was the understatement of the year," I said. "She was driving the wrong way down the boulevard and nearly sideswiped a car. But did she get a ticket? No. Just me."

"Be glad you got those tickets," Mayhew said. "Patricia planned to follow you, cut you off in the alley, and shoot you. It was Fourth of July, remember, and nobody would have noticed a shooting with all the firecrackers going off. She just might have gotten away with it. But when she saw the police stop you, she figured she wouldn't have a chance right then. She said she was going to kill you later."

"Then she got Margie drunk the next day and found out I was on the wrong track, so she didn't try again," I said.

"Right. While you were getting those tickets, she went back to the alley and picked up all the casings she could find, then threw them down the corner sewer. It's been a dry summer, so we recovered most of them."

"Find anything else down there?" I said.

"Yeah, three purses, five credit cards—all canceled—and a plastic Ziploc bag of pot, ruined by the water," Mayhew said.

"The local thugs have been busy," I said.

"Here's what I want to know," Mayhew said. "What dweeb would buy a twenty-two pistol on the street when it wasn't fully automatic? Why did she waste her time getting it from those kids? She could have bought the same thing at any Wal-Mart and paid a lot less for it."

"Gee," I said. "Thanks for that bargain hunter's tip, Officer Friendly. Patricia didn't know anything about guns, and she'd probably never been in a Wal-Mart in her life. The kids at the trouble house took advantage of her ignorance. Besides, Patricia always bought used if she could. It was one of her recycling principles."

"Good thing she didn't know anything about guns," Mayhew said. "That saved your life. Those cheap semiautomatics are easy to jam. She pulled the trigger too fast too many times, and a casing got hung up in the slide that's supposed to spit them out."

This conversation about how close I came to getting killed wasn't doing much for my appetite. I was glad when Mayhew's beeper went off and he had to go. It was odd to think that I was alive because a cop who hated me was eager to write me a fistful of tickets and the kids at the trouble house had ripped off Patricia. I ordered a second round of buttered wheat toast and crunched on it for consolation.

Patricia's family got her a fancy lawyer, and she's trying to plead insanity. It's harder to get away with insanity these days in Missouri, but in my opinion—and remember, my degree is in journalism—Patricia was battier than a barn owl. Of course, she did have the presence of mind to shove that flamingo into Caroline, to make it look like Margie was the killer. Maybe Patricia wasn't so crazy after all. I'll let a jury figure it out. Personally, I don't care what they do with her, just so she doesn't get out and get me.

Patricia did enough damage. I had eight weeks of boring physical therapy before I could move my elbow properly again. It still doesn't bend quite right, but it's not like I'm a relief pitcher for the Cardinals. It does enough for me to get by. It got me off the recycling section, too. So it was almost worth it.

And that was that. Except my life hasn't been the same since. I miss Lyle terribly and think about him all the time. Once, in an elevator, I saw a man whose hair curled over his collar like Lyle's does, and I felt like someone had punched me in the gut. Another time I thought I heard him talking at a table behind me in a restaurant, but when I turned around, it was a fat, bald man who somehow had Lyle's voice. He seemed puzzled by my look of disappointment. I would remember little things Lyle did, little funny kindnesses. I wondered if his living room, so beautifully furnished with family antiques, still had the beat-up UPS box sitting next to the couch. His cat Montana loved sleeping in that box, and Lyle refused to move it.

I missed his hands and his lips, and I missed his smell of coffee and sandalwood soap, and most of all, I missed our conversations. He was my best friend as well as my lover, and he always understood me. Except for that one thing. He couldn't understand how I felt about marriage. Sometimes I have to literally hold one hand with the other to keep from calling him, but I don't. I'm strong. He's not blackmailing me into marriage. I don't need to get married. I'm through with men. Forever. Who needs them? Dina had the right idea with Stan the cat. I'd keep a cat, too, but I like to sleep alone. Lyle's cat, Montana, really knew how to take over a bed. I wondered how he was doing. I'm talking about Monty, of course, not Lyle.

Mrs. Indelicato won't forgive me for breaking up

with Lyle, so I keep away from her confectionary. I could get frostbitten, going into Mrs. I's store. It's not as convenient, but I shop more at Schnucks these days, because there isn't room in the confectionary for me, Mrs. I, and all her disapproval.

When I need company, I walk over to North Dakota Place and break a lemon bar with Mrs. Meyer on her screened-in porch. We sit and rock and listen to the sad end-of-summer sound of the cicadas, and she gives me all the neighborhood gossip. She's the one who told me that Sally married the nice accountant after her face-lift healed. "Although I don't know if he married her because of it or in spite of it," she said. "Sally is a very attractive young woman, and that face-lift has left her skin stretched too tight, in my opinion. I don't think she needed it, not that she asked me. I don't understand young people. Always talking about the natural look, except when it comes to their own appearance."

We both ate another lemon bar and solemnly agreed with each other, although I wondered if I'd feel the same way about face-lifts in another ten years or so. Mrs. Meyer, in her white tennis shoes and flowered housedresses, had the courage to let herself age gracefully. I hoped I would.

Mrs. Meyer also told me the trouble house family moved out the day after Patricia's arrest. "The police were over there asking questions about where Patricia got that gun," she said with great satisfaction. "Must have scared them. The whole bunch took off in the middle of the night, and good riddance. I watched them load a pickup full of furniture and appliances. Packed it so high they had to tie everything down with rope. They loaded up three beds, an almost new couch, some lamps and tables, a stove, and a refrigerator. I thought that was odd. That was a furnished apartment they were renting, you know. But I didn't call the landlord. Couldn't even if I'd wanted. The landlord un-plugged his phone at night."

"One of those, huh?" I said. The city was plagued with landlords who ducked their responsibilities. "Let me guess. He lived in West County."

"Chesterfield," Mrs. Meyer said. "In a great big new house. On a very quiet street. You can bet he doesn't put up with the noise like we had to. Dina found his address and phone number in the city records, and we all started calling him to complain about those people. His tenants were selling drugs, and guns, and had loud music blasting late at night. Ooh, you couldn't believe the pounding sound and the filthy language that so-called music used. But the landlord didn't want to hear about that. All he wanted was his rent check. One Sat-urday night at two A.M., when we were awakened for the second night in a row, we all called. The landlord must have heard from ten or fifteen neighbors. After that he unplugged his phone when he went to bed, so we couldn't bother him. So I couldn't call him when his tenant drove off with all that furniture, and it wasn't my place to call the police."

"Right," I said, knowing Mrs. Meyer called the po-lice about as often as most people dialed time and tem-perature. She fed them lemon bars and wrote nice letters to their superiors about how helpful the officers were, so she got a pretty good response.

"The next morning I called the landlord at his office and told him his renters had left and he'd better secure the front door, because it was wide open. He drove right over here. When he found out his renters had hightailed it with his furniture, you could hear him yelling all the way back to Chesterfield." Mrs. Meyer grinned. "They owed two months back rent, too. There is a God, and she is just."

During another lemon bar session, Mrs. Meyer also told me the latest Dale and Kathy rehabbing disaster.

Actually, *I* ate the lemon bars. She was busy knitting something yellow. "Dale and Kathy patched all the cardboard-covered holes in the walls, except for one on the third floor. Dale was going to fix it. He was about to plug in his screw gun, when he noticed something odd. It wasn't a regular wall receptacle. It was a cheap brown extension cord, papered right into the wall. He followed the cord around, and found it was a series of extension cords stapled into the molding. The previous owner had been running a TV and a fan off that crazy arrangement. It's a wonder their house didn't burn down. Dale and Kathy only used that floor for storage, and they never noticed the extension cords before. I don't have to tell you they had an electrician over there right away."

"I guess they're going to be busy fixing up the third floor now," I said.

"No, not really," Mrs. Meyer said, and smiled. "They're both working feverishly on the second-floor nursery. Kathy's expecting. They've been trying for some time, and they're both deliriously happy about the baby."

"They're always deliriously happy," I said, sounding somewhat churlish.

"That's because they don't need or want the same things you do, dear," Mrs. Meyer said, calmly knitting. "You would be miserable with a husband and children. You know that, don't you?" Then she abruptly changed the subject. "I'm knitting this for the baby," she said, holding up something that looked like morning sunshine with arms and legs. I wasn't sure what it was, and I was ashamed to ask. I guess I'm not cut out for family life.

I don't hear much from Dina these days. She called once or twice to see how my elbow was healing, but she is busy with her new job at the mayor's office. The last time I heard from her, Dina asked if I still wanted to contribute something for Caroline's flowers. I told her I'd given Margie a ten-dollar bill the day of the memorial service. Dina called Margie, who said she'd forgotten it, and she'd bring it right over.

Margie no longer calls me with funny story ideas. She called once to thank me after Patricia was arrested and gave me an antique silver cigarette case as a present. I don't smoke, but I like the case. Mellow old silver has such a lovely sheen. I leave it out on the coffee table, except when Jinny comes to call. It's not that I believe Margie stole this one from Jinny's friend. I just don't like complications.

Nothing much changed at the *Gazette*. Most of the staff was busily backstabbing everybody else or working to turn out a third-rate paper in a first-rate city. I kept out of sight, wrote my columns, and enjoyed the wacky tales my readers told me. They kept me sane. But the best story didn't come from a reader. It was the saga of Charlie's wife. Excuse me, ex-wife. The woman we'd dismissed as a dull little sparrow had been canny as a hawk. While Charlie had been busy skirt-chasing at the *Gazette*, "the Wife," as he called her, had been quietly taking courses at Midwestern State University, so she could complete her degree in art history at his expense. The Wife, who was actually named Natalie, had a plan. She confided it to a friend, who told the whole world after Natalie's divorce. Natalie wanted to get a job in the university's art department as soon as she had her master's degree. She knew two instructors would be retiring that same year, and she had a little pull with the college board. She was pretty certain she could swing a low-level instructor's job. As soon as she did, she planned to divorce Charlie. Instead, he divorced her first. Because Nails was pregnant and he needed to untie the knot fast, Natalie's lawyer was able to negotiate a hefty cash settlement and monthly

maintenance. She used some of the money for a make-
over, a new wardrobe, and a health club membership.
The rest she spent opening the small, chic Showcase
26 in the hot new Clayton arts district. Tina, our City
Hall reporter, told me the twenty-sixth was the day
Natalie's divorce from Charlie became final, but that
could have been a coincidence.

The Showcase 26 opening was quite an event,
thanks to heavy hype on the *Gazette* arts page. Charlie
ordered the *Gazette* arts reviewer to give the show, a
display of feminist origami, a favorable review. Charlie
was terrified that if the gallery failed, the judge might
up his maintenance. With two kids in college and one
on the way, he couldn't afford any more debt.

Even the bitchiest *Gazette* staffer said Charlie's ex
looked stunning that night. Natalie's hair was streaked
blond, her body looked tanned and toned, and her
short, low-cut black Ungaro showed off trim legs and a
first-rate boob job. What a change. When she used to
make public appearances with Charlie, she always
wore long gathered skirts and artsy loose tops. Babe
claimed he could see the face-lift scars around her
ears, but he always said that when a woman over forty
looked good.

Several people noticed Natalie was being particularly nice to Nails. At eight months, Nails's wardrobe
choices were somewhat limited, and she'd opted for
the sweet impending motherhood look. An unfortunate late-stage waddle and a natural tendency to sweat
made her look more frump than mother figure. But
Charlie's ex-wife brought Nails a cool nonalcoholic
drink with her own hands and praised her outfit. Several people overheard Natalie say "Those little ducks
around your collar are so retro, my dear. I can't tell
you how much I admire a woman who has a child
after age forty. Late-night feedings and diapers were
almost more than I could handle at twenty-five. But

you'll be surprised how fast the time will pass. Why, Charlie will be seventy-two-years old when your little one graduates from college."

Nails did not seem comforted by this revelation, but with less than a month to go before the birth, I doubt if anything made her comfortable. Babe insisted that he heard Charlie hitting on his ex that same night, when Natalie was alone in the gallery office, and she turned him down. But you can only believe about half of Babe's tales.

We did know for sure that Natalie is dating a Clayton lawyer. That wasn't a surprise. Clayton, with its huge county courthouse, was overrun with lawyers. But this one was Charlie's worst nightmare, a libel lawyer. Natalie knew many intimate *Gazette* secrets from years of listening to Charlie rant about libel suits, and Charlie was worried she'd impart them to her new lover. She never mentioned the subject to Charlie when he called to ask about their two college-age children. I wondered if Nails had to listen to Charlie go on about potential libel suits, his ex-wife, and her lawyer lover.

I won the Nails Is Nailed baby pool. The money was almost enough to cover my court costs and fines from my alley escapade, but it couldn't help with the year's probation. I was supposed to be grateful because all the tickets had been combined and knocked down to two: speeding and exceeding the speed limit in an alley. The fact that I was running from someone who was trying to shoot me was not considered a mitigating circumstance. The judge said he couldn't show favoritism to a *Gazette* reporter. I wished the *Gazette* had shown more favoritism and supported his honor in the last election. I might have had a lighter sentence.

Three days after the birth Smiley Steve posted the baby's picture on the office bulletin board. I'd watched

my mouth for a while and was back in the good graces
of my mentor, Georgia. She was in a good mood, anyway. The *Gazette* book club went on hiatus when Nails
went in to have the baby, and with any luck, the club
would stay that way and Georgia would never have to
finish *Ensheathe and Ensnare*, etc.

I'd run into Georgia in the hall, and the two of us
stared at the red, angry-looking creature in the hospital photo.

"The kid's bald and has a pot belly, so he must be
Charlie's," I said.

"All babies look like that," Georgia said.

"Well, with Charlie's record for monogamy, maybe
they're all his." Georgia was about to think up something sarcastic when Smiley Steve came by, collecting
for the baby present. I threw in five bucks before Georgia made me give more.

"What are they calling the baby?" Georgia asked
Steve.

"Van would be a good name," I said, remembering
where the parents had their tryst in my neighborhood.
Smiley Steve looked puzzled. Georgia gave me a glare
that should have peeled the makeup off my face. For a
small person, she has a powerful presence.

The child's name was Charles Junior. We all waited
for Mother Nails to return from maternity leave. I was
sure she'd dump the kid with a nanny as soon as possible and get back to causing trouble at the *Gazette*. But
she didn't. Two weeks later, posted next to Charlie Junior's pot-bellied picture, was this announcement:

"Ms. Nadia Noonin is resigning as editor of the *Gazette* All Business section, effective immediately, so
that she can devote herself full time to parenting. She
will contribute a monthly column on child rearing to
the *Gazette*." It was signed by Charlie himself.

Nails giving up her career for a kid? I was shocked.
I also didn't believe it. That woman didn't take up with

Charlie because she wanted a husband and child. She got pregnant and married him to advance her career. Something had gone wrong with her grand plan. We found out what it was soon enough. I heard a version of the same story from Babe, our gossip columnist, and Endora, the one *Gazette* reporter who really did move in St. Louis society. Two sources are enough to confirm any story. Here's what Babe and Endora said happened:

Charlie and Nails's fling went unchecked, until it finally embarrassed the publisher personally. He'd been spending most of his time at the home office in Boston, so he had no idea the scandal his managing editor and business editor were causing, and no one at the paper wanted to wise him up. When he finally came into town, a couple of his pals sat him down at the Petroleum Club and explained the facts of life to the man. It turned out Adam Eichelberg, the president of the Eichelberg Company, the one Nails repeatedly attacked in her column for sex discrimination, was a friend of these men. They didn't appreciate their pal Adam being pilloried in the press as a woman-chasing sexist pig while Nails and Charlie were licking champagne off each other at the Opera Theatre. The publisher was steaming when he finally heard the Charlie and Nails stories. They made him a laughingstock in the sanctuary of his club. He called Charlie on the carpet and gave him a choice: She goes, or he goes. Or they could both go. The publisher didn't much care.

Charlie cared. Nails went.

"He sold out his own wife to save his career," I said to Georgia.

"You sound surprised," she said. "You've known all along that Charlie would betray anyone." I knew it. But his capacity for double-dealing always amazed me.

I wasn't surprised when Marlene the waitress gave

me the final chapter to Charlie and Nails's love story. I came in for my usual one morning at Uncle Bob's and she was fuming. She couldn't even wait for me to sit down before she blurted, "Charlie was in last night, without the Queen of Sheba." That was her nickname for Nails. He must have done something really bad. Marlene was still furious. I could tell by the extra pink that stained her pretty Irish complexion.

"Nails is at home these days, devoting herself to nurturing and parenting," I said.

"He's in here, devoting himself to hitting on my waitresses," Marlene said. "He came in late last night. He told Shelley, my youngest and most innocent server, that she had beautiful eyes."

"That line is older than he is. What did you do?"

"I sent Shelley over to wait on a table for twelve," Marlene said, "which kept her busy, and I personally waited on Charlie. I told him an important managing editor deserved the attentions of a more experienced server. He did not look happy. He left his usual fifty-cent tip."

"Exactly the right amount to buy yourself a *Gazette*," I said.

"Hah," Marlene said. "Don't have to. You won't believe how many *Gazette*s get left behind in the morning. People read them and throw them down. They almost never leave *The New York Times*. They like that paper."

Sigh. The readers didn't love us. Well, that wasn't anything new. And Charlie was back to his old habit of catting around on his wife. That wasn't new, either. Now the woman who'd been sneaking around with a married man could sit at home and wonder where her husband was. I guess that was justice. But I wondered why Nails paid for their little romp and Charlie didn't.

Charlie could break his promises, but Lyle stayed true to his word. He never called me. Not even when the *Gazette* reported that I'd broken my elbow during my encounter with Patricia. I thought surely he'd come see me then, or at least call. But he didn't. Instead, he sent flowers, my favorite peach roses, with a card that said "Call me if you change your mind." It made me so angry, I tore up the card. But I kept the roses until the petals fell off. Then I threw them away. I won't call him. I haven't cried, either. Not once. I'm proud of that. I sit up night after night, wrapped in my grandmother's yellow-and-brown afghan, watching old movies and reading until my eyes are bloodshot. But I don't cry. I didn't want to be married. I won't be forced into it. I got what I wanted. Well, I did, didn't I?

Sometimes, when I can't sleep, I wander around the neighborhood. Some people might think that's crazy, walking alone at night. But I don't care. I seem to be drawn to North Dakota Place. That's where my life started unraveling. I walk on the green boulevard and watch the moonlight shimmering on the angel fountain. Sometimes I think I can see Johnny Hawkeye skimming across the grass, and Otto on his ladder, laughing, and Caroline yelling at him. So I wasn't very startled when one night, about two A.M., I saw a wheelbarrow coming up the sidewalk, pushed by a sturdy woman in cutoffs. It must be Caroline, restlessly patrolling her street. North Dakota Place did seem supernaturally well tended lately. Even in eternity, Caroline couldn't stop caring for it.

I kept walking on the boulevard grass, even though I knew this would upset Caroline, dead or alive. I wasn't afraid of her. "The dead don't hurt you, the living do," my grandmother used to say, and since it was the pain over Lyle's loss that kept me awake most nights, I agreed.

But it wasn't a dead woman pushing the wheelbarrow. It was Margie, browned and more muscular than I'd ever seen her. "Hi," she rasped. "I kept thinking about mulching those trees I just put in at the end of the boulevard, and then I thought, why wait till morning? I have other things I can do then. I couldn't sleep. So I got up to do it now."

"You've been keeping up North Dakota Place, haven't you?" I said.

"Someone has to," Margie said. "I've been meaning to have a talk with you, Francesca. Could you please keep off the boulevard grass? At least give the new grass a chance to get started. I'm not yelling or demanding. I'm asking you nicely. I spend all my time cleaning out the fountain and raking and weeding and planting and picking up and I'm not going to get anywhere with you stomping all over my grass."

"Sure," I said.

I was right after all. Caroline was alive.